Borrowed Time

Jenni Daiches

Vagabond Voices
Glasgow

First published in October 2016 by
Vagabond Voices Publishing Ltd.,
Glasgow,
Scotland.

ISBN 978-1-908251-69-5

Printed and bound in Poland

Cover design by Mark Mechan

Typeset by Park Productions

The publisher acknowledges subsidy towards this publication from Creative Scotland

ALBA | CHRUTHACHAIL

For further information on Vagabond Voices, see the website, www.vagabondvoices.co.uk

With thanks again to Faith Pullin and Colin Manlove, and to all the dogs.

Borrowed Time

January 2014

Kenspeckle. In the old days they'd have called me a witch. An eccentric white-haired woman living in the woods, where the branch of a sycamore scratches at the window, where sometimes in the dark an owl hoots, where hectoring crows strut on the rough grass and stare. But I have dogs, not cats, and it's not quite accurate to say I live in the woods, although there are trees and up the hill behind me the pines and birches thicken.

Kenspeckle. The odd old woman with dogs. I am a stranger, but I've been here long enough to have learnt a few new words, and for others, long buried, to come to the surface. My grandfather pointing out the birds as we walked through the fields that surrounded the village near Edinburgh where he had always lived – mavis, lintie, peesie. You could smell the coal and hear the constant clank of coal trains carrying it away. I tried not to gawk at the black-grimed men on the street. They were the only black men I ever saw.

I live in a garden. It was once a very large garden, divided by a low wall. A lawn and flower beds near the house, then the wall and steps down to the kitchen garden. In the corner furthest from the house is an old railway carriage. That's where I live. I am the old lady who lives in a railway carriage. Perhaps I imagine the sidelong looks, the children whispering.

The big house is a solid three-storey stone villa, built not long after the canal was opened in the early nineteenth century. I've been told it was built for the mistress of a local landowner who made a fortune in the Caribbean from where he imported a black woman whom he kept in style. His wife and family lived in a mansion a few miles away, now decayed and roofless. Its windows gape, eerie and

3

empty, and trees grow out of its gaunt walls. But I can see the windows lit, chandeliers, women in rustling silk, servants shadowy. Or mornings with the mist licking the moor, the men in tweeds with guns under their arms. A shaggy pony with the carcass of a deer slung on its back, its head and antlers hanging in defeat.

In a fold of the hills behind me, among the pines and birches, the bracken and thick clumps of nettles, are the few stones that remain of a group of cottages. The landowner, rich on sugar and slavery, decided to improve his estate which meant getting rid of many of his tenants. They went to Australia, I believe. I walk up there often with the dogs and loiter among the tumbled stones. I can see where the hearth once was. There are times when the forlorn emptiness of such abandonment suits me. I have become acquainted with emptiness. Life fills and fills as the years accumulate. At least, it does if you're lucky, if you have a purposeful occupation and people to love. But there comes a point when for most – for all? – substance begins to drain away. People disappear, and the feeling grows that you live in a territory whispering with shades and spectres.

Beyond the settlement there are standing stones and rocks with cup and ring marks. To be there in a smirr of rain, the sky low and occluded, is to feel a phantom presence. I lose myself sometimes, if I stand long enough with the dogs snuffling in the undergrowth, drawn into an ancient past which diminishes my own few decades of life. There were places in England where I felt stalked by history, but never so intensely and yet so imprecisely as here, making my way up the hillside past a blackened hearth telling of daily labour and the etched rock that speaks of the need for so much more than daily labour. I can feel my skin tingle, and I am glad of the dogs' company. But this is not my country, and these more ancient hauntings have never been flesh and blood presences, though strangely easier to understand.

After the war – at my age the war, towards the end of which I was born, is always the Second World War – the stone villa was lived in by a family called Gordon. William Gordon was an animal feed merchant and had a shop in the town. In the summer months the family moved out of the house and lived in the railway carriage, while the house was let to holidaymakers. The house looks out across a single-track road to the canal, and from the back you can see the river winding through the moss and the gnarled hills to the side and beyond. From the upstairs windows you can glimpse the sea, and to the east, if the day is clear, you can see the rising mass of Cruachan. On a fine day in winter it has a crisp white outline, but today the cloud is low. Somewhere I have a photograph of my son, my elder son, on Cruachan's snowy top. He's wearing a red woolly hat and dark glasses, and the sky is intensely blue.

I have been in the big house several times and was once shown round its neatly furnished rooms, but most of the time it's empty. I was told William Gordon's unmarried daughter lived in the house, which was sold when she died some years ago. No one seems to know when the railway carriage appeared. Looking at it now it seems rooted and oddly natural. It helps me towards the beginning of belonging.

The year after Tim died I got into our car, which had become my car, and drove north. It was an impulse, or perhaps rather a compulsion. It wasn't planned, but something made me do it. Something made me pull out a suitcase from the cupboard at the top of the stairs and hastily pack some clothes and books. I'd hardly ever travelled on my own, but I had Tim's maps and made myself sit down and examine them. Tim loved maps. He would study contours and declivities, and the way roads and railways obeyed and sometimes defied the landscape. He saw maps in three dimensions. If we take that path, he'd say, planning a walk in the Yorkshire Dales, we'll get a good view across the valley.

I opened the car bonnet and checked the oil and water. Tim always insisted on a rug on the back seat and a plastic box of emergency rations. These hadn't been touched for years, so I crumbled up the ancient cereal bars for the birds and put in a packet of digestive biscuits I found in a tin. I made sandwiches and a flask of tea. Tim never travelled in winter without a snow shovel, but it was June. The orange plastic shovel stood in the garage next to the foot pump and petrol can. The dial on the foot pump wasn't working but I took the petrol can. I felt Tim's shadow as I made my preparations. He was always methodical, unhurried. He liked to get things ready. When he'd loaded the car he would stand with his hands on his hips, his head tilted, thoughtful. Then he'd give the slightest of nods. If it was a working trip he'd say goodbye at the kitchen door, a quick kiss and a pat on the shoulder. If we were going somewhere together he'd watch while I got my coat and my bag and locked the door. Ready for the off? he'd say. Ready for the off. He would have wanted to prepare for his own death.

I double-locked the front door and I drove away from our red brick house in the late morning, stopping to shut the gate. Pink and purple lupins had spilled beyond the garden. I drove away from the village, about halfway between Leeds and York, where I had lived for nearly forty years, where Tim and I had brought up our children, and in twenty minutes was on the A1 heading north. I didn't really know where I was going, in spite of the maps. Just north. Tim may have shadowed my preparations, but he wouldn't have been happy at my lack of destination. Tim always had a destination, though he didn't always reach where he wanted to go.

My mother was born near Edinburgh. As a child I'd spent holidays with my grandparents in their bright new council house, built in those busy, constructive years that followed the war. When my own children were small we once spent two weeks on Skye, and perhaps Skye was at the back of my mind as I headed north. An island. A refuge, perhaps, with

6

the protection of water. A bridge wouldn't be difficult, Tim said as we queued for the ferry. In those two weeks, it had rained almost every day, but every day too there were sunshine and rainbows and hen harriers quartering the moor close to the cottage we rented. The children, four of them, explored the shore and the rock pools, clumped through heather in their wellington boots and fell into bogs, spotted live deer and a dead sheep, and seals basking on the shore. And Jake, twelve years old that year, gazed at the Cuillin, rising dark and barbed and commanding through the cloud, and asked if we could all climb to the top. When you're older, his father said. Lucas, aged four, stopped on the stony path and said, my legs are tired.

After the children were in bed, Tim and I sat outside in the delicately light evening and sipped Talisker. I remember the translucent glow of the sky. A picture had reassembled inside my head, although I knew that to go back to places where you were happy, before any of the bad things had happened, was not a good plan. The children in bright colours, red and orange and yellow. Tim relaxed, his long legs stretched out, his hand reaching out to take mine.

I drove steadily but not very fast. Cars and trucks flew past me. A few miles past Scotch Corner, almost instinctively I turned off the A1 on to the A68 and the traffic fell away. It was the route my father used to take on the annual drive to Scotland. There was a long stretch of straight Roman road. I pulled in at a lay-by, rolled down the window and ate a cheese sandwich and drank tea from the flask. I could smell grass and hear birdsong. On the other side of barbed wire black and white cows stared, their jaws moving slowly and steadily.

Every other day I take the dogs and walk the two miles to the Co-op in the town. Two years ago the old Renault gave out and I decided not to replace it. I bought a bicycle instead though I don't use it often because with the dogs it's better to walk. The town isn't large, perhaps 10,000 people, with most of the shops on the one main street: a butcher's, a fish shop, a baker's, and I go to them too. I take my small rucksack. I plan my shopping so there isn't too much to carry on any one journey. Heavy things, dog food and wine, I order online. Most of the delivery men know me now, though at first my address baffled them. There are no house numbers. My address is just The Railway Carriage, Achnabarr. Achnabarr is the name of the big house. There may once have been an older settlement there.

The railway carriage has a lean-to at the back where I stack my firewood and store bits and pieces, dog food in a plastic bin, a case of wine turned on its side. Anyone could raid the bottles, of course, but here I don't worry much about such things. When I go to the town or up the hill with the dogs I don't lock my door.

A glass of wine every night is my only luxury. I've never smoked, and I don't eat a lot. I've never gone in for designer clothes or spent much on the house, but I don't consider books and music luxuries, although in the early days of marriage, when money was scarce, buying a book was a treat. Sometimes I avoided telling Tim that I'd spent money on books. He read, of course, but not in the same way as I did, not avidly, not needfully, and except for thrillers on holiday, mostly non-fiction. I am lost without a book. A room with no books disturbs me. I am a frequent visitor to the library in the town. They know me there, and they tell me when new stock has arrived. There's a young man I particularly like, who always greets me cheerfully. Hello there, Mrs Billings, he says, his accent Glasgow though he told me his parents are from Bengal. How are you doing?

I grow vegetables in the old kitchen garden. It's not my land, but the Turnbulls, who now own the house, are keen for me to make use of it. They are not around very much and have no interest in gardening. They live in Stirling where they both work for a big insurance firm, and are here

8

for occasional weekends and a few weeks in the summer. I'd never been much of a gardener. Tim cut the grass and trimmed the hedge. I planted spring bulbs and sweet peas and petunias in pots round the front door. But my first spring in the railway carriage I dug and hoed and pulled out mounds of weeds. I slashed back the brambles and bracken. I uncovered gooseberry and blackcurrant bushes, and a straggle of raspberry canes. I raked the earth and put in seeds and tried to ignore the stabs of pain as my hips and thighs objected to the unaccustomed work. I was out every day looking for green shoots, and then suddenly they appeared, pale green hints of lettuce and spinach, fronds of carrot, sturdy spears of peas and runner beans, purple-veined beetroot leaves.

A broken-down greenhouse had almost disappeared in a tangle of brambles. Kirstie from down the road helped me salvage it. She's a clever girl, Kirstie. She has a good eye and is handy with a hammer. Although some of the wood had rotted and most of the glass was broken, shards embedded in the undergrowth, she reconstructed half a greenhouse where I've been growing tomatoes and peppers. Her reward is a share of the produce. I have shelves of jam now, and my little freezer is well stocked.

Kirstie teaches maths at the high school. She and her two nearly teenage daughters are my only neighbours, except when Brian and Moira Turnbull are here. They are pleasant enough, and have invited me in for a meal two or three times, but we don't have much in common. They tell me I should spend some time in Glasgow, for the music, the theatre, the shops. It's only two hours in the car, they say. Or there's the bus, they add when they remember I am now without a car. They are often in Glasgow themselves and seem anxious to assure me that they are cultivated people. They have no children, and I wonder why they bought such a large house which is so little used or why they drive a large SUV when they don't really go anywhere except here and flights to exotic destinations abroad. Sometimes they have guests, but only once, at New Year, did the house seem full. I was invited to their party, but left as soon as I decently could after midnight. Their friends were lawyers and accountants, and I found conversation difficult. I got bored with myself as I explained several times that after forty years in Yorkshire I now lived in a railway carriage in the garden. Each time there was the same reaction. What fun, one woman said. A railway carriage, said another, what a charming idea. Perfect for weekends.

As the oldest person there I felt I had a licence to leave, in spite of protests that it was far too early. I walked across the garden in the thin shoes I had scarcely worn since leaving Yorkshire. Frost glinted in the moonlight. I let the dogs out and stood at the door of my railway carriage and looked back at the lit windows of the big house and wondered if anyone noticed the strange old woman at the door of her fun and charming residence.

The next morning I looked out of the window to see a small figure standing in the garden. It was staring at the railway carriage. I watched it for a while. It didn't move. It was wearing a thick jacket, a woolly hat and a scarf tied round its neck. I opened the front door and the dogs barrelled out. Cleo charged straight up to the small figure, which silently held out an ungloved hand but continued to stare at the railway carriage. I followed the dogs into the garden. It was cold but there was no wind. A pair of dark blue eyes looked at me from under the woolly hat. Hello, I said. Is that your house? I nodded. Did it use to be a train? Yes, I said, it's a railway carriage. Do you sleep in it and everything? I nodded again. Does it have a toilet? Yes, it has everything I need. Can I see? Come on in, I said. What's your name? Gregor Black. That's a good name. I'm staying in that house – he gestured backwards. Mum and dad stayed up until midnight but I wasn't allowed. Well, perhaps when you're older. I'm six. *I'm clever as clever. I want to be six*

10

forever and ever, I said. The grown-ups are still in bed and I haven't had any breakfast. I stepped back through my doorway and he followed me. He inspected my entire home, kitchen, bathroom, living room, both bedrooms, without saying a word. Finally he said, I'd like to live in a railway carriage. Would you like some toast? He looked thoughtful for a moment and then said, No thank you. I expect they've got up now. I looked across at the big house but there was no sign of life.

He stood at the open front door. How did it get here? Did an engine pull it? I don't know how it got here, but there are no railway tracks so it can't have been pulled by an engine. There might have been tracks in the olden days. There might, but I don't think so. He stepped down into the garden and looked about him as if hoping to find traces of tracks. Then he shook his head. It's a mystery, he said. It is indeed. A mystery. I like mysteries, I said. He turned and made his way across the garden. Cleo rushed up to him again and this time he paused to stroke her head. Then he began to run and in moments was through the French window of the big house.

Near Corbridge I found a bed and breakfast and stopped for the night. That evening I walked by the Tyne eating fish and chips. There were paths that criss-crossed a stretch of meadow and a few clumps of bushes. The Romans were at Corbridge, a supply base a couple of miles south of Hadrian's Wall. I suppose the river was useful to them. We'd stopped at Housesteads on our way back from that Skye holiday, and walked along the wall for a mile or so. Tim explained to the children that the wall was not the division between England and Scotland, that England and Scotland were relatively recent definitions, that the border had often shifted. And now it was a line on the map, not a line on the landscape. It was a grey day. We tramped unevenly for a while and looked north at hills dark under low cloud. The

Scotland we had just left seemed forbidding and almost sinister, as it must often have seemed to the Romans.

I stood by the river and scattered the last of my chips for the ducks. A fisherman on the far bank cast an invisible line into the brown water. I remember the feeling I had then, a sense of achievement that I'd driven that distance alone, found somewhere to stay and food to eat, as if I were an explorer dependent for survival on the resources of the wilderness and the skills of a hunter. Since Tim's death the world had sometimes seemed like a wilderness. I didn't know where I was. I would wake up in the darkness and for a tiny moment I would be in my childhood bedroom in the Sussex country town where I grew up, or in the attic flat in Burnley where Tim and I had spent the first years of our married life, where our first two children were born. But there was no mum and dad, no Tim, no child. Just heavy enclosing darkness and now a growing chill as the light faded.

But in a green meadow by the Tyne there was a hint of a new beginning, indistinct, like a reflection trembling in moving water.

The next morning I carried on, with the green and brown hills looming larger as I approached the Border. I was on Dere Street, following the Romans north through Redesdale with the Kielder Forest to the west. The road straight, blind summit after blind summit, and the landscape emptier. The Catcleugh Reservoir spread away to my left as the road climbed towards Carter Bar. At the summit there were several cars and a coach parked and a clot of people with cameras, but I didn't stop. Memories of crossing the Border in our black Ford Prefect flooded back, my elder sister and I on the back seat, my mother's jubilant, We're in Scotland! My father, A foreign country girls, you'll need to learn the language. The same exchange every year, the same look of reproof from my mother, the same rumbling laugh from my father, the same giggles from their two daughters.

The Eildons, look, my mother would say when the distinctive blue-grey hills came into view, and I could see them now to the northwest. And every year my mother would add, Walter Scott country. We must go there sometime. But we never did.

I skirted Edinburgh on the bypass, passing the sign to my grandparents' village. For a moment I was tempted to stop, to seek out my grandparents' council house and walk to the end of the street to where the fields began. But it would all be different, the mines and the railway long gone, the smell of coal, and I was reluctant to encounter change as well as reluctant to stop. So I carried on and took the Stirling road, and when I saw a sign saying Loch Lomond I followed it. I wasn't, after all, heading for Skye, or at least not directly. I was going somewhere I had never been before. Green fields stretched on either side, studded with cattle and sheep. I caught up with a tractor, its driver glancing neither left nor right, his square shoulders immobile. The tractor lumbered slowly for several miles before turning in at a farm gate. At Buchlyvie, I stopped at a café and had a bowl of soup. I drove on west, through Balloch and up Loch Lomondside, the mountain on the far shore bulking clear in the afternoon sun. The water shimmered, a pearly blue-grey. My mother and father met on the summit of Ben Lomond. They liked to tell the story of how they were youth-hostelling, each with a group of friends, climbing the mountain from different sides, and as my father toiled up the final few yards there was my mother standing by the cairn on the summit, the wind blowing her fair hair, laughing. It was August 1937. Two years later, with war on the horizon, Mairi Elizabeth Ewing became the wife of Raymond Henry Letford. As a child I loved that story. I loved the picture my father painted of my mother on the summit, laughing and windblown. It was so vivid I almost saw it as a photograph, but there were no photographs. I often imagined myself on that mountaintop, a clear sky, and turning to see a figure approaching, stalwart, a pack on his back and a steady upward stride.

Romance on a mountaintop. I grew up believing that that was how love and marriage should begin, an instant attraction between two people in a beautiful landscape.

And we walked down the mountain together, my father would say, And when we reached the road there was a butcher's van, so we bought sausages and cooked them for our tea in the youth hostel. And my mother would sit, her chin in her hands, smiling and almost shaking her head, as if, perhaps, Raymond Letford was making it all up. Was it really like that, mum? Did you really meet on top of a mountain? Yes, pet, we really did, and we really did have sausages for tea, which we fried in a big black frying pan on an old kitchen range. And we made toast. And we sat and talked until everyone else had gone to bed.

At Tarbet I was pulled to the west, ignoring the turning that would have taken me to the northern tip of the loch. The road began to climb and mountains reared ominously closer. Although the sun was shining and the lower slopes were green, higher up the rocky crags were bare and dark. Apart from a few cars on the road there was no sign of human life to relieve the emptiness. Thin streams fell down the mountains' flanks, white and almost perpendicular. I saw birds of prey hanging above, black against the blue sky. Not eagles, surely, but buzzards perhaps. I felt a frisson of excitement, but I tried to keep my eyes on the winding road. After the steep climb, a long descent down to the head of another loch, where there were some scattered buildings and a field of sheep.

I spent that night in an old ramshackle hotel in Inveraray. I ventured into the bar and ordered a gin and tonic, and sat there in the hushed stillness reading a *Scotsman* that had been left on a table. There was no one else there. The girl in tight jeans and triple earrings who had served me disappeared. The crackle of each turning page of the newspaper seemed as loud as a pistol shot. The clink of ice in my glass was like a peal of bells. Then I heard voices and people streamed in, their accent familiar. They were from York-shire, a coach party from Huddersfield as I learnt later. I felt mildly annoyed as I watched them crowd to the bar, where there was no one to serve them, and discuss loudly what they would have to drink. In seconds I was enveloped in a haze of talk and shifting chairs – is this chair free, love? – thanks, I'll have a pint of bitter – bitter? won't get that here – lemonade shandy for me, Bill. I shrank into myself, but could no longer focus on the words on the newspaper's page.

The next day I was up early and ate a huge breakfast in an empty dining room. As I finished a couple came in and sat at the table furthest from mine. They nodded in my direction, but showed no inclination to speak, to me or to each other. I had my map beside me, out of date but I guessed the roads wouldn't have changed much. I decided to continue on the road that edged Loch Fyne. As I poured myself a third cup of tea the first of the coach party came in, four of them, and spent several minutes loudly deciding which table to sit at.

Now, four years later, I walk to the loch shore sometimes, but I go more often to one of the little lochs, up the hill and among the trees. The dogs like it there. If it's rain-ing, and it often is, there's shelter under the pines and the muted sound of rain on the branches is soothing. I've been there today, trudging through the damp leaves that have been lying since autumn. There was frost this morning, but later the sun was bright and a hint of real warmth filtered through the bare branches. It's the end of January, and it's not beyond belief that spring is approaching. In the garden snowdrops are showing a sliver of white. From time to time my foot crunches on a pine cone. The trees near the path are widely spaced, but away from the path they are dense and within minutes you're struggling to find a way through bracken and wind blow. I find it hard now to clamber over fallen trees and tangled roots. My limbs won't move as freely as they did once. I have to be careful when I get out of bed in the mornings as my legs are stiffened with arthritis.

By the time I was down from the hill the chill was creeping back and the dogs were wet and muddy. I rubbed them down in the lean-to, where I keep a collection of old towels. We were glad to get into the warm. The heat comes from the little stove where I burn wood and peat, which Harry from the farm up the road brings me. I get my eggs from Harry too. You wouldn't trust Harry to look at him. He's thin-faced, unshaven and with bad teeth and black fingernails, and is never without a dirty baseball cap, but he's good to me. He was the second person to knock on my door after I moved in, with a gruff offer to supply eggs, potatoes and firewood. Once a month I walk up to the farm to pay him, and sometimes speak to his wife Alison, whose dyed red hair flames incongruously above the frayed man's jacket she wears when she feeds the hens.

I'm now settled on the sofa, me at one end, the dogs at the other. The dusk closes in. I won't be out again today. I'll read, I'll put some music on, a Boccherini guitar concerto perhaps. It was Lucas, my youngest child, who introduced me to Boccherini. I'll have a go at the crossword in yesterday's paper. I'll watch the TV news. Soon I'll cook something simple and pour a glass of wine and read some more. I'll let the dogs out for five minutes before I go to bed.

In eight months' time I will complete my threescore years and ten. I'm into borrowed time now, my mother said on her seventieth birthday. She had three years of it. Death came fast after a diagnosis of bone cancer. She was reduced to little more than rotting bone before she died. Tim and I sat on either side of my father at the crematorium. He was stunned and silent as a man he scarcely knew stood up and encompassed his wife's life in five minutes and told him how wonderful she had been. He was right, of course, but it didn't seem right to hear it from him. Perhaps it was the emptiness of what now seemed like a large house that made my father appear diminished and crumpled. There was a look of bewilderment which never quite disappeared. I would visit two or three times a year, and he always came to us for Christmas. He was better then, brightening at the children's noise and messiness, but he couldn't be persuaded to sit down at the piano, which I kept in tune in the hope he would be tempted. Lucas, my only musical child, played occasionally but lost interest when he took up the clarinet. So it was there mainly for dad. Once or twice I saw him run his hand over the closed lid. And once, when Lucas, Melchior in that year's school nativity play, was singing "We Three Kings" I saw his fingers play a silent accompaniment on the arm of his chair.

They warn you, don't they, not to do what I have done, to uproot yourself late in life and distance yourself from the support you are likely to need. I don't know why I have done this.

1944

On 11 April 1944 a bomb fell on the house of Raymond and Mairi Letford in a country town in Sussex on the London to Brighton line. The house had been built only ten years earlier, and the Letfords had moved into it a month before war was declared. It still seemed new and fresh, with a modern kitchen and a gas cooker. Raymond Letford was not in the house. He was flying a plane that was dropping bombs on retreating Germans. Mairi was there with her three-year-old daughter Miranda, who as an adult spoke sometimes of dust and broken glass. She remembered the crunch of glass under her feet and the taste of dust on her tongue. The bomb was dropped by a German plane shedding its load as it began the journey home. Not a direct hit, but it caught the back corner of the house and left a large hole where a privet hedge had divided the Letfords' garden from their neighbours'. Mairi Letford was four months pregnant. She had shards of glass embedded in her upper body. Small scars, like bird tracks, on her shoulders and the back of her neck remained for the rest of her life.

There had been no warning. Mairi and her daughter were in their beds when the bomb fell. Bleeding from the embedded glass, Mairi ran into the bedroom next door where her daughter lay wide-eyed and totally silent, and snatched her up. She stumbled down the stair, avoiding chunks of ceiling and leaning away from the splintered bannister. She stepped through the rubble and plaster dust and through the front door, which swung on one hinge, and out on to the paved path, where she stood rocking her child and humming *greetin for a wee bawbee tae buy some Coulter's Candy*. She had no idea how long she stood there before the neighbours appeared and led her into the house next door where several windows had been shattered by the blast, and gave her sweet tea and tucked the little girl up under a rug on the sofa.

One side of the house was badly damaged. For a week or two mother and child continued to live in it, sleeping downstairs on a sofa and camp bed. There was no gas and no water. Mairi trudged back and forth between next door's kitchen and her own with buckets of water. Their neighbours lent them an old electric ring which took forever to boil a kettle, and brought in hot food. Marie swept up the worst of the dust and debris and papered over the broken windows. The kitchen was intact, although crockery had been shaken off shelves and smashed. She knelt on the floor to sweep up shards and splinters. In the mornings she half-filled the kettle and set it on the electric ring before getting herself and her daughter dressed. She made tea and then porridge, stirring it slowly as she gazed out into the back garden scattered with broken glass and slates and fragments of brick. The two of them sat at the kitchen table and ate their porridge, which tasted of dust. All the time she kept the little girl under her eye. Every time they went upstairs to the bathroom Mairi feared that something would collapse or fall.

Mairi clung to normality – what alternative was there? Each morning she tidied the bedclothes, fetched water, washed dishes, stood in queues, and tried to remove the interminable dust. It was cold. In the evenings after Miranda was asleep, she sat with a blanket round her shoulders and tried to read. But then Raymond's parents came and insisted that Mairi and Miranda move in with them. Though not entirely convenient, and not quite reconciled to their son's union with the daughter of a Scottish railwayman, they thought it their duty to take in his family. They stood on the doorstep, both of them, in coats and hats with the car in the drive. We'll help you pack, they said, but then looked at the stair with the bannister hanging and were clearly relieved when Mairi suggested that they remain on ground level. She left Miranda with them in the living room, and went upstairs herself, but instead of packing she sat for a long time on the edge of the bed she shared with her husband, still covered in dust and broken glass. His shirts were folded in the drawers, his trousers and jackets hanging in the wardrobe. But she would have to leave his things. She pulled a suitcase from under the bed and filled it – underwear, skirt, blouse, jersey, nightdress, clothes for Miranda, toothbrush, soap, flannel. The baby? But surely by that time she would be home. She sat down again, her hand on her belly.

Norman and Hilda Letford lived on the other side of town, in a bigger house with a view out to green fields. Mairi and Miranda had a bedroom each. Mairi wrote to Ray that they were none the worse for their experience and comfortably installed with his parents. They were occasionally able to speak on the telephone. It could have been worse, she said. The house is damaged but still standing. We'll get everything sorted, said Ray. He wrote his wife a letter twice a week, always adding a message for his parents. His letters were reassuring but short. He said little about how he was spending his time. In June he had a weekend's leave, and on the Saturday, he and Mairi and Miranda walked the mile from his parents' house to their own damaged home. The windows were boarded up and in the garden the grass was growing through the scattered wreckage. It will all get sorted, Ray said cheerfully. I'll come over tomorrow and cut the grass. He eyed the debris that would have to be cleared first. We'll have it all sorted in no time, you'll see.

On Monday 18 September in the house of her parents-in-law Mairi Letford gave birth to another daughter a little earlier than expected. A midwife was present, as was Hilda, in her dressing gown as it was three in the morning, and too fidgety to be of any great help. From time to time she retreated from the spare bedroom to smoke a cigarette. Downstairs Norman Letford was drinking whisky in his pyjamas and also smoking. He was a wine merchant and had sources of supply of both whisky and cigarettes. The birth was straightforward, though Mairi wished for her own mother rather than the uncertain assistance of her mother-in-law. Her own mother was four hundred miles away, and more worried about the son fighting somewhere in Holland than she was about the daughter producing a new life in Sussex. The son did not survive the war. The news of Kenneth Ewing's death came five days after the birth of Sonia Victoria, a sister for Miranda Elizabeth, mother and baby doing well. Why Sonia? Mairi always gave a gentle laugh when she was asked. I was reading *War and Peace* at the time, she said. I wanted her to be Natasha, but Ray felt that was too Russian, even though the Soviet Union was our ally, so we settled for Sonia. Victoria – well, obvious I suppose. Miranda is Shakespeare of course, and Elizabeth is my mother's name, and my middle name. Names are important, don't you think? They should have meaning. They should connect. And she looked thoughtful, her pale hands folded quietly, and added, names are like a message for the future. She would in later years comment incredulously on the names chosen by some for their children.

Norman and Hilda couldn't understand why their daughter-in-law spent so much time reading. She went back to the house regularly to collect books, which she piled neatly on the floor of her bedroom. They were mostly undamaged, but smelt of destruction. She had bought *War and Peace* in a second-hand bookshop in Edinburgh shortly before her marriage. She was reading it for the second time.

On the last day of 1943 Raymond Letford had had a week's leave. The Russians were advancing. Miranda's birth in 1941 had been an act of defiance. She was conceived early on in the Blitz. Then the Germans invaded the USSR and advanced on Moscow. The birth of Sonia was an act of hope. Ray and Mairi no longer agonised over the wisdom of bringing another life into the world. Their daughters were heralds of a new age. And meantime Mairi worked as a volunteer in a local nursery, her baby in a pram, and regarded the room full of toddlers as proof of faith in the future rather than hostages to fortune. She watched two small girls as they spilled a box of coloured bricks on to the floor and began to build, only for another child to knock down their towers. It's a bomb, the boy said, holding up a toy airplane.

At the moment his second daughter was born Raymond Letford was somewhere over the English Channel. It was the day after the launch of Operation Market Garden, the attempt to capture the crossing of the Lower Rhine at Arnhem. Sonia Victoria Letford was a week old when British troops withdrew. A setback, but by the time she was a year old the war was over, and on that first birthday Lord Haw-Haw was sentenced to death for treason. Mairi watched her children carefully. She wished she could prevent the imprint on their lives of war.

Raymond Letford came home physically unscathed, but it was some time before the family returned to their partially repaired house. Sonia and her sister Miranda grew up in that house, which never quite regained the sheen of 1939. Sonia did not remember the drabness that seemed to coat it like the layers of dust that her mother worked so hard to remove, but in her teens there were still items of utility furniture bought to replace what was damaged. She remembered her mother's pile of mending, which never seemed to diminish although she spent many evenings with her needle. She remembered the excitement when her mother bought new winter coats for her daughters, matching coats in dark red with brown collars. That Christmas the girls were given winter boots, with warm linings and zips.

For years Mairi Letford felt the house to be shabby, but by the time Sonia started primary school you would perhaps not have guessed that the pleasant, airy, comfortable, if now less ornamented, house had received a bomb, except that a blackened streak descended from the guttering down part of the back wall. Mairi insisted that it should not be painted over. Some of the rubble from the crumbled walls was incorporated into a rockery at the far end of the back garden. A fragment of the bomb was displayed in a glass-fronted corner cabinet in the living room.

Occasionally Ray Letford had a nightmare that his wife and children were buried under a heap of rubble, which looked not as if a bomb had dropped but as if there had been an earthquake in some hot, Mediterranean country. In his dream, his hands scrabbled desperately. Many years later Ray would show the bomb fragment to his four grandchildren and would tell them the story of what happened to grandpa and grandma's house when he was dropping bombs on France. The grandchildren would hear the story several times, and it always ended the same way. Who knows, their grandfather would say as they stood round the cabinet in the corner, maybe one of my bombs landed on a French house just like this one. The grandchildren were all familiar with pictures of bombed houses. They knew, even if the pictures did not show this, that amongst the broken brick and crumbled concrete there were probably dead people. Their grandparents wished them to understand the random nature of miracles.

At first the grandchildren thought that pictures of the smoking ruins of destroyed cities belonged to the past, but gradually they came to realise that people's homes were still being shattered by explosives falling from the sky. Sometimes, when the family were watching the television news, Sonia their mother would say, Every baby is a war baby, and their father Tim would reach across for her hand and say, It's true, there are plenty of people having it worse than we ever did, than our parents ever did.

Mairi Letford, whose older brother was killed somewhere in Holland, brought up her daughters to be aware of how lucky they were. There was a comfortable amount of money. They were well-looked-after and well fed. Even with shortages and coupons, they were dressed in good clothes. Grace Letford was also good at mending. They went to good schools and were encouraged by their parents who praised them when they did well. Their mother was gentle and serious and read a lot of books, their father exuberant and prolific with jokes and shaggy dog stories. Well yes, Sonia would say if anyone asked, I had a happy childhood.

February 2014

I inherited my mother's angular, bony frame and prominent cheekbones, and age has if anything accentuated both. I have her blue-grey eyes. Like her in her last years my cheeks have grown more hollow and my face more grooved. Her fair hair faded to grey and then white, as mine has done. My hair, once thick and smooth and light brown and always cut short is now white and shoulder-length. When I came here I stopped going to the hairdresser and I trim it myself when it gets too long. From early childhood I had a habit of running my hand through my short hair so that it stood on end for some seconds before falling back into place. I still do it, but without the same effect. I wear it tied back at the nape of my neck but strands always escape. It makes me look severe, I know, as well as untidy, and when I release it at night and brush it in front of the mirror my bones seem to sharpen and the lines on my face deepen. The witch in the railway carriage.

But children do not call me names when I pass, although they stare sometimes. I am wearing jeans and hiking boots, a dark red anorak, a knitted hat if it's cold. I have taken up tapestry, almost accidentally. I was once with Clare when I admired a tapestry kit. Maybe I should take up tapestry when I retire, I said, half joking. When the time came, Clare presented me with a tapestry kit, an oriental design in beautiful colours. It was neglected for a long time, but after Tim's death I found it and examined it properly for the first time. I began, inexpertly, to stitch with the coloured wools and found it strangely soothing. My thoughts could float undisciplined as patterns took shape. I completed a rather lumpy cushion cover, and tried again. My third attempt was almost acceptable. I began to design my own patterns. I sketched out designs with coloured pencils, most of which never got further than shapes on paper.

There's a wool and craft shop in the town, a tiny place stuffed with a huge range of wool and random craft materials, run by a frail old woman with white almost transparent skin. She sits behind the counter with her knitting needles going. There is never anyone else serving, and I suspect the shop will go when she does. I browse amongst the colours and buy whatever takes my fancy. One day I'll create something good enough to give as a present, but it's playing with the colours that intrigues me most, and the meditative rhythm of the needle, in and out.

The dogs were an accident. We never had dogs when I was growing up, just guinea pigs and goldfish. The first dog was intended to be temporary, a black undefinable animal with a Labrador face and ears and deep brown eyes. She belonged to an elderly man who broke his hip. The dog needed looking after while he was in hospital. It was Kirstie who told me of the predicament, and who suggested that I might enjoy having a dog for a while. So Cleo came to the railway carriage, and as it happened she came to stay, as her owner never regained enough mobility to take her for walks, and died a year or so later. Six months after Cleo joined me, a young half-starved collie cross was found wandering in the town. The local vet telephoned, and I found myself with a second dog. Jet took a few weeks to settle, but he and Cleo are good companions now, to me and to each other. They provide the rhythm of my life. I had perhaps not acknowledged before the satisfaction of having living creatures to care for, or recognised that I was missing the patterns they impose. It was a while before I appreciated the way they occupied some of the empty space which at first I had wanted to be all mine.

Until Tim died, there was always someone to look after. My children, my parents intermittently as they grew older, my husband, my husband's parents, the people of all ages whom I've taught over the years. There was never a choice, and it sometimes felt like a burden. There were times when I longed for the burden to fall away. Even Tim could sometimes be too much for me. There were times when his presence seemed louche and awkward, filling a space that I wanted for myself. There were times when I longed for all of them to disappear. My sister Miranda chose not to burden herself. There were times when I envied my sister Miranda.

On the day I parked my car beside the canal and walked in the sunshine of a late June afternoon it came on me, not perhaps for the first time but with striking clarity, that everyone I had cared for was lost or distanced. I was free. They had all gone. They had all left this life or were far away. It was a free-dom I hadn't fully recognised and would not have chosen, in spite of those moments in the past when I felt imprisoned by the people closest to me. And when I saw the "For sale" sign and pushed open the gate and followed the paved path past a large house with blank windows and on to the far end of an extensive and neglected garden I knew at once that there was no reason to remain in my red brick Yorkshire home. A railway carriage. Why not? There it was, paint peeling and a rhododendron thick with purple flowers threatening to block what seemed to be the front door. The door was fastened with a large padlock, but I peered in through dirty windows. There was no furniture except for two old kitchen chairs in a space that must have been two compartments knocked together. I could see a sink, an old electric cooker and some shelves. More windows revealed three more spaces, a living room probably, and bedrooms. In the last room there was a cardboard box on the floor and on top of it an old copy of the *Beano*. That was as much as I could see.

I walked round to the back and found the lean-to and a room with a frosted window built on at the kitchen end. I guessed it was a bathroom and smiled at the frosted window. Only someone on the hillside with powerful binoculars could possibly see in. Clumps of nettles and brambles reached almost to my height. The brambles were in blossom.

I returned to the front door and stepped back. I noticed the missing wheels, the way the carriage now seemed rooted in the garden. *Faster than fairies, faster than witches*. But this railway carriage wasn't going anywhere. Whatever its his-tory, it would never again be flying by painted stations. And yet there was just that hint of a previous existence, *Each a glimpse and gone forever*. How on earth had it made its way to a tiny canal-side hamlet in the Scottish Highlands? If no one were to buy it, if no one were to look after it, surely it would slowly disappear into the earth.

The estate agent in the town was closed by the time I got there, but there it was on a card in the window alongside a dozen more conventional properties for sale. The railway carriage was "full of character with potential as an ideal holiday home". I walked round the corner to the Argyll Hotel and booked a room. It hadn't been my plan to stay overnight. I thought I would drive on to Oban, but here I was, eating a meal of lasagne and soggy chips and drinking two glasses of red wine. I'd intended to read my book, a copy of Neil Munro's *The New Road* that I'd found in an Inveraray charity shop, but couldn't concentrate. I felt strangely excited.

Twenty-four hours later, after a night of not much sleep, it was all arranged. The estate agent explained he couldn't leave the premises as his assistant was on holiday, but he gave me a key and I returned to the railway carriage. The rusted padlock resisted my efforts with the key, and I had to make several attempts before I could get in. Inside it was dirty and smelt of damp, but I felt a surge of blood through my veins. I looked around the living space, hung with cobwebs, and could see how comfortably it could be arranged. A good clean and a lick of paint. I began to think of colours. Between the kitchen and the bathroom was a utility room ideal for a washing machine. There was plumbing – I turned a tap and brownish water spluttered out. There was an electricity meter although no power. There was an old wood-burning stove in the living area. I spat on a tissue and rubbed a clean circle in the window dirt. I could see the unkempt kitchen garden, the tidier lawn reaching to the house, overblown roses, French windows and a patio. The excitement was almost painful, like the return of blood to frozen hands. I wanted the railway carriage so badly I forgot the mental list I'd made of what to look out for, and walked so fast back to the car I was almost running. The main street in the town was busy and it took some minutes to find a place to park. When I burst in through the estate agent's door I was out of breath.

There was nothing eccentric about me then, except my urgent desire to possess a damp, dilapidated railway carriage. My hair was fashionably cropped. I wore neat cotton trousers and a flowered shirt and carried a shoulder bag with cash and credit cards, a diary, keys, comb and pocket mirror, a small packet of tissues, a phone. A blue scarf was thrown over my shoulders. A retired professional, neat if not trendy, though semi-professional might be more accurate, as I never worked full-time and was never promoted. Year after year I did the same thing, with variations it's true, but never breaking the mould. If there had been opportunities for adventure, I failed to spot them. And I did not look for alternatives to my steadily contained existence. My frustrations were not strong or long enough. I had a husband, children, a solid and comfortable house.

I stayed in the Argyll Hotel for three days, reluctant to take myself away from my discovery. I drove down the west coast of Kintyre and walked on a sandy beach. The sea was calm and almost emerald, withdrawing gently from the shore. I scrambled up a couple of small hills. I looked across to the dark slopes of Jura. I knew that George Orwell had written part of *Nineteen Eighty-Four* on the island, and had often told my students of the way he embraced the remote and the difficult. Was that what I was doing? But not so very remote, surely, and not difficult either. It could be done, so why shouldn't I do it? It's our beginning, Tim said as we climbed the stairs to the dusty attic flat in Burnley that became our new home. We looked out at the hills through the dirty windows. There was excitement then too. Threadbare carpets, skimpy curtains, the stains on the kitchen sink did not matter then.

I watched sailing boats moving skittishly in the breeze and seals lolling on sunny rocks. I walked up and down the little town's main street and noticed its shops and the view from the loch shore down to Arran. I bought postcards to send to my children and went in to the post office for stamps, but

I didn't tell them what I had done. I didn't say, my name is Sonia Letford and in a few months I'll be in here often. But all the time I was picturing myself in this strange new territory, in a place I would make my own. I sat on the sand of an empty beach and hugged my knees.

In the early years of marriage I had sometimes imagined what it would be like when Tim and I were old. There would be only the two of us, the children away with their own lives, but not too distant. We would have grandchildren and they would visit, but most of the time we would not need to share our space except with each other. We would do things together. We would go to the places we had gone as a family, to Swaledale, to the cliffs at Robin Hood's Bay, to the hamlet high above Ullswater where we twice spent Easter, once with snow on the ground. But now was not, after all, a time for revisiting places of happiness. I didn't go to Skye.

I drove back to Yorkshire and put my house up for sale. I still hesitated to tell my children. I treasured my secret, but the rush of freedom I felt as I began to get rid of a lifetime of possessions did not drown out the guilt. There was a rush of anxiety too, which shivered through me sometimes at night, with a warning voice. Was I rash? Crazy? Inconsiderate? Did I know what I was doing? To that last question I would answer, in my most optimistic moments, No, of course I don't, but that's the point. The exhilaration of risk could be wonderful.

It was like saying yes to Tim when he suggested marriage on Brighton beach. It was a chilly, breezy April day and we were sitting on the stones, from time to time chucking one into the water which lapped a few yards away. It wasn't a proposal exactly. We could get married, was what Tim said. What do you think? Yes, we could, I replied, casual, without a thought. And so we did. But first we walked to the end of Brighton Pier and stood hand in hand in the breeze and a surge of adventure ran through me like an electric shock. Tim and I living together, making a life together, children. He put his arm around me and held me so tightly against his spare body that it hurt.

I would soon graduate. I did not have a career planned, just a vague notion of working at something not too uncongenial. When an acquaintance of my mother who worked on a women's magazine mentioned they were looking for new recruits it seemed like a good idea to apply. I went to London for an interview, in a smart linen dress and carrying a white handbag, and was offered a job. My role was to read and draft answers to the agony aunt letters. I did it for a year, and by the time I left I was practised at combining pragmatism and reassurance. My boss encouraged me to think of it as a career. Most of my small salary was eaten up by the cost of commuting from my parents' home. Miranda was vastly entertained by her younger sister's employment. She threatened to write herself to ask for advice.

And I am here now, in my railway carriage. I made my choice and did not allow myself to pause, to ponder consequences, to reconsider. I would, no doubt, see less of my children and grandchildren. But my son and my grandchildren were thousands of miles away. I had visited them once, and twice, before the children were born, Lucas and his wife had returned to England. I would, I assured them, make the journey to Auckland again, but my son would never set foot again in the house he grew up in. He protested. My daughters protested. What was I thinking of? Clare arrived from London with a plan. Buy the railway carriage by all means, as a holiday home, but don't sell the house. She even offered to help out financially. She'd put some of her own money into the railway carriage. Clare was doing well in London, working for a company that ran training workshops for big organisations. She spent a weekend reluctantly clearing her old bedroom. That Sunday afternoon three couples came to view the house while she hovered disapprovingly.

Harriet phoned from Cambridge, on her mobile, between lectures. I'm worried for you, mum. Don't do anything you might regret. By the time she arrived in Yorkshire the house was sold to a young couple with a toddler and a baby. As they walked through the house the father held the infant, only a few weeks old, against his shoulder. Look, Charlie, this could be your room, and this one, right next to yours, could be mummy and daddy's room. They stood in the kitchen looking out into the garden, smiling. We could have a swing and a climbing frame, they said. They could have been me and Tim with Jake and Clare all those years ago, when we piled out of our old Mini and gazed at the red brick house standing solidly in its spacious garden. Were we seriously thinking of buying such a house? Was this the kind of life we were going to have? Was it possible that our life could expand to fill two reception rooms, a spacious kitchen, four bedrooms and an attic "with potential"? The prospect was almost overwhelming.

The toddler began to grizzle and the mother picked her up. I gave the little girl a digestive biscuit and she held it in her fist, not eating but staring at me as if I couldn't be trusted. We're moving to Bristol, said the people who sold us the house, to be near the grandchildren. We've found a very nice bungalow. I'm moving to Scotland, I explained. Oh Scotland, said the young woman brightly, how lovely. It's so beautiful. We went to Aviemore once to learn to ski, but I don't suppose we'll be doing much of that any time soon. And her husband smiled more and shifted the baby against his other shoulder.

When I told Harriet that I had accepted the couple's offer she was standing motionless in the doorway of her room, her back to me. In one hand she held the rag doll that had been her favourite. There were loose threads where the doll's features had been stitched, and one eye was gone. When at last Harriet spoke it was to ask what I intended to do with Lucas's stuff, and with Jake's. There were still things of Jake's in the attic. She turned to look at me, almost accusingly. You can't get rid of Jake's things, she said. I had thought that too, once. But maybe, I said as gently as I could, maybe now was the time. And dad, what about dad? Her voice rose. She stood, one hand on the door frame as if she needed support. I can't keep this house as a mausoleum, I said quietly. I could see she was distressed, but went on to say, Don't you think it's time for a new beginning? It could be the best thing for me.

Harriet looked startled. I thought you would want to stay here. It's our house. I can't imagine it not being our house. You'll be going to a place that dad was never a part of. Yes, I said. Yes, I think that's the point. You want to escape from memories, reminders of dad? No. There's no escape from memories. I just… I searched for the right words. I suppose I just want to be somewhere else. Harriet looked down at the doll she held in her hand and took a deep breath to steady her voice. My God, I thought, I'm being so selfish. You're not going to get rid of everything? I shook my head. Not everything, I said.

What did I keep?

Books. Some of Tim's engineering books. They didn't mean much to me but they were his. Jake's collection of Arthur Ransome, because I'd loved them as a child and he loved them too. I kept the trophy he had won for cross-country running, and letters, not many, he had written to me from university. I kept the picture he'd drawn of his dad when he was seven. We liked it so much we had it framed. I kept most of Tim's tools, although I didn't know what they were all for. The thought of someone else using them disturbed me. In different circumstances I would have given them to Jake or Lucas. The girls took no interest in them, which I regretted because I liked the idea of a daughter following in her father's footsteps. Tim was always a little bemused at their career choices. And photographs. There were several boxes of photographs.

Harriet wandered round the house frowning at the piles of stuff that would go. She took a few things herself, and so did Clare. There's not much space in a railway carriage, I said. Lucas sent emails from Auckland asking for things to be kept. He wanted his dad's favourite chair and Jake's cricket bat. I agreed to put a few things in store, although it seemed unlikely that Tim's chair would ever make the journey to Auckland. I sold the dining table and the six chairs, the Welsh dresser and the large leather sofa, most of the bedroom furniture. Bed linen, clothes, crockery and a stack of board games went to charity shops. I weeded out clothes, my own as well as Tim's and clothes long abandoned by the children. Toys I'd kept for grandchildren to play with went to a local nursery. Bricks and Lego, Jake's electric train, Harriet's farm with all the animals, Lucas's Action Man. Clare hired a car and took away the doll's house Tim had made for the girls. Gradually the house emptied. At the end of each day I looked around as the space grew and felt a deep sense of satisfaction. Not just of satisfaction, of renewal. I hadn't realised the therapeutic value of less stuff. I began to pack the things I was going to take, and as I packed I discarded more. My mother-in-law's pretty Spode tea set. Sherry glasses. Tablecloths and napkins. What use would there be for them in a railway carriage?

Books. I was ruthless with the books. A second-hand bookseller from York came, selected, and gave me a few hundred pounds. They went into cardboard boxes, the books I'd had as a student, most of the books I'd used in my teaching, paperbacks I knew I would never read again, reference books. I watched as the boxes were loaded into a van. The books I was keeping I dusted and packed carefully. At the end of the day my hands were black. One night I came to a halt like a stopped clock. I had not eaten. I was kneeling on the floor with a book in my hand. The book slipped out of my fingers and I sat back on my heels staring at the black window, my mind a blank. I had not drawn the curtains. Anyone passing tall enough to peer over the hedge would have seen a woman kneeling on the floor apparently in a state of deep meditation and surrounded by boxes. I was light-headed, and for a moment when I got to my feet thought I would faint. I grabbed the back of a chair and surveyed the chaos. I could do no more.

In the last week the emptiness expanded and the rooms grew larger, but my world seemed to shrink. I moved from the kitchen, where I ate odd meals, trying to use up the contents of the freezer and ancient tins in my cupboard, to the bedroom which now contained only the bed and a small chest of drawers. I wore the same clothes every day – suitcases were already packed. For days I went without a bath or shower. I was almost too tired to wash my face. The night before the movers came to pick up the few remaining pieces of furniture, the stacked boxes, two trunks and several black bin bags of odds and ends, I sat by the window and looked out into the garden as dusk fell. It was early October. I watched the apricot glow of the sunset and felt, for the first time since I'd set this whole enterprise in motion, a heavy sadness. I'd poured the remains of an elderly bottle of sherry into a mug and sipped it with tears running down my face. I'd stripped the house of almost everything. I'd sold off my old life, thrown away nearly forty years. What are you thinking of, mum? Are you sure you want to do this? Where exactly is this place you're going to? You can't sell the house, you can't, it's our home. My children's voices echoed through the empty rooms and called across the garden as the sunset faded. The football kicked through the open French windows, the paddling pool on the grass in the sunshine. Clare playing Pink Floyd at full blast, Lucas practising the clarinet. Jake shouting, Where are my football boots, and Harriet muttering her lines for the school performance of *Twelfth Night*. You have your own homes now, I said out loud. And Jake. He would have been settled by now. Settled. My father giving me a hug when I told him

Tim and I were going to get married. It will be good to see you settled. Every father wants to see his daughter settled.

I'd shown them on the map. I'd shown them exactly the place I was going to. I'd shown them the road through the Rest and Be Thankful Pass, down Loch Fyneside. The hills, the canal, the shore, the islands, the town. I had taken photographs of the railway carriage hemmed in by brambles and nettles, but these I did not show them.

What are you trying to do, mum? Clare asked. Isn't it a bit late to reinvent yourself? I smiled. You look just like grannie, she said. It's never too late, I said. And who knows how much time I have left? I want to make the most of it. Don't say that, mum. I'm being realistic. It's such an enormous risk. It's an adventure. Are you going to tell me I'm too old for an adventure? No, no, she protested, of course not. There was a pause. But is it the right adventure? We just want to be sure it's right for you, she added a little sententiously. I hugged her. I know you do, love.

The movers arrived at eight. It took them barely an hour to load the van while I filled my car with suitcases, an electric kettle, some basic supplies and a bucket full of cleaning things. I watched the van depart and for a moment wondered if that was the last I would see of its contents. The possibility did not disturb me greatly. I was hardened now to the notion of loss. It was nearly ten when I locked the door. I left the key with the estate agent in Wetherby and drove for seven hours, stopping twice to drink coffee and eat a sandwich. I spent the night again in the Argyll Hotel and was at the railway carriage at nine sharp the next morning. A fine rain was falling and a puddle had gathered at the doorstep. The rhododendron was larger and more intrusive than I remembered. Without its blooms there was something bullying about its encroachment. There were a few wizened brambles clinging to the thorny bushes. When I opened the door the smell of damp and dust greeted me. Cobwebs still hung from the ceiling. It wasn't as if I had expected them miraculously to disappear, but it hadn't seemed so bad in June, in the sunshine, with the purple rhodies blazing alongside. I left the door open and walked through to the far end of the carriage into the second bedroom, then turned and walked back. My footsteps rang on the bare floor. My new domain.

I expected the van at any time. I threw off my jacket and began at once to sweep and dust. The water that ran out of the hot tap was cold and still brownish. I found the electricity meter and with some trepidation pulled down the on switch, then located the immersion heater but it took an hour before the water was even slightly warm and by that time the van had arrived and the unloading had begun. Everything had to be carried through the garden from the front of the big house where the van was parked. I gave the men a large tip. It was clear they thought I was off my rocker. You going to be all right, love? they asked as they pocketed the notes. You going to live here?

I stood by the single-track road and watched the van depart. It passed lock number seven on the canal and the cottage that I would later learn to be Kirstie's. At the bend of the road is another cottage and beyond that, out of sight, a small cluster of houses and a hotel. The little shop and post office which had once been there had long since gone. A pair of mallards puttered on the canal, trailed by a string of half-grown ducklings.

I turned and made my way back through the garden of the big house and down the path to my new home. The movers had piled boxes in the lean-to as there was no space inside. I would have to take them in one at a time to unpack. I gripped the box at the top of the heap, but it was too heavy to lift. It was labelled "kitchen". I opened it and pulled out baking tins. Baking tins? How likely was it that I would bake? I shoved them back into the box and went inside. Suddenly I felt desperately tired. I sat down on the small sofa that had been placed under the windows of my new living room and gazed in bewilderment at two armchairs and a coffee table that seemed not to belong there. It was all beyond comprehension. I had made it all happen but couldn't grasp how. It wasn't real. I had been transported into a strange and unfathomable world.

I don't know how long I sat, pinned to the sofa by some undetectable force, but when my thoughts came into focus again it was getting dark and the chill and damp had seeped through me. I got stiffly to my feet and foraged in a bag I'd dumped in the kitchen for a bottle of wine and a glass carefully wrapped in a tea towel. I was prepared – Tim would have been proud of me. I returned to the sofa with a glass of wine and watched as the last trace of light faded from the sky and darkness blotted out the garden. I wanted Tim to see me. I didn't want him to be there, because this was the start of my new life without him and he had to be banished, but I wanted him to see me, and smile, and say, You're doing a good job, love. You've got a lot of work to do and it will all be different, but keep going. Remember Brighton beach. Yes, we could, and we did. How exotic and unreal the prospect of married life seemed then, and yet we sailed into it regardless. We giggled sometimes as if it were all a joke, a game. Our preparations for the wedding were minimal. I went to London and bought a cream-coloured wool suit in Jaeger's sale, which on the day I wore with red shoes and a scarlet handbag. In the photographs the jacket of Tim's suit looks a little too short in the sleeves.

I poured myself a second glass of wine, knowing that before I drank it I should at least make up the bed. But my limbs were unwilling to be put into action. It took a huge effort of will to stand up and walk to the space that was now my bedroom. The bed stood naked and unappealing. I pulled bedclothes out of a black bin bag and roughly covered it. I returned to my glass of wine. It did not occur to me to eat anything, although I had planned to heat a tin of soup. After the second glass of wine I just had strength enough to dig out pyjamas and fall into bed. I lay awake for a long time, shivering even with a sweater over my pyjamas, until at last I fell asleep. When I woke it was light, the birds were singing, and I was very hungry. I rolled stiffly out of bed and padded barefoot on the cold floor into my new kitchen.

I put the kettle on and stepped outside, disturbing a little coterie of chaffinches that had gathered on the path. They fluttered and flashed away. There was not a sign of human life. The big house stood robust but empty. It was cold but the sun was shining and the sky was almost cloudless. A blackbird was helping himself to the remaining few berries on a rowan tree. I looked down at my bare feet on the mossy stone flag, pale, vulnerable, and not in keeping with this new, strange, northern place.

It took several weeks to put things to rights. I cleaned every inch of the interior and painted the walls. I shifted furniture, warning myself to take care even as I heaved and tugged. If my heart were to stop I wondered how long it would be before I was discovered. The prospect didn't worry me unduly but my limbs ached with all the activity. I unpacked the boxes in the lean-to and carried the contents inside. I made a collection of items I had no space for, or, as I now realised, no need for, and piled them into the car to take to the local charity shop. The books were a problem. There was nothing like enough shelf space, so I stacked the surplus in the second bedroom. The towers of books were still there when my daughter Clare came to stay.

I'd watched my reduced possessions carried from the van into my reduced space. I'd left so much behind, and yet I felt I'd shifted the balance of the scales, a single individual, her boxes of books and crockery, a few pieces of furniture and in a world perspective an infinitesimal shift from south to north, a tiny corrective to the southward flow. My own daughters had released themselves from their Yorkshire upbringing and gone south. But I had come north, continued the journey I had begun when I married but had reconnoitred as a child when every year we set out to drive from Sussex to Edinburgh, through London, the North Circular, the A1, staying overnight at The Swan in Wetherby, no distance at all from where I would spend so many years of my life.

A journey to my mother's country, where as a child I felt they did indeed speak a foreign language. I often found it hard to understand my grandmother and grandfather and the people in the street who greeted my mother, and I noticed that my mother's language changed, that her accent deepened and she used unfamiliar words when she spoke to her parents or her old school friends. She seemed to acquire an extra dimension, which fell away when we returned to the house in the south of England which was the focus of her life. Mairi and Ray were married in an Edinburgh registry office and then took the train to Pitlochry where they spent three nights and climbed Ben Vrackie. At the end of their last day, the sleeper to London and a lunchtime arrival at their new house, the house that five years later would receive a bomb.

Scotland was different, exciting sometimes when we visited the city and walked up the hill to the castle ramparts and looked across at the silver firth and the distant hills, but puzzling. My mother was not the same as other people's mothers. Other people did not make a journey every year across a northern border. Other people did not spend a week of every summer in a place that revolved around the digging of coal and the rumble of coal trains. Other people did not have a grandfather who worked on the railway or a grandmother who let her grandchildren make pancakes on an iron griddle. We took it in turns to drop a spoonful of batter and watch the air bubbles form before we turned each pancake over. It was one of the few things that Miranda and I did together.

Red brick gives way to grey stone. The grass takes on a

different shade of green. The hillsides climb more steeply, the rivers run more swiftly.

We'd drive into Swaledale sometimes, Tim and I and the children when they were small, and walk up to the abandoned lead mines above Gunnerside. The children liked it there. We'd eat our sandwiches beside an old rusted winch and what was left of decaying buildings. Once Jake fell into a stream and we sat on the hillside in the sunshine waiting for his trousers to dry as he pranced around in his underpants. That was before Lucas was born. Jake must have been six or seven. Perhaps Jake's love of high places began then, on that grassy slope, running headlong downhill in his still damp jeans. Or perhaps it was a legacy from his grandparents' mountain romance. Ben Lomond, the beacon. Ben Vrackie, the speckled mountain. But I did not know then the meaning of the mountains' names.

You look down over the dale, the sheep scattered over green grass criss-crossed by stone walls, the river fringed by trees. The solid stone rectangles of field barns. Harriet reaches up her arms to be carried. Tim lifts her on to his shoulders and she squeals and waves both hands in the air. A breeze stirs her fine brown hair. Clare demands to be carried too. But you're a big girl, Harriet's too little to walk very far, but you're a big girl. The corners of Clare's mouth turn down. I picture the dales always green, dotted with white, newly shorn sheep, and lit by gentle sunlight. As we regain the road a gang of rooks breaks away from the trees and swirls blackly above us. We have promised that we'll stop for fish and chips on the way home.

I was painting the surviving stretch of carriage corridor when there was a knock on the door. A young-looking woman with a thick mane of reddish curls and clear grey eyes was on the doorstep. She smiled. I thought I'd come and say hello, she said. I'm Kirstie, your nearest neighbour. I can see you're busy – I had a brush in my hand and paint on my fingernails – but why don't you come over for a cup of tea sometime? But I invited her in, there and then. She looked so pleasant, smiling, friendly. You've made it really nice, she said as she settled into a chair with a mug of tea. It's transformed. I used to peer in the windows sometimes. I rather fancied it myself, to be honest, but with two growing girls it was a non-starter. I could imagine myself living here though.

The damp was obliterated by the smell of fresh paint and of the wood burning in the stove. I smiled. Kirstie was my first visitor, and wonderfully said what I wanted someone to say. I looked around at the bright cream walls. I need to make curtains, I said. She replied, Do you have a sewing machine? I shook my head. You can borrow mine. You'll probably have to go to Oban for fabric but I know a good place there. I'll come with you if you like. And she did. We went in her car with her two daughters in the back, both silently plugged in to their MP3 players. Ellie was about to be thirteen. Jess was eleven and had her mother's thick, copper-tinged hair.

At the end of November I phoned Clare on my mobile, standing out in the road to get a signal, and suggested that she spend Christmas with me. But she had already accepted an invitation from friends in Shropshire. I'll come for Easter, she said. I phoned Harriet. Perhaps she and her partner Matthew would like to come? It's an awfully long way, she said doubtfully, an awfully long drive in the middle of winter. I suppose it is, I conceded reluctantly. But we'll come in the summer, she said quickly, that would be lovely. We'll come in the summer for a nice long visit.

A few days later I ran into Kirstie in the Co-op. She invited me for Christmas dinner and I accepted. We sat in her kitchen and ate roast duck as the darkness closed in. Afterwards the four of us cleared the table and washed the dishes, then sat down again and played Cluedo. I didn't have the dogs then. Kirstie wanted to walk me home, but I had my torch and insisted I was fine on my own. It was a clear, cold night with stars scattered across the blue-black sky. It wasn't late, but there was no one else on the narrow road. As I walked it was as if I was drawing a thread between two small islands of human existence. The big house loomed dark and empty. I was glad I'd left a light on in my railway carriage, a beacon to guide my return.

Last night it snowed. I woke to the garden smoothly white. When I let the dogs out they dig their noses into the snow and run round in excited circles, leaving erratic trails of prints. Later, there are my own prints crossing the garden and returning. In the early evening, as dusk is falling, it snows again and soon all the prints are gone.

1954

On her tenth birthday Sonia Letford had half a dozen friends for tea. All girls, they arrived in party dresses and played games before sitting down to sandwiches and cake and jelly and ice cream. Her mother had made red and yellow jellies in individual fluted moulds. Sonia's sister Miranda was thirteen and considered herself too old to take part except as an organiser. She regarded Sonia with a critical eye. In her pink party dress she looked even more gawky than usual, her legs thin, her wrists bony. Miranda had her father's glossy brown hair and long lashes and was proud of her burgeoning curves. And she was clever, top of her class in most subjects. She had already announced, shortly after having her tonsils out, that she intended to be a surgeon, scornful when the response was, perhaps a nurse, dear. When her attempts to boss the younger girls made no impression she retired to her room, but came back downstairs when it was time for tea. She didn't sit at the table but hovered and passed plates with an air of superiority, helping herself as she did so. When the younger girls had left the table she sat down with her mother and drank tea.

When Raymond Letford got home from work he wrapped his younger daughter in an almost suffocating bear hug, told her she looked beautiful in her pink dress, and sat down at the piano and played and sang "My Darling Clementine" and "She'll Be Coming Round the Mountain". The girls, apart from Miranda, all joined in. Mairi sang too, as she washed up in the kitchen. Now her younger daughter was ten. It didn't seem possible.

Sonia would not have another birthday party like it. The next year she was at grammar school and the pattern of friendship changed. No one had parties any more. A birthday outing to the pictures with a few select friends was more acceptable.

Sonia's best friend in primary school was a small, curly-haired girl called Wendy, an only child whose father commuted to London every day and whose mother worked in a local bank. She was the only working mother Sonia knew, although a few of the girls had mothers who worked in the local Boots or Sainsbury's, and one mother had been an ambulance driver during the war. Sonia and Wendy made up elaborate stories about a fictitious family of ten children and numerous horses and dogs. In this family they were twins, Wendy a boy, Sonia a girl, and as the eldest of the siblings led the troop of children and animals into all kinds of adventures. They galloped imaginary ponies through the patch of woodland at the back of the house. They broke up gangs of criminals and rescued wounded and abandoned creatures. Wendy often came to Sonia's house after school, as her mother didn't return from work until after five o'clock. Mairi felt sorry for her, but in fact she was a cheerful child and always polite. She liked to help in the kitchen, and once Mairi and the two girls spent a Saturday afternoon baking empire biscuits. The best bit was spreading the jam and the icing and topping each one with a glacé cherry. Wendy had never heard of empire biscuits. Sonia and Wendy also made up a secret code in which they communicated to each other, often sitting side by side on the sofa writing elaborate messages which they then exchanged and painstakingly deciphered. On one occasion they got into trouble at school for passing each other incomprehensible notes. Ray Letford laughed and laughed when he was told about the episode.

Sonia was also friendly with Vivien, whose father had been killed in North Africa. Vivien lived with her grandparents and was rather vague about the whereabouts of her mother. She had a much older brother who was a policeman. Vivien's grandparents ran the local hardware store and lived above the shop. Sonia was allowed to ride her bike to the shop, which was useful as Vivien's grandfather was good at adjusting brakes and mending punctures. The shop seemed to overflow into the flat upstairs and there was always something interesting to look at. Vivien's grandfather would often be sitting at the kitchen table with something in pieces in front of him.

Sonia passed the eleven-plus and went to the local grammar school, but Wendy was sent to boarding school. For a term or two Sonia and Wendy wrote each other letters in code, and during the first Christmas holiday Sonia was invited to spend the day at Wendy's house. After lunch Wendy's father taught Sonia how to play backgammon. Wendy was full of stories of girls with exotic names and eccentric teachers and goings-on in the dorm. But gradually the coded letters petered out. Wendy had new friends to stay during the holidays, or went off to stay with them. When Sonia said to her parents that she wished she could go to boarding school her mother was shocked and her father put an arm around her and said, But think how much we'd miss you, love.

Vivien did not pass the eleven-plus so she too went to a different school. For a while the two girls continued to see each other. Vivien would turn up sometimes at the Letford house, always unannounced, and sometimes, if she was in that part of town, perhaps on an errand for her mother, Sonia would look in at the hardware shop and she and Vivien would take their bikes to the park. But after a few months they saw less and less of each other. We don't see much of Vivien these days, Mairi commented, who'd have thought that schools would make such a difference? But she knew they did. She knew that schools had always made a difference. She herself had won a bursary to George Watson's Ladies' College. Her school blazer made her conspicuous on the village streets and she hated the walk from the bus stop to the cramped terrace where she lived with her parents and older brother.

At Sonia's school there was a group of girls who had ponies, and Sonia hovered on their margins. Eventually she was allowed into their horsey games because she came up with good ideas. For her eleventh birthday her parents gave her money for riding lessons, and she liked to pretend that her favourite pony at the stables was her own. It was a brown pony with black mane and tail and a rather ungainly long back, but he was lively and could jump, unlike some of the animals who had to be kicked into a canter and could hardly haul themselves over a pole laid on the ground. But she could never really belong with the pony-owning girls who were members of the Pony Club and went to gymkhanas. They were quite nice to her when it occurred to them, but she was never invited to visit their homes or to have a shot on their ponies. She would watch and hope as they cantered figures of eight in a muddy field, but she was of no significance to them. Without a horse she was, most of the time, invisible.

Miranda wasn't the least bit interested in horses. She regarded her younger sister's enthusiasm with condescension occasionally spiced with contempt, but Sonia was used to Miranda's disdain. It had always been there, from earliest consciousness. It seemed as natural as her father's geniality and her mother's quieter but sometimes distracted love.

45

Sonia knew she would never have a pony of her own. She knew that however deeply you longed for something, it would not necessarily be yours. No one told her that. She worked it out for herself. We're so lucky, her mother would say sometimes, we're so lucky to be all of us together. We could have been killed, Miranda would add sententiously, we could all have been killed, even you Sonia, before you were born. And dad could have been shot down, and that would have been the end of that. Sonia looked at her sister propped against the kitchen sink in a flowered circular skirt and her hair loose and luxuriant. But we weren't, she said. Oh don't be so literal-minded, Miranda said scornfully. Don't you have any imagination? Why would I want to imagine us all dead? Well, we will all be dead one day, and Miranda swung out of the room. Don't mind your sister, said Mairi, but Sonia sagged on to a chair and thought how hopeless and unfair it was, having a big sister who was beautiful and brainy and always managed to have the last word.

Miranda was nearly fifteen. She had discovered anthropology and had given up the idea of becoming a surgeon. Sonia sometimes wondered if it was necessary to become anything. She rather hoped it wasn't, as she had no idea what it was she wanted to be. After all, her mother wasn't anything. Wendy was going to be a nurse, she said, and Vivien was going to take over the shop. Sonia couldn't follow her father as a wine merchant because she was a girl. The pony-owning girls were going to be showjumpers or vets. Without a horse, there was no hope of becoming a showjumper, and probably little chance of becoming a vet either. Do you want to be a vet? Vivian asked doubtfully. Not really.

You go for it, Raymond Letford said to his elder daughter. You're a clever girl. Your teachers say you could aim for Oxford. You go for it. And Mairi looked up from her book and smiled her agreement. Yes, pet, she said, you make good use of that brain of yours.

On the day rationing ended, 4 July 1954, Ray Letford's

father Norman had a stroke. He had been reluctant to give up his shop, although his son was eager to take over, and his only concession to age was sometimes to go home early and sit in the lounge dozing over *The Times*. He still made an annual trip to vineyards in France and Germany, sometimes Italy, taking Ray with him. On these trips his energy and alertness returned. It was shortly after getting back from that year's trip that he collapsed. Now he needed help with everything. Half his face had slumped and his speech was slurred. At weekends Ray took his father out for a run in the car and the girls took turns to accompany him. They drove to the Downs, sometimes as far as the coast. Each time Norman would say very little about the passing scenery, but worried about squandering petrol although petrol rationing had ended four years earlier. Sonia found it hard to understand what he was saying.

They would find a place to have tea and help the old man out of the car and into the tea shop. It was an embarrassment for Sonia, the fuss, the effort to guide her grandfather past tables and chairs and people's feet, the stares as Norman Letford tried to lift his teacup with a trembling hand. Ray leant forward to wipe drips and crumbs from his father's shirt, clean on that morning, and neat tie, and Sonia wondered how he could be so matter-of-fact. She dreaded the Sundays that were her turn. Sometimes Miranda successfully argued that she had homework to do so Sonia had to take her place. Miranda's schoolwork was always a priority. Sometimes her mother insisted that Sonia accompany her when she went round to give her mother-in-law a hand. Grace Letford was too thin. Anxiety seemed to have stripped away her once substantial flesh. Sonia did not like to look at her sharp wrists and stringy neck. Old age was horrible. Surely her own mother and father would never become like grannie and granddad. Surely they would never mumble and shake and spill food and need two hands to lift the teapot.

Later that year Mairi's mother died of cancer. Her father now lived in their council house alone. He manages wonderfully well, Mairi would say if anyone asked. Two or three times a year she took the train to London, the tube from Victoria to King's Cross, another train to Edinburgh, to spend a few days with him. When the whole family came on their annual visit he dusted the bedrooms and made up the beds, and cooked mince and tatties or his speciality, ham and haddie with a poached egg. In the kitchen he was slow and methodical, assembling everything he needed before he lit the gas. The fish on one plate, bacon rashers on another, eggs in a bowl. Every morning he set out for the messages with a list and a string bag and came back with the *News Chronicle* and whatever else was necessary – bread, onions, a pound of shin of beef so Mairi could make a stew. Sonia would accompany him on his daily expedition, reassured that although there was always a smell of stale tobacco and of something slightly sour which she could not identify he walked briskly and when he poured boiling water into the brown teapot he lifted the large kettle with one hand. The sleeve of his jacket was rather greasy.

Ray Letford took his father-in-law into town to arrange the rental of a television set. What do I want with a TV? he grumbled. I like the radio. But when the television set arrived and Ray triumphantly switched it on he was enthralled. He delightedly watched *Para Handy* and *The White Heather Club*.

He no longer took his two granddaughters on the tram all the way to Corstorphine to go to the zoo. Even Miranda, until she became a teenager, liked the zoo, although she complained about the uphill walk to the top where the zebras and antelope were. He no longer took them to Waverley Station to get on a train and cross the great bridge to the Kingdom of Fife (how grand it sounded) with the ferries moving on the water far below, and on to Aberdour. It was a long walk down to the beach, and a long walk back again. In an old canvas knapsack he carried a flask of tea and sardine sandwiches wrapped in greaseproof paper.

With her tenth birthday passed Sonia had before her the prospect of the eleven-plus. Miranda had sailed through. With Sonia it was perhaps touch-and-go. Just do your best, love, her father said, but privately he thought it a shame that his elder daughter was so clever and promising to be so pretty, while his younger daughter was not so bright and looked as if she would always be awkward. It doesn't bother me that she's not academic, he would say to his wife, but Mairi Letford saw herself in Sonia. She saw an incipient elegance in the long limbs and high cheekbones and a thoughtfulness in the blue-grey eyes. Mairi Ewing had collected a very respectable degree from the University of Edinburgh and her husband admired her intelligence. Her parents were proud of her. Aye, they would say, she'll be a teacher mebbe. A teacher! Sometimes she wondered if she might find employment somewhere but she never did, although she helped with her husband's paperwork. She sat at the dining room table with her reading glasses on and a slight frown and a pencil in her hand as she checked columns of figures. She enjoyed it, and he said he could not manage without her.

Throughout Sonia's childhood there was a photograph on the top of the upright piano. It showed Raymond and Mairi Letford on their wedding day. She is wearing a dark calf-length dress and a flowery hat, and is carrying more flowers. Her smile is thoughtful. He wears a dark suit and a white shirt. His thick hair is swept back and he is grinning. Beside the photograph are pictures of their two daughters, as infants, then the two of them together in a photographer's studio, in their best clothes and each holding a doll. Then in school uniform. In every picture the contrast is striking.

Sometimes Sonia held up both hands and examined them. They are my hands, she would think, but how do I know they are mine? What makes them do what I want them to do? How do I know I am me? Suppose there was a mistake and I am really someone else? Suppose Miranda isn't really my sister? Supposing I don't have a sister? Suppose I actually have a brother who got separated from mum and dad in the war and doesn't know he has a family? All the things that are part of me may be not me at all. The front door when I open it and go into the hallway. My mother in the kitchen. My father holding a glass of wine to his nose, his rather loud voice, My girls, where are my girls? Maybe we aren't his girls. Maybe Miranda is his girl but I'm not. Miranda must be his girl because she looks like him. Her mother looking up from the cash book, removing her spectacles, smiling, Peel some potatoes, pet, will you? Sonia regarded her hands as if they were not attached to her at all. My body is not me. The real me has nothing to do with these odd white limbs that propel me from place to place and handle objects, books, pens, dishes, the potato peeler. The real me is somewhere inside, with my heartbeat, or in my head. Where in my head? And she'd shut her eyes and try to focus on a place deep within, a mysterious essence which she could never locate however intensely she tried. Sometimes she tried so hard it hurt.

She's very like you, Grace Letford often said to Mairi with a slight hint of disapproval. But Sonia thought her mother was beautiful. She often wore trousers, which showed off her smooth slim hips. Sonia did not think that she herself would ever be like her mother, who sometimes put her arms around both her daughters and said, We're all war babies, and she would laugh quietly. War babies are special. But she spoke sometimes of her Uncle John who died in the year she was born, and of her brother Donald. We're lucky, she'd say. None of us died in the war. We were bombed though, mum, Miranda would say. I was bombed. I remember. Do you, pet? Was it dreadful for you? But the thing is, we all survived, didn't we? Dad came back without a scratch. Not everyone was so lucky. We could have died, though,

Miranda said, almost resentfully, as if to have survived was in some way a cheat, as if the possibility of death was a badge of honour.

Miranda considered herself more of a war baby than Sonia. Sonia had not been bombed. Sometimes Sonia wished she had been born just a few months earlier. She wished that she too could say, I was bombed, I remember. But then she would think, I was bombed, actually. I did exist when we were bombed. Otherwise Miranda couldn't say that I could have been killed before I was born. You have to exist before you can die. But she understood that Miranda liked to talk about death. Even when she was quite small she would say to visitors, Our house was bombed. Mummy had broken glass all over her and she could have been killed. And then she would widen her deep brown eyes and add, *I* could have been killed. Sonia wasn't born yet – she can't remember the bomb. It was Miranda's trump card. Memory wins. Sonia was excluded from the club of we were bombed.

Well, double figures, Ray said to Sonia on her tenth birthday. Two daughters into double figures. Soon I'll have two teenagers – what a terrible thought. Next thing, you'll be wanting boyfriends and lipstick. He rolled his eyes. Think of that! Mairi, are we going to let our daughters go out with boys? And Mairi laughed and said, If I hadn't gone out with boys I'd not have met you. And I'd have married somebody else and you girls wouldn't exist, he said. I might have had a load of boys instead. I suppose you'd have preferred that, said Miranda coldly. No, no, boys are nothing but trouble. Give me girls any day. And Sonia, who with some relief had changed out of her party dress which was scratchy round the neck, tried to imagine not existing. Never being born. Or bombed as a baby, which was almost the same thing. Did Miranda have similar thoughts? If she were to ask she'd get a scathing reply. Perhaps one day she would ask her mother, who was sitting with an open book on her lap, not reading but smiling her quiet smile. She was tired. A dozen ten-year-olds romping around the house. It was a relief to sit down with a book, even if she did not read. There were many things Sonia intended to ask her mother, but for most the right moment never came. Then it was too late.

Sonia went upstairs to her small bedroom. There was a bed with a candlewick bedspread, a chest of drawers and a bookcase. Miranda had her own desk but Sonia did her homework at the dining room table, sometimes alongside her mother with the accounts. The family only ate in the dining room on special occasions so Sonia could leave her schoolbooks spread about. Sometimes at the other end of the table there would be a jigsaw, and Mairi would leave the accounts and work away at it while Sonia finished a fractions exercise or wrote a composition. Imagine an island, Miss Mitchell had said. Sand, cliffs, a hill, palm trees. Imagine being cast away on that island. Coconuts, fish, birds. Sonia carefully explained how she would fashion a bow and splice splinters of stone on to arrow shafts. She would make a fishing line from the hair of a wild goat and fish hooks from bone. She would throw sticks at the coconuts to bring them to the ground. She would build a shelter out of branches. She would need a knife. A pony on the island was not likely, but there might be a dog, left behind when a ship called in for water. A dog would be useful.

For Christmas that year Sonia received a pair of jodhpurs, a Pony Club annual and riding gloves. By the end of the day she had read the annual from cover to cover. She saved her pocket money for extra riding lessons. She was learning to jump on Teddy, the brown pony. He had a thick rough winter coat and when she laid her cheek against it she breathed in his horsey, leathery, earthy smell. One day Teddy, who usually flew over the two-foot jumps, inexplicably swerved and deposited Sonia on the muddy ground. It was the only time she fell off in her brief horse-riding career. She was quite proud of the bruise on her shoulder, which took a long time to fade.

March 2014

March is drawing to a close. There was a frost this morning, but the sun was warm and the frost soon vanished. By midday it was warm enough to be out without my woolly hat and gloves. The dogs and I walked as usual beside the canal's brown water into the town. In almost every garden the daffodils are out and the tulips beginning. There is blossom out too, and green buds. It's good to see the colour returning. I realise I am a little weary of the muted browns and smoky greens of winter, although they contain such variety.

It's not been a bad winter, very little snow, but age makes the cold wind harder to bear. It used to annoy me that Tim's mother always had the heating turned on high, but now I understand. To get out of bed into the cold is hard. If I put a lump of peat on the fire last thing at night there is still a welcome heat when I get up in the morning. I have learnt by trial and error how to deal with my little stove, but sometimes the smoke leaks out, and there is a perpetual thin film of ash on all the furniture.

On wet days I sometimes don't go into the town, even if it means running out of milk or bread. Then I fall back on oatcakes and peppermint tea. But today is beautiful, the birds singing, sparrows diving in and out of hedges, an unafraid blackbird foraging in dead leaves beside the path. At the top of the main street I look down across the loch, rippled by a light wind. There is still a messy fringe of weed and plastic left by winter storms that drove the tide high on to the grass.

I go to the fish shop and the baker. On the way back a yacht chugs slowly past us, flying a Greek flag. It's early in the year for traffic on the canal, especially a boat all the way from Greece. There must still be people in Greece who can afford expensive yachts.

I spend the afternoon in the garden. The grass has started to grow. There are hillocks of dead leaves and the dried remnants of last year's summer plants. There's enough warmth in the sun to be out without my jacket, digging the vegetable patch and pulling the last of the beetroot and parsnips. The dogs mooch around as I work, sniffing in corners, the collie digging his own holes in bursts of furious activity. The rhubarb is through, nakedly pink, and the lilac is beginning to show pale green buds. The slow rhythm of the work is almost like meditation and thought drifts in a pleasantly unfocused way.

I am in the garden for nearly two hours, digging and weeding and clearing paths, but my legs are aching now. If I bend and crouch too much I get a sharp pain in my right thigh. I go inside to make tea, and sit at the window with my mug in both hands. Sometimes I sit for as long as an hour staring through the glass but seeing nothing beyond the images inside my head. Tim will be there, and Jake, my mother's smile, my father's voice, a tune on the piano, all so nearly tangible yet phantoms. "Swing Low, Sweet Chariot" – that was a favourite song and we always let my father sing the first verse on his own in his gravelly baritone before my mother's light contralto and Miranda and I joined in. The pain of their nearness is baffling. My sister turns away. She did not always tolerate the singing. She keeps her distance now as she always did. Her rich dark hair falls over her shoulder but I cannot see her face. Is it the face as I last saw it? Her luxuriant hair was reduced to short, wispy fronds when I saw her that last time.

I look down at the mug in my hands, half-full of luke-warm tea. When I am very old, it will be like this perhaps, reduced to immobility, the heat turned up, memory floating, senses eroded, with all that lies beyond the window's glass unreachable. Colour, the fresh green, the bright yellow of daffodils, tulips just showing a purple edge, my only connection with spring, all life worth the name happening

54

elsewhere. How will it be when my mind is content, or per-haps not content, with blurred reverie, and if I have visitors will I remember who they are? Will Kirstie and her daugh-ters come? I must keep moving. I must do more before the arrival of that ominous threescore years and ten. My aching legs and that twinge in my back must be ignored. When I am very old, will I be here between these walls? Will I ever be very old? It's not something I relish, but the alterna-tive is death. I don't relish that either. Even in a very small world colours and birdsong are a source of pleasure.

Clare has been on the phone. We'll do something for your seventieth, she says. There's no need, I say, it's just another birthday. Harriet and I thought we would take you for a weekend break somewhere. Where would you like to go? Nowhere, I say, knowing that it sounds ungrateful, even truculent. I don't want to go anywhere. And anyway, I have to be here on the eighteenth. Why? Clare sounds irritated. I have to be here to vote. Vote? There isn't an election coming up, is there? The referendum. Oh, right, of course, so it's on your birthday? Well, get a postal vote. You don't have to do it in person. I don't reply. I don't want a weekend break, I don't want to go anywhere. I don't want to get a postal vote, I want to slip the little piece of paper into the ballot box in person. And yet I'm touched. My daughters want to give me a holiday. Perhaps I should let them do that. So, Clare asks, how are you going to vote? I don't know, I say. It can't be that important if you haven't made up your mind. I have six months to think about it, I say, there's plenty of time. I half expect Clare to say, But any-thing can happen in six months, but of course she doesn't. And of course it can.

My first spring here I still had the car and had not yet acquired a dog. The evenings grew lighter and longer, and I often went out late, sometimes just into the garden, some-times a little further, to watch the last glow fade in the sky. One night in June a decision took shape which had been lurking in the margins of my mind for a long time, and two days later I set off and drove north to Oban, where I'd been a few times to go to the big supermarket and wander by the harbour, and once with Kirstie for curtain material. This time I didn't stop but continued on an unfamiliar road. I followed the shore of Loch Linnhe and on through Fort William. Away to my right were the Glencoe mountains and Ben Nevis. I had photographs of Jake on the summits of mountains which became familiar names – Aonach Eagach, Aonach Mor and Aonach Beag, steep ridges, big and little – and although I could hardly imagine the pleasure they gave him I liked to listen as he talked, and was amazed at how easily these names rolled off his tongue. My great-grandmother was a Gaèlic speaker, my grannie told me. She knew no English when she first came to the city. There was one mountain, though, whose name I never heard from Jake.

On through the Great Glen and then west. I spent the night at Kyle of Lochalsh and thought about crossing to Skye. But he never tackled the Cuillin. He talked about it. He remembered seeing as a small boy the looming mass of mountain dark against a sky blue one minute, muffled with cloud the next. He remembered the sudden rain and pulling over his hands the sleeves of the orange cagoule that was too big for him. He remembered wading through burns in his wellies. Another time for Skye, I thought, another time for happy families. So on north to Lochcarron and into a landscape of grim scoured heaps of rock still streaked with snow. I stopped somewhere near the shore of Loch Torridon. I ate half a bar of chocolate and spent a long time staring out into the water, which on that day was a deep, mesmerising blue.

I knew I had to go yet further north but I was finding it hard. Water seemed more friendly than mountains. I was unwilling to turn away and get back into the car, and when at last I did I sat for a long time with my hands on the steering wheel and the window down listening to the sound of the ripples at the water's edge. But whatever the reluctance, whatever the invisible barrier, there was a pull.

More names came to me as I followed the road east and on through Glen Torridon. The huge sandstone ramparts of Liathach bulked ahead, impossibly steep surely, with the fingers of snow glinting in the sunlight, yet I remembered so clearly Jake's excitement as he described the climb, the narrow ridges linking the summits, the total, bone-crushing weariness at the end of the day, the triumph. Liathach, mum. I could hear his voice. You need to go there one day. Forget Ben Nevis. Liathach, the grey one, is the mountain of mountains. And here I was. I wanted this to be Jake's mountain, his memorial because it seemed to contain his voice, but it wasn't, it couldn't be.

I stopped the car. From where I was I could see no track, no possible route up the formidable rock. Yet I knew that he and his friends had climbed it – was it at the end of his first university year? And was it coming down Liathach that the cloud came suddenly and wrapped itself around them so they nearly lost the path and each other? Or was that another, perhaps less daunting mountain where it was still all too easy to lose your way? His voice, earnest. That's what people don't realise. It's easy to die on a little hill if you don't take care. But don't worry, mum. I'm careful. All serious climbers are careful. It's the amateurs, the strollers, who go for a wander up a mountain on a sunny afternoon without proper equipment, who get into trouble. You really don't need to worry.

I believed him. I worried a little, sometimes, and I was always relieved to get a phone call to tell me he was safely down from another summit. But I saw his boots and ice axe and his first-aid kit and I believed him.

At Kinlochewe I turned to follow the long arm of mysterious Loch Maree. They'd climbed Beinn Eighe too, now looming above me. The sky had darkened and the ancient rock seemed heavy with menace. The far side of the loch was dominated by another great slab of mountain. I stopped the car again and walked down to the edge of the water. There was no wind. The water stretched to the far shore without a ripple, almost black. I'd read somewhere that there were kelpies in Loch Maree and I imagined their ears and nostrils lifting out of the water, their heads and necks and a long tangle of manes. I walked through tall pines on a carpet of pine needles that silenced my footfall.

We sat round the table in our Yorkshire kitchen and listened to Jake's mountain tales. His siblings pretended indifference, but I knew that they liked to hear him. He was a good storyteller. Tim and I would exchange looks. He's dramatising, our looks would say, our mountain boy is hamming it up. It's not the Himalayas he's talking about here. It's only Scotland. But we'd seen the Cuillin, we'd seen the way a mountain darkens the water it towers above. We'd seen our little troop of children diminished by the scale of height and emptiness.

I stopped at Gairloch and found a bed and breakfast. That evening I walked on the beach and was caught in a sudden squall and shower of rain, but when the rain cleared everything was very still, the freshened air, the water. A few moored boats hardly moved. The sun set, a fierce but blurred red. The next morning Mrs Mackenzie gave me two boiled eggs from her own hens and home-made oatcakes.

I walked out to the car in soft, moist air and drove on under a silvery grey sky, climbing over the moors, summits stretching on either side, to Loch Ewe and past the pink sands of Gruinard Bay. Then I was driving alongside Little Loch Broom and the sun came out. We'd found it on the map, Tim and I. We had to force ourselves to look, but there was something pleasing, even comforting about the loch's name and we did not want to move our eyes from the finger of blue. The mountain itself suggested nothing of comfort. When its jagged ridge appeared my hands tightened on the steering wheel. At Dundonnell I pulled into a lay-by. There was one other car, a white Toyota. On a weekday in June someone was perhaps somewhere on the mountain's creviced flank.

I'm not sure how long I sat in the car alongside the peaceful loch before I made a move, and I'm not sure how I came to be on the track that led towards An Teallach. But I did walk along it in warm sunshine, the air filled with the smell of broom, wheatears flitting just out of range. There was a scattering of tormentil, like yellow confetti. Through the thin soles of my not very robust trainers I could feel the hardness of the ground. There were stretches of muddy path which showed recent boot prints. I felt foolishly ill-equipped and hoped I would not meet serious walkers with rucksacks and climbing boots. I knew I could not go far, but there was An Teallach's massive spiny back lit by the sun and at the same time almost unreal, like a mirage. An Teallach, the anvil. It might have refashioned my son.

I walked for about a mile and then sat on a lump of smooth warm rock. I stared and stared at the mountain. It seemed astonishingly new, as if its wildness were freshly minted for my eyes, but I knew it was old and savage. I did not want to look at that terrible jagged edge, but had to. With binoculars I might have seen some tiny figure, black against the vivid blue of the sky, but I saw no human life.

For years I had thought about coming to An Teallach, but Tim would not do it. We'd all climbed Scafell once, the only time the whole family had climbed together, but I wouldn't be climbing any mountains now. The little hills near my new home had to be enough. This was as far as my pilgrimage would take me. I got up stiffly from my warm rock and made my way back to the road, my thigh muscles resisting being on the move again. The white Toyota was gone.

In a kind of dream I followed the road to Inverness, an incongruous city with Boots and Marks & Spencer and Tesco, in a place where, I felt, there should not be a city, where the landscape and the open sky surely should deny streets and shops and car parks. But I parked my car and bought a sandwich in Marks & Spencer and sat by the river to eat it. I had been on the road for only a few days but it seemed a lifetime. And in a sense it was. In a sense I had travelled for all the years since Jake climbed his last mountain. I felt worn out, as if I had been constantly on the move. I felt that my daily existence had no relevance. The journey had begun – where? When I left my Yorkshire home a year ago, not knowing where I was going? When I set eyes on the railway carriage? Or way back, in the hallway of our red brick house with the telephone in my hand? When Tim Billings appeared on a stretch of tarmac somewhere between Reading and Slough? Or when Raymond Letford tramped up the last few yards to the summit of Ben Lomond and was delighted by a young woman smiling as the wind lifted her hair? What had driven me to leave a place of warmth and happiness, a place of love and protection, where my children had grown up, where my eldest child had sat in the kitchen and talked of mountains with his peat-brown eyes shining? I sat by the River Ness eating a sandwich as if that was what it had all led to, my journey's end.

I joined the heavy traffic on the A9 and headed south. I noted the hospital sign. I had not gone to the hospital. I had stayed at home with my younger children. My younger children needed me, and I needed them. They were all in the car with me when I drove Tim to York to get on the train north. We stood in the station concourse, a tight little group, Clare clutching my arm, Lucas watching his father walk away from us, his face swamped in bewilderment. When I saw Harriet's tears I couldn't stop my own. The compound of grief and guilt – to let Tim go alone – was so crushing a burden that I could scarcely believe the blood still flowed in my veins. The four of us stood like statues long after Tim had vanished, while the flow of people parted round us as they went about their business.

Now it was done. I could go home now. Wherever the journey had begun, now it was completed, and I had no doubt, as I forked right and on through Glen Spean, where home was, a home of my choice and my making, however accidental the choice had been.

Tim would have balanced the pros and cons. Okay, he says, you want a new direction, a new life. That's fine – but don't forget that relocation won't change who you are. What will you gain and what will you lose? A new environment, new friends perhaps, new interests. And on the debit side, old friends, security, familiarity. You'll be further from your children and will almost certainly see less of them. Tim was remarkably silent when my decision was made, though it was less a decision than a compulsion, but then, driving home, I heard him clearly. Is it Jake or your mother that's drawn you to Scotland? he asks. But it's not an either-or, I reply indignantly. At the same time, I knew Tim really wanted to know. Tim always wanted to know. He wanted clear answers to straightforward questions. He wanted unequivocal statements. We could get married. That was a real possibility. And we did get married. That was a fact. We stayed married for more than forty years. Man and wife. He still really wants to know.

I hear him now. Well, love, you're going to have to vote in six months' time. And I know you will vote, because you always do. So give it some thought. This is important. Whatever changes Scotland is going to change the whole country. You do realise that, don't you?

My reinvention as the old woman of the railway carriage might compel me to vote for Scotland's independence, to confirm a rediscovered identity. I hold to the land of my mother's birth, the land whose mountains my son chose. Yet in the twenty-first century to draw a firmer line on the map, a blacker line... You're in a different country now, girls. But I prefer to blur distinctions. I have chosen to live a long way from my daughters but I do not wish to increase

61

the distance. They already feel I am too far away. Yet here I am, no going back (but they would protest – Why not, what's stopping you?). However it happened, I have chosen to make my home in the Highlands of Scotland, not in a city where I can pretend to be cosmopolitan, expand my Yorkshire clipped wings. I should, perhaps, be ready to throw in my lot with the possibility of an invigorated, perhaps even fairer, society. That's what some say. The achievement of a fairer society in Scotland will benefit everyone. Tim is right. I will vote, I've never not voted, but how I will choose is another matter. Some might say that my past record on decision-making is not impressive. Not that I've made bad decisions, rather, I've allowed them to happen without much help from me. Even the decision to come here.

You're not Scottish, says Clare, not really. I agree. Though in another time and another place I would not have been able to escape my mother's identity, and after all my great-grandmother was a Gaelic speaker. But I live in Scotland, I say to Clare, that's what counts. Do you *feel* Scottish, mum? No, I say. I feel... But I stop, because I am not sure I can explain to my daughter how or what I feel. It is as if those detached limbs I contemplated as a child have been restored to me. I am myself now, occupying my own space. The space moves with me, changes shape, changes size. Fortunately civil society has devised other ways of determining the right to vote. Unlike prisoners, strangers who pay their taxes are allowed to have a say. Think of all those people, Clare says, born in Scotland and now living somewhere else who can't influence the future of their own country. Yes, I say, but they have chosen to go and I have chosen to come. Maybe they had no choice. Maybe, but I had a choice. This is where I am now, and irrespective of how I am labelled I have a vote. I hear at the other end of the telephone an exasperated sigh.

I have a vote, but that is not the same as having the means to make a decision. I know I am not, really, a part of this place. I know that however content I am, I never will be.

Two years ago I left the dogs with Kirstie and went to London. The bus took me to Glasgow, retracing part of the route that had brought me to my new home, and then the train took me south and the hills and stone walls gave way to red brick and mock Tudor and neat hedges and untidy dumping grounds. I sat on the tube from Euston to Kennington clutching my small case between my knees, struggling to breathe, struggling to convince myself that I was not alien, that I could speak the language, that I did not have to study the A to Z to remind myself of how to get to Clare's street.

I got to the surface of the earth in a swirl of bodies and confidently set off, pulling my little wheelie case behind me, bumping over the cracked pavement, breathing in the clotted London air, but there was no familiarity. It had been three years since I'd been in London, since I'd last stayed with my elder daughter, but it was important that I did not hesitate. I did not wish to expose myself as an outsider. It began to rain. Was I going in the right direction? I stopped under a café awning where people were sitting outside smoking with coffee cups and wine glasses in front of them. I gave in and pulled my A to Z out of my bag and glanced around. No one paid me any attention as I surreptitiously peered at the open page. All I could see was a blur of lines and tiny print. I had to fish in my bag for my reading glasses which made the crowded page slightly more legible. It took several minutes to find Clare's street – second on the left, but it was further than I remembered. A tiny upstairs flat. I would be sleeping in Clare's bedroom while she took the sofa. When she opened the door she had her jacket on. I'm only just in, she said. She embraced me and kissed my cheek. You're wet, she said. It's so good to see you. Yes, my daughter, I thought, but said nothing. She shrugged off her jacket. Tall, slim, straight brown hair cut so it fell to her chin in a sleek swath. She wore a hip-hugging black skirt and an olive green tight-fitting top. Silver earrings dangled from her ears. She asked how the journey had been and opened a bottle of Pinot Grigio.

I spent three days with Clare. London rattled me. I tentatively purchased an oyster card and felt obliged to trail exhaustedly around the city, to Tate Modern, the British Museum, the Portrait Gallery. In spaces that had in my younger days been familiar to me I now felt lost. I was bombarded by people and noise and smells. In the British Museum shop, looking for presents for Kirstie and the girls, I found myself wedged in by a group of Spanish students. I had no existence. They closed in, unconscious of my foreign presence, then suddenly dispersed, still untouched by my insubstantiality. At the National Film Theatre, decades ago a favourite haunt with always a sense of anticipation, of excitement, I sat in the café and ate a salad, battered by conversation buzzing from surrounding tables. Just stop for a moment, please, stop and take note of the stranger in your midst. But of course I did not want anyone to take note of me, I wanted to remain anonymous, unidentified, unremarked. In my Yorkshire village I was Mrs Billings, wife of Tim, mother of Jake and Clare and Harriet and Lucas. To a few neighbours I was Sonia. In my Highland town everyone knows the witch of the railway carriage although they may never speak to me and I don't know their names. I tried to smarten myself up for London. I trimmed my hair and tied it neatly back. I bought a new jacket in Oban. Nevertheless, I feel I am marked as an outsider, someone who doesn't belong and does not know her way. Someone who has forgotten how to speak the language. Someone who cannot move along the street, descend underground, board a bus, with confidence and purpose

I let myself into Clare's flat with the key she had given me and looked for clues as to my daughter's life. There were books by authors I hadn't heard of, muted beige pictures on the walls. Most of the names on her CDs meant nothing to me. With some relief I spotted Bach and Mozart, Billie

Holiday and Miles Davis. This was music she'd heard as a child. Mozart and Miles, her father would say, what more can you want? The kitchen was as small as my own but tidier, with matching crockery in terracotta and sets of elegant glasses. Stainless steel saucepans hung in a neat row. In the fridge were several bottles of white wine, cheese and prosciutto, half a jar of pesto, some tomatoes and mushrooms, and a supermarket package of sirloin steak. Our dinner. A thin smoky grey vase stood on the windowsill, which looked out on to small back gardens, mostly covered in slabs of paving.

I wanted to know about Clare's life but I wasn't sure how to ask. She talked mainly about her job. She had recently been to Frankfurt, and a trip to Hong Kong was a possibility. She mentioned her boss frequently, Jack his name was, but I found it hard to follow the intricate dynamic of office politics. Her laptop was open on the kitchen table and even as she was grilling steak her phone was in her hand. Twice it jangled into life and she spoke rapidly into it as she turned the steak and delved in the fridge for salad dressing. Later, it bleeped a message which she glanced at as we ate.

On Friday night we went to a concert at the Festival Hall, a Czech string quartet playing Dvořàk. Clare had remembered that I was particularly fond of Dvořàk. Thank you, I said afterwards, that was a perfect choice. Mum, she said, taking my arm, don't you miss this sort of thing? Wouldn't you rather be somewhere you could get to concerts and galleries? I don't need them every day, I said cautiously, not wanting to offend, not wanting to spoil the lingering vibration of the strings. And besides, I am not without music. I can listen to Dvoràk any time I like, and we do have concerts, you know, visiting musicians. And galleries. And touring theatre companies. We are quite civilised. But it's not the same, Clare protested. I mean, you enjoyed tonight didn't you, listening to music you love played by first-rate musicians? Wouldn't you like to be able to do that more often?

We strolled arm in arm through streets still warm from summer sun. No, I said after a pause, it's not the same. I like it though. I squeezed her arm to show her I wasn't ungrateful. We walked in silence for a while. Then Clare asked, Shall we get a taxi? No, let's walk. It's not so far. Let's just walk home. So we did, but we spoke very little and I realised she was slowing her usually brisk pace to match my slower progress. It was an opportunity I let slip, to ask her, Are you happy? What is your life like? Is there a man in your life? Do you think about marriage, children? (It will soon be too late for children.) I'm not sure why, but somehow walking through the warm streets with their acrid smell of grime and fumes I wasn't able to find a voice to utter the words that rattled in my head.

I am baffled sometimes at how to communicate love when the obvious words seem cheap and overused. Tim and I did not go in much for terms of endearment. At some point in our forty years together we stopped professing love in words, except on birthday cards. All my love, Tim, XXX. Once we were married, we were never apart long enough to write letters, though I have the few letters we exchanged before that day. If Tim was away for more than a day or two he'd send a postcard, always signed off in the same way. Missing you, he'd write in his loopy scrawl. XXX.

The next day I caught the train to Cambridge to see my younger daughter. A Saturday. Harriet met me off the train. She and her partner Matthew live in the upper part of a Victorian house in a broad street fifteen minutes from the station. We walked, trundling my little case. It had been raining and the pavements were wet, but the sky cleared as we walked and there was a faint rainbow. Harriet carried my case up the stairs. The flat was much bigger than Clare's, on two floors, with a spare bedroom as well as a large study. From the spare room there was a view to the botanic gardens. Harriet and Matthew share the study. There is a desk at either end, and they sit at their computers with their backs to each other.

Matthew likes to cook and that night spent much time in the kitchen, humming as he ground spices for a curry. I like Matthew, though I find him slightly comical. He has a narrow delicate face with dark short-cropped hair and round spectacles. He teaches medieval history at the university and talks a great deal and with boundless enthusiasm about church politics. When I pay attention I find it quite interesting, but my thoughts often drift. I don't think he notices, although occasionally he pauses, removes his glasses, holds them arm's length from his face, replaces them.

Harriet and I join him in the kitchen where there is a captivating smell of garlic and spices. Harriet whips cream for a pudding. Matthew's sleeves are rolled up revealing pale skin although it is summer, and a thin froth of hair on his forearms. Harriet in contrast is quite tanned. She stands propped against the worktop, the bowl of cream held against her pale yellow T-shirt, beating vigorously with a hand whisk. There is a splatter of cream on her khaki trousers. Her hair is thick and straight, like my own, but a little darker than mine once was. I notice a couple of grey hairs – she's only thirty-eight. And what about a child for these two? Is it too late for Harriet also? Do they want a child? They've been together for seven years, so probably not, or if they do it's not worked out for them. I can't ask Harriet about this. My grandchildren are on the other side of the world.

Matthew leans over a hot pan and breathes in deeply. Harriet dips her finger into the cream and licks it, puts the bowl down and unscrews the cap from a bottle of Sauvignon. She half-fills three large glasses and sits down opposite me at the kitchen table. Cheers, she says, lifting her glass. It's lovely to have you here, mum. I smile. It's the first time I've been in the home she and Matthew share. They have been in it for about a year. Do you like the flat? It's lovely, I say. We can walk to work. We thought about a place out of town, but this makes much more sense. Matthew measures rice and water into a pan. Won't be long, he says cheerfully. If it's nice tomorrow I thought we'd go to Ely Cathedral. I haven't been since I was a student, I say.

I'd gone to Ely just once during my three years at Cambridge, with my friend Dilys and two boys who had a car. It must have been the end of my first year at the university, after exams. I didn't know the boys very well. Dilys had gone out with Jeremy a couple of times and Keith was Jeremy's friend. Let's go to Ely, somebody said, so we did, driving too fast along the A10 with the windows down, sweeping past church spires and fields on either side of the road green with wheat. A few miles to our right was the River Cam, a river we thought of only as a stretch of sluggish water winding through Grantchester meadows and on past the backs of colleges. We had no idea where it began, or that we whizzed past the place where it joined the Ouse which took its waters through the Fens to the Wash. We did not think of rivers as lines of connection. None of us had ever been to the Wash.

The square tower of the cathedral rose from the flat land. Jesus, it's big, said Jeremy. Dilys giggled. We left the car in a side street and walked up a slight rise and through a grassy park towards the cathedral. The massive structure almost overwhelmed the small town. I don't like cathedrals, Keith muttered. There's something scary about them. You're meant to be scared, said Jeremy. You're meant to be awestruck and overwhelmed by the power of God. You're meant to feel very small and insignificant. Unless you're a bishop or something, in which case you bask in the building's magnificence.

And I was awestruck when we went inside, dazzled by the colour and the light, the radiant stained glass, the gold and red and deep green. The light's intensity was heightened by the precise and elegant divisions of the octagonal vault. Jeremy was silenced. We were all silenced. We wandered aimlessly and separately. The interior of the building seemed to glow with a kind of passion. I sat for a while.

My family had never been churchgoers, my father out of indifference, my mother because her own parents had been freethinkers and socialists. I had been to carol services with the school and once went to evensong in King's College Chapel. You have to do it once, said the acquaintance I went with, and I couldn't argue with the magic of the place, the delicate interweaving of the music and the high latticed roof, as if the music was in some way creating the space.

When we emerged into the daylight and walked across the grass with crows loud above us, Dilys in particular seemed chastened. Maybe I should start going to church again, she said, without further explanation. She took Jeremy's arm and they walked a little ahead of me and Keith, who said quietly, I was brought up a Quaker. I find all this too much, really. It makes me feel a bit sick. Do you still go to meetings? I asked, curious. Sometimes. Makes you think, though, Jeremy said, but didn't enlarge. True enough, I thought, but what does it make you think about? Do believers absorb the glow of all that stained glass and think of God, or ponder how they can be better people? Do they feel enhanced or diminished?

We found a pub, the entrance down a few steps. I remember Keith, who was tall, ducking through the low door. The boys ordered pints of bitter. I had half a pint of cider and Dilys ordered barley wine. I've always wondered what it was like, she said. We bought our own drinks the first time round, but then Jeremy paid. He was the car owner and seemed to have money. How much did we drink? I can't remember now, but a while later we were sitting in fading light on a low wall beside the cathedral eating chips from vinegary paper. Jeremy stood up jiggling the car keys. Time to hit the road. Keith got unsteadily to his feet. I can't stand up, Dilys said, and Jeremy and I had to pull her up. Jeremy laughed. It's powerful stuff, that barley wine. We walked down the street to where we'd left the car, Jeremy and I on either side of Dilys, Keith placing his feet carefully, all of us except for Dilys laughing at nothing. When we reached the car, Keith leant against it, spreading his arms across its roof. It seemed to take forever to get us all in. In the back seat Dilys slumped and closed her eyes. Jeremy drove very slowly out of the town. It was nearly dark.

After a few miles a weak voice came from Dilys's corner. I think I'm going to be sick. Bloody hell, Dilys. Jeremy pulled up and Dilys stumbled out of the car. I didn't move but heard her retching. Keith got out of the car and wandered off into the dark to have a pee. Jeremy sat in the driver's seat with his head resting on the wheel. It started to rain. Jeremy raised his head and shouted, Get back in the bloody car. Stop messing about. Keith reappeared and Dilys clambered back into the car, wiping her face with her sleeve. I gave her a tissue.

We set off again, Dilys apparently asleep. I could see Jeremy's hands gripping the steering wheel. Headlights appeared and rapidly disappeared. Take it easy, Jeremy, Keith muttered. Were we going fast? A bend, Jeremy's foot on the break, the swivel of the car as the tyres failed to grip, the lurch on to the verge, the thud as the front wheels tipped into the ditch. Dilys screamed. Did I scream too? No seat belts. Blood on Keith's forehead.

A car stopped. Someone found a phone box and dialled 999. We didn't move – we couldn't move. It was a two-door car and the doors were jammed. Jeremy was groaning. Dilys reached for my hand and I gripped hers tightly. It seemed like hours that we sat, shocked and silent until the police and an ambulance came and somehow they got us out of the car. I don't recall much else, except for the bright lights in Addenbrooke's Hospital and sitting on a red chair. Dilys and I had minor bruises but Jeremy had several broken ribs. In spite of a lot of blood, the cut on Keith's forehead wasn't serious.

They kept Jeremy in overnight. Keith, Dilys and I left the hospital and walked shakily along Trumpington Street. It was late and we were without our gowns. We were in no state to dodge the bulldogs out on the prowl for delinquent undergraduates. At the top of Silver Street Dilys and I parted from Keith and walked down to our college building where we had adjoining rooms. The door was locked of course and we hadn't signed out. It took us ten minutes to wake a fellow student by the time-honoured method of throwing pebbles at a window. She came down to the front door, bleary-eyed in flowered pyjamas, and let us in. A few days afterwards term was over and I went home. I never told my parents, who were anyway distracted by the news that I had gained commendable exam results, not brilliant, but no one expected me to emulate my sister. My bruises were already beginning to fade. No comment was made.

Some months later I saw Jeremy in Market Street. We said hello but paused only briefly to enquire politely after each other's health. Dilys had given up on Jeremy, but she had a coffee with Keith. His head had healed but there was still a tiny scar. He said he hadn't seen much of Jeremy. At the start of the next university year Dilys and I found ourselves living in different buildings, the luck of the draw rather than choice. But we saw less of each other, and that by chance rather than intention. By the time we gained our degrees we had drifted apart, and made only half-hearted efforts to stay in touch. I have no idea where she is now.

Here is Harriet, leaning her elbows on the table. We have finished our curry and Matt is opening a second bottle of wine. Matt and Hat, Clare calls them, and I think I detect a touch of envy. Harriet is saying, Mum, why do you have to be so far away, so remote? Why don't you come and live in Cambridge? We could find you a nice little flat close to us. A strand of hair has fallen across her slightly flushed cheek. She looks so young. Yes, says Matt, filling my glass. There's plenty going on in Cambridge to interest you. And it's easy to get to London if you want something more exciting. I am laughing and shaking my head. He means well, my not quite son-in-law. My daughter is looking at me, concerned, her pebble-grey eyes wide. I am sure she really would like me to be living nearby. I worry about you, mum, she says. My dearest girl, I say, surprised at myself as it's not the way I usually address my daughters, you shouldn't worry. And I want to tell her how I feel about where I am now (not here in Cambridge, but where I more really am than anywhere else) but cannot find the right words, so I turn to Matt and say, But I have no wish to go to London. If Clare wasn't there I'd probably never go to London again. Why should I? And his face mirrors Harriet's concern. Never go to London again? Is this the first inkling of senility? Matt grew up in Cricklewood.

I am sitting between them, the two pairs of eyes looking at me as I laugh again (Is it the wine? they are thinking). I'm not going to uproot myself again, I say confidently. No, my transplant is complete and one hundred percent successful. (I'm not sure how true that is, but it will do for the time being.) And it's not so very far. Must be all of five hundred miles, Matt says earnestly. It's not the distance in miles, Harriet says. It's just so different. Exactly, I say. That's why I'm there. Five hundred miles takes you to a different place. A day's drive. Your brother is on the other side of the world, about as far away as you can get. And you know something? In some ways Auckland is less different from Cambridge than rural Argyll is.

We drive to Ely. I am sitting in the front next to Matthew at the wheel. I am trying to remember what the road was like all those years ago. The fields seem unchanged, low and flat, with an occasional undulation and wheat beginning to ripen. There are patches of green, and black and white cows, and a paddock of horses. Out of sight to the east the Cam runs as it did before. It's fifty years since I went to Ely, I tell them. And I tell them also the story of the accident. I never knew about that, says Harriet. Did dad know? Oh yes, of course he knew, I said. It wasn't that serious, just a bit of a shock. But you've never talked about it. I've not given it much thought. But it does return sometimes, the sickening lurch of the car leaving the road and that terrible silence, probably lasting only seconds, before an awareness of life returned. And then Jeremy's voice, Jee-sus. A pause. Is everyone all right? Jee-sus. It hurts to breathe. It comes back to me now, but all I say to Harriet and Matthew is that the car went off the road and we were all a bit bruised. Nothing serious. I remember now that it was my upper arm that was bruised, and my shoulder ached for several weeks. Jeremy's broken ribs must have caused him a lot of pain. I was nineteen years old.

There is the cathedral dominating the huddled town. With some difficulty we find a place to park. These days, Matt says as we walk towards the building that dwarfs everything around it, these days we build towering edifices to glorify Mammon. I can't decide whether it's preferable to glorify God. You can argue that neither is for the greater good of humanity. If you're a believer, Harriet says, of whatever kind, you could probably make a case for either. If it's not God that makes the world go round, it's money. We are crossing the park that surrounds the cathedral. But God, says Matt, or his lieutenants, needs money to create grandeur like this. It's all about power and authority. Do you think the poor sods who lugged the stone felt their souls improved by carrying out the work of God? Maybe not, but those who carved the stone and made the stained glass, they probably felt the better for it. If creativity is the expression of the soul perhaps it brought them closer to God. Is creativity an expression of the soul? Matt asks. It's as good a way as any of locating the soul, I say. Hmm. Tracking backwards, as it were. And then Harriet says, out of the blue, I'm sure for Jake climbing a mountain was an expression of the soul. There is nothing to be said in reply, but I wonder why the cathedral has prompted Harriet to think of her brother. She was sixteen when he died. Was there some association between the grandeur of cathedrals and the grandeur of mountains? As if in answer to my unspoken question Harriet said, John Muir thought of mountains as cathedrals. They made him feel closer to God and invincible, which is a good way to feel even if it's not true. Matthew took Harriet's hand.

We had paused to gaze at intricate carved stone. The original building on this site, Matt was saying, was a monastery founded in 673 by a woman called Etheldreda. It was destroyed by the Danes. Seventeen years after Etheldreda died, her body was dug up and astonishingly had not decayed. It was reburied inside a stone sarcophagus and became a shrine visited by pilgrims. It's often the way these things begin. A site accumulates layers of meaning, often overwhelmed by the final manifestation. Who thinks of poor old Etheldreda now?

We knew nothing of Etheldreda, Dilys and I, Jeremy and Keith. We just submitted to the light and colour and complexity created by later generations, and then cheerfully went on to drink too much. Towards the end of the tenth century, Matt went on, it became a Benedictine community, and a few decades later work began on the cathedral. The monastery was dissolved by Henry VIII and a lot of the carving and stained glass destroyed, but it was refounded a couple of years later. Some things stubbornly refuse to be obliterated – I find that reassuring. And now… We stood beneath the octagon, bathed in bright, fragmented summer sun. There's nothing quite like it, is there? You do almost want to say, thank you God. Thank you all those nameless hundreds of haulers of stone and hewers of wood, Harriet said. Matt put his arm around her shoulders and shifted his gaze from the splendour above him to her face. I watched as they smiled at each other. If I'd helped to create something like that, Matt said, I think I'd feel pretty damn good. You'd have located your soul, I say. The location of the soul, says Matt, now there's an interesting debate to be had.

The next day Harriet and Matt are off to work. Teaching is over for the year but they have meetings. From the second floor window I watch them walk down the street, each carrying a black bag with a laptop, books and papers. They are wearing almost identical clothes, jeans and light jackets, and walk almost in step. I can't help thinking of them as children, like the two in the Start-rite advertisement setting off down a long empty road in their new shoes. And I am thinking also of the men and women who taught me, Dr Harding in her tweed skirt, settled in her armchair with her head back and her eyes half closed as she listened to me reading out an essay on *Tristram Shandy*. The men in suits and gowns whose lectures I erratically attended but often did not attend to.

Later I go out. I spend the day retracing once familiar routes, but am baffled from time to time by new buildings and redefined streets. Street names and college names echo in my head and much is unchanged, which makes the sudden appearance of unexpected concrete slabs that much harder to absorb. Trumpington Street, Silver Street, King's Parade, Trinity Street. Some of the colleges now charge for the privilege of wandering through their grounds. I am outraged at this – something essential to the city has been lost. No more shortcuts through college grounds without paying a toll. No more sense of the colleges as part of quotidian thoroughfares for people who had no connection with them. Town and gown divided even more.

My eyes follow a girl in a yellow jumper flying along the Backs on a bike. Why it's me on my old Raleigh with my scratched leather bag of books. Where am I going? To the library? To college for lunch, shepherd's pie and rice pudding? Back to my room to write an essay on John Donne? I've never taught John Donne. *Moving of th' earth brings harms and fears.* There are moments when the past hurts, not because it's painful but because it's gone. What harms and fears did I think of then? A car goes off the road. We are bruised and frightened. For a while, perhaps, we go more carefully. But that girl in a yellow jumper flying along on her bike, is she going carefully? Is she worried about the essay she has to write, about her future if she doesn't make the grade? Or perhaps her boyfriend has dumped her and her world has juddered to a halt. How I ached for Tim when I thought there was never a chance he could be a part of my life. How he filled my thoughts, even when I was in the company of others. And that first embrace. I feared, of course I did, that I might lose him. I did not think that he would die. I closed down thoughts that one of us would likely have to live without the other.

There are punts on the river. The sluggish water is the familiar muddy brown nodded over by drooping willows. All along the Backs there is a smell of mud. If you dabble your bare feet in the water you can feel it. I am tempted to do that, to bring back the sensation of my toes sliding into mud, but of course I don't. Here I am not the eccentric railway carriage witch but an unremarked older woman of no particular distinction.

That first day when my father said goodbye and the door closed. He had driven me from Sussex, the car loaded with suitcases and boxes, my record player and transistor radio. My mother helped me pack, reminiscing about her own beginnings as a student, but she lived at home and took the bus every day to the university. She was nervous, she recalled, the daughter of a railway conductor, unsure of herself, in those first few days at once disappointed and awed and charged with excitement. The lecture rooms were drab and some of the lecturers aloof, as if it were no concern of theirs whether their audience took in their words. But it was a new and wondrous world nevertheless. The sheer magic of men and women talking together, my mother said, sitting on my bed beside my open suitcase, smoothing the jersey that lay folded on her knee. The discussions, the ideas flying back and forth – the people I met seemed so clever. It took me a while to realise that I was quite clever too. She laughed and reached out for my hand. You won't have that problem, pet. I know Miranda always seemed the clever one, but you've done wonderfully well. We're very proud of you. Oxford and Cambridge, my goodness, I never dreamt of such a thing when you were babies. My father had opened one of his good bottles when I got the news that I'd been accepted by the college of my choice. He eased out the cork, his eyes bright with anticipation, poured an inch of red liquid into a glass, held it to his nose and breathed deeply.

After my father left I stood in the middle of the floor and regarded my neatly stacked belongings. There was a narrow bed, a wardrobe and a chest of drawers, a desk and chair. The walls were bare and the bookcase empty. There was a rather threadbare carpet on the floor. I could hear cheerful voices outside my door. I went to the window and looked out on to the street, just in time to see my father's car departing. I stood there for a long time, watching the flow of bikes and people, lost. When at last I turned there were my possessions exactly as before, still neatly arranged, untouched. I pulled out some books and half-filled the empty shelves. More than twenty years later I would watch my elder daughter do exactly the same thing. Footsteps in the corridor. I slowly crossed the room and opened the door. There was no one there. All the other doors were closed, the voices gone.

For most of the day I am walking aimlessly. I peer through college gates, enter those that allow visitors without paying. I remember things, moments, images, sensations, some memories so fragile they are no more than indistinct clues I cannot bring into focus. I make a wide circle, along the Backs, up Bridge Street, past the Union from which women were excluded, down Jesus Lane, drawn by some invisible string through the entrance to Jesus College (no payment required) to staircase D where once I and others were given sherry by a young left-wing fellow of the college. Was that the occasion I cycled back to Silver Street escorted by a young man called Conor who asked me out? We went to see *Spartacus* at the Regal. Nothing came of it. I try to picture Conor. He had a thatch of yellow hair, but nothing else of him survives.

I walk back along Trinity Street and stop in Heffers Bookshop where I buy a copy of a novel by a young writer whose name appears on book prize shortlists. I go into the Copper Kettle for coffee. Memory and reality simultaneously clash and corroborate. Half a century ago at my finger tips and yet beyond reach. I open my newly purchased book and begin to read as I sip my coffee. On that first day, too, I sought the comfort of books, until there was a knock on the door and before I had time to say come in, it opened to reveal a long-haired girl with a heart-shaped face. Hello, I'm Dilys, she said, in an accent I couldn't identify. I'm going out to explore. Want to come? So we went out, and walked up Silver Street, over the bridge and up to Trumpington Street. We passed the bikes stacked against the wall of Peterhouse and more outside the spacious entrance to King's. Everywhere there was movement. Where are you from? asked Dilys. From Sussex, I said, thinking the name of the town of my birth would mean nothing to her. I'm from Nottingham – D. H. Lawrence country – and she laughed. We wandered through another gate. Wow! said Dilys. Trinity Great Court, I said. We were overtaken by two tweed-jacketed men. We walked round the court and out again. We found a Woolworths and each bought a kettle, a teapot, and blue and white striped mugs. That will do for a start, said Dilys.

I can remember what I was wearing on that first day. A grey skirt and a pale blue jersey with a collar. I had a cream-coloured leather jacket which I'd bought with earnings selling wines and spirits, and a paisley-patterned scarf which my grandmother had given me. Do you have a bike? Dilys asked. I nodded yes. It had come in the back of the car, with the front wheel removed. My father had reassembled it for me before he left and it was now in the bike stand outside the Silver Street building. I don't, Dilys said. I'm told I can get one cheap at the police auction. We bought tea and milk and biscuits and walked back to Silver Street. Dilys filled her kettle and set it on the gas ring at the end of the corridor. We sat in her room, Dilys cross-legged on the bed and me in the only armchair, and drank tea and ate rich tea biscuits. Here's to us, Dilys said, raising her blue and white mug. Here's to a brilliant student career.

You do realise, she said later, that we're outnumbered ten to one? We can take our pick of the most likely to succeed. Only if they pick us. Oh come on, Sonia. Don't you find it a bit overwhelming? I said. There are so few of us and we're excluded from so much. Oh, you mean the Union business. Who cares about that? That only matters if you aspire to be a Tory politician. Or to marry one. Well, I think it's important. We may think we have an advantage, being in demand, but really we don't. A university should be a place of equality. Doesn't bother me, Dilys said, and anyway it's all going to change.

The next day I return north. Harriet sees me on to the train. We'll visit later this summer, she promises. After we get back from the conference in Prague. She looks very young, standing on the platform as the train pulls out, her hair pulled back in an untidy ponytail, the sleeves of her checked shirt rolled up to the elbow and a loosely tied red scarf round her neck giving her the look of an American pioneer. She smiles and waves. Tears come to my eyes. Parting from my children is always hard. If I lived here, I tell myself as the train leaves the city behind and rolls through fields of ripening wheat, the parting would not be so hard. And why not return to a place I once knew well? Perhaps, before Scotland, I might have considered it. But not now. It's too late now.

Three times after leaving Yorkshire I got together with my friend Colette. Colette taught French in Leeds University's extramural department, as it was called then. That's how I met her, because I taught there too, English literature evening classes twice a week most years. That was my career, that and occasional lectures at other institutions. That was where my vague aspirations as I read and listened and took notes and wrote essays at the University of Cambridge had led.

Colette was small and slight with fine tobacco-brown hair and violet eyes. There was a vitality about her; her slender fingers were always on the move. She always seemed poised for rapid action, and she spoke rapidly, in both English and French. Her father was French, in Britain with the Free French army during the war when he met her mother. They met on a train, and she loved the story of how my parents met. On top of a mountain! She clapped her hands. Colette was very popular with her students, many of whom were old enough to be her parents. Although she moved with an air of impatience, she was very patient with them. We were roughly the same age and took to having a drink together after our classes. Her kindliness shone through her rapid-fire talk. Over the years we had got to know each other well.

Let's meet somewhere halfway, Colette suggested. I still had the car, so drove south, crossing the Clyde on the Erskine Bridge and on through Lanarkshire and Ayrshire to a little place on the Solway where we stayed at a nautical inn and walked on the sand. We stood at the water's edge and looked across to England. I have never been here, Colette said. I've had several stays in the Lake District but I never thought of crossing the border. Never been to Scotland? Oh yes, to Edinburgh, twice, but this is very different. But I had never stood on the edge of the Solway Firth either, or looked at England, grey and hazy, from across the water. Colette's gold sandals sank into the wet sand and a breeze stirred her shoulder-length hair, from which the grey had been eliminated, and the dangly earrings she was never without. To the west a deep red sunset bled through a wide arc of sky. Colette had pushed her unnecessary dark glasses to the top of her head. She took my arm. She had mentioned offhandedly a pain in her right leg and was limping slightly. Arthritis probably, I said, like me. We walked a little unevenly on the wet sand, two old crocks. Crocks, Colette laughed, I like that word. Crocks. *Deux vieux clous.*

We turned and walked slowly back to the nautical inn where we sat in the bar and had a nightcap. We're in Scotland, we must drink whisky, Colette insisted. She held her glass of Ardbeg up to the light, took a delicate sip, and frowned. I think I like it. She took another sip and closed her violet eyes. I think so. And then with her scratchy laugh that was quite unlike her crisp but airy voice she said, This was such a good idea, Sonia. I like it here, yes, I really do. I will come again, with Oliver perhaps, although it's hard to persuade him to go anywhere. And this time she took a more generous sip of whisky and set her glass down with a sigh of satisfaction. And we will do this again, just the two of us. But Sonia. You must do something with your hair. I'm not sure it was a good idea to let it grow.

Colette did not drive. I had picked her up from the station at Lockerbie but suggested that I take her to Carlisle to get the train back. It was raining when we left to drive through Annan and across the border at Gretna. Back in England. Back in England for the first time since I had left nine months before, but not an England I knew. It was a road I was travelling on for the first time. The hills rolled away to the east, border country unknown to me. A sign by the road announcing England, just as at Carter Bar, then Carlisle and the River Eden and the Cumbrian hills. Beyond, I knew from the map, was a road that peeled off the M6, a road that would take me through Settle and Keighley, to familiar names, Airedale, through Wharfedale to Wetherby and the village I'd lived in for all those years, known and comfortable. But at Carlisle's railway station I hugged Colette and said goodbye and watched as she limped through the barrier. It was still raining when I drove off. I took a wrong turning and found myself on a minor road heading towards Penrith. At a farm gate I manoeuvred the car round to face the north.

The following November there was an email message from Colette. Sorry about the email, she wrote, but there's no good way to let you know that I've been diagnosed with bone cancer. The words skated off the screen. I read them again, and a third time. I saw her on the sand, cheerful, the wind stirring her hair, but with pain in her leg. Arthritis, I'd said. I heard her voice, every word beautifully articulated with a hint of something not quite English, a whisky in her hand. We will do this again.

I got up and went to the window. There was a gusty wind, and for some time I watched as leaves were snatched and spiralled through the air. I was going to phone, but it was too hard. I returned to the computer and wrote one short sentence. I am coming to see you. Two days later I was on the bus, then the train to Leeds. I didn't feel able to drive. Colette had never married, although she had a devoted companion called Oliver who had a curio shop in Whitby. For decades she had spent most weekends there. In the winter Oliver sometimes shut up shop and joined her in her Leeds bungalow, but he didn't like to travel. Colette's students knew something of this, enough to speculate, which amused Colette. Who is this man? Am I living in sin? That's the question on all my students' lips, she would joke, her violet eyes dancing, her fingers dancing. It would be such a shame to give them the facts. The facts are quite dull, really. I like to think of their imaginations running riot, though sometimes I wonder how much imagination they have. Sometimes I mention *mon ami*. If I'm feeling naughty, I drop in a little bit more for them to chew on.

Oliver was with her when I arrived. He was a quiet, contained man, always with a slight frown as if in a state of perpetual puzzlement. He shook my hand with some formality and carried my small case into the spare room, and apart from offering me a cup of tea, said little. The next day he returned to Whitby. He kissed Colette on the doorstep of her bungalow and patted her shoulder, then got into his car and drove away. Colette waved. There was something reassuring about Oliver's matter-of-fact departure and Colette waving him off as if he were heading for a day at the office.

I stayed with Colette during her first chemotherapy session. Her slight body looked a little thinner, her face a little drawn, her eyes less bright, but only in her movements did she betray her illness. She struggled to get up from a chair and for a split second there was panic in her face if she couldn't lay hands at once on her stick. Her fingers were still. Sometimes just walking from one room to the next seemed to exhaust her. The chemo left her so fatigued she found it hard to hold a book. She sat very still, as if gathering up every ounce of energy for use when next she had to move. But then she would talk, almost as readily as before, and the spark would return for long enough to believe that all would be well.

After a week she insisted she was feeling better and persuaded me to return home. Oliver was with her again when I left, but I could not help thinking that if I'd stayed in my nice brick house near Wetherby I would have been able to see her every day, do things for her, take her out if she felt like it. When I hugged her she felt even frailer and more brittle than she looked. I'll be back soon, I said. I'll be in better shape next time, she said cheerfully. I've persuaded Oliver to book tickets for the Playhouse. And so I left her, leaning against the door frame, pale but smiling, a yellow scarf tied round her wispy hair, her silver earrings trembling slightly.

I wasn't back soon enough. She'd kept from me the true extent of her illness, though I should have guessed – I'd seen it all before. But I wanted to believe in her power to stay alive. I wanted to believe that attitude could make a difference.

It was late November when I saw her in Leeds. It snowed, and then there was Christmas and the start of a new year. We emailed almost every day and spoke on the phone. Each time she assured me that all was going well. I'm planning to come in February, I said. When Oliver phoned I knew as soon as I heard his Yorkshire voice that it could not be good news. I booked the train south from Glasgow but Oliver phoned again. It was too late. You will say a few words, won't you, Oliver said. She wanted that.

Again I was on the bus to Glasgow, the train. I watched the drab winter hills pass, snow on the heights and sheep grey against muted browns and greens. The night before the funeral I lay sleepless in the same bed I'd slept in two months before, when Colette was sick and frail but alive, and we could talk when her little bursts of energy masked the draining of her spirit. Oliver seemed adrift and awkward. He had lost weight and his hair was thinner. He joked in his quiet, dry voice, You'd have thought it was me getting the chemo, but I couldn't laugh. You're not planning to wear black, are you, he added anxiously. No, I reassured him. I had dug out a bright top and even found some clip-on earrings to wear in her honour. When he saw me ready for the crematorium Oliver smiled. She's got her own favourite earrings on, he said, the jade ones I bought in Hong Kong years ago. I remember them, I said. They were very pale green, almost translucent.

At the crematorium I sat beside Oliver in the front row. The only family were two cousins of Colette's, who had come from Lille. I was surprised to discover that Oliver's French was quite fluent though flavoured with Yorkshire. He sat leaning forward slightly, his hands clasped on his knee. When he got up to speak he was calm and measured. Someone I didn't know from the university also spoke, and then it was my turn. I looked at the surprising number of people sitting in front of me, a blur of faces, and took a deep breath to steady my voice. I said that Colette was a wonderful friend, an inspiring colleague, known her for more than thirty years, will be hugely missed... What are the right words to convey loss? Tim, Jake, Miranda, mother, father. The people you love disappear until you disappear yourself. But I didn't say that. I described walking on the Solway shore, watching the sunset and listening to the last calls of the seabirds, and drinking Ardbeg in the nautical inn. That's how I'll remember Colette, I said. That was how I wanted to remember her, but I saw her, the flesh drained from her face, her knuckles white from her grip on the door as she said goodbye. I spoke words that did not relate to the lasting image, and wondered if she knew it was the last goodbye.

There was music, Vivaldi's cello concerto and Mozart and Georges Brassens, and afterwards people gathered at a nearby hotel. Oliver bustled among them, seeming to gain strength from his role as host, and words of admiration were murmured at his courage. I spoke to one or two people I recognised. One or two others politely asked me about my friendship with Colette. I heard myself say, She was my closest friend, and she was, for much of my adult life, and now she was gone. She had a way of tipping her head back when she laughed her rasping laugh, her earrings shaking. You can't replace friends. I surprised myself by saying that to a man I vaguely recognised. They leave a void that can't be filled. He nodded, and held his glass out to be filled as Oliver passed with the wine bottle. I took the opportunity to move away.

You can marry again – it's been suggested that I should. You can put another man in the place of your husband, in your home, in your bed, and you can do the same things together that once you did with someone else. It won't be quite the same, of course, and probably you wouldn't want it to be the same, but his position in your life is the same. It is much harder to replicate friendship. Oliver filled my glass and kissed my cheek. Perhaps he had noticed that I said more than I'd intended to an almost stranger. What about her house, someone asked him. Oh it will go on the market. Colette had it all worked out. I wasn't surprised. Colette could appear fay and disorganised, but in fact was hard-headed and thorough. Of course she would have it all worked out. And Oliver would retreat to his flat above the shop in Whitby. I don't suppose there will be anyone else for Oliver, although people are full of surprises. Who but Colette could have sustained a relationship like theirs? I envied it in a way, and I think she envied mine. That appreciation of what the other had was part of what held us together. For each of us it was a kind of vicarious living of another life.

So I lost Colette. I left the hotel and took a taxi to the station where I boarded an evening train that carried me north again. I arrived in Glasgow too late for the last bus so spent the night in a Travelodge. Next morning the early bus took me onward. I was familiar with the journey now, out along the Great Western Road through Anniesland and on to Clydebank, and then north to Balloch and Loch Lomond. It was a grey day with a sharp wind that whipped spurts of white on the loch's surface. The summit of Ben Lomond on the far side was lost in cloud.

1964

Sonia Letford and several thousand others had been walking the tarmac road for more than three hours. Her feet were sore – she suspected the start of a blister and it was only the second day. She was hungry. They walked under a grey sky, although it had not yet rained. A despondent silence had fallen over the people she was walking with. Then there was a ripple through the ranks. Tea and sandwiches! They rounded a curve in the road and there, laid out on a row of trestle tables on the grass verge, were plates of sandwiches and urns of tea presided over by women in hats and raincoats. Local church, someone muttered. The column broke up and little groups sat on the grass with paper cups of hot liquid and ham and orange cheese layered in white bread. The Cambridge University banner was propped up against an ash tree. Dilys pulled chocolate out of her knapsack and shared it out amongst the three or four sitting near her. Then she shook out a cigarette from her packet of Gitanes and lit it. Sonia didn't smoke, but she liked to breathe in the unmistakable smell of a French cigarette.

A tall young man in a black leather jacket approached the group followed by a girl with a cascade of dark curly hair. Someone called out, Tim, you lazy bugger, where have you been? I'm a working man, not like you layabouts, was the cheerful rejoinder. Typical that you manage to miss most of the worst stretch. Reading to Slough is a killer. Came up from Lancashire yesterday – got here as soon as I could. God almighty, what are you doing in Lancashire? In gainful employment – what you do when you grow up. You two still together I see. Of course. But Kath is working in London now so it can be tricky. So what are you up to now, Kath? I got a job at Transport House. You did? Well, good for you. Must be interesting. Any inside stories we should know about? Any cats to be let out of bags? She made a face and tossed her head. Sonia watched and listened until the two of them moved away. She noticed the tall young man's thicket of brown hair, his black-rimmed spectacles and his long, lanky stride as he picked his way among the groups sitting on the grass. She watched the girl, whose unbuttoned coat revealed what looked like a kaftan in vivid red and purple. She was wearing high black boots.

The call came to move on and Sonia got reluctantly to her feet. The banner was raised. Dozens of circular peace signs and black "Nos" on yellow were held aloft. The cavalcade shuffled off. A slow walk for half a mile, a stop – Why are we waiting? – then movement again, the marshals urging, Close the gap, close the gap. Stop, start, slow pace, fast. Five, six, seven abreast, then twos and threes. Dilys dived into a shop to buy more chocolate and didn't reappear for half an hour. I marched with Liverpool for a bit, she said, they were singing some great songs. They trudged through suburban Slough. Curious passers-by stopped to watch and a little group of people clapped and shouted Bravo! and Ban the bomb! Join us, join us. It began to rain. Up ahead a band was playing. The sound faded and was replaced by bagpipes.

They spent the night in a primary school. Desks had been pushed aside to make room for sleeping bags. Sonia unrolled hers and lay down at once, flat on her back, eyes shut, her feet throbbing. The floor dug into her shoulder. We're going for something to eat, Dilys said. Have you tried out the kid-sized lavs? Sonia didn't move or open her eyes. The buzz of voices around her was a confused gabble. There was a blend of smells, school disinfectant, sweat, wet clothes. A foot prodded her ribs. Come on, Son, I'm starving. Sonia pushed herself up to a sitting position and looked around the hall. Everywhere human shapes, sitting, lying down, picking a way between heaps on the floor, queuing for the toilets, clinging to radiators to get their clothes dry. Her eyes at last focused on Dilys, hands in pockets, long blonde hair darkened by the rain, and the little group impatient for food. Someone reached down and pulled her to her feet. Onward and upward. She struggled into her wet anorak and followed them back out into the rain.

When they returned there were sleeping bodies all over the floor. Sonia waited her turn to have a pee, crouching down on a miniature toilet, and brush her teeth – she didn't bother to wash – and threaded her way back to her own few square feet of space. As she wriggled into her sleeping bag she noticed a tall figure a few yards away. He knelt on the floor and peeled off his jersey. Sonia watched as he wormed his way into a double sleeping bag that was already occupied. She couldn't see, but it had to be the girl in the kaftan who had tossed her head of thick curly hair. The hard floor pressed into Sonia's shoulder blades. The dustiness of the floorboards filled her nostrils. She slept fitfully, waking often and easing her limbs in a vain effort to find a more comfortable position. There was no silence, but a constant erratic drone of shifting, shuffling, coughing, low voices, tears even, Sonia thought at one point.

The next morning the girl in the kaftan stood almost regally by the window, one hand resting on the windowsill, her head tilted back, her hair tumbling behind her, her elegant profile illuminated. She looked as if she were posing for a Pre-Raphaelite portrait.

They marched on to London and through London's endless suburbs. Some bystanders clapped, others booed, but the marchers shouted Join us! to both and sang defiantly. *Men and women stand together, do not heed the men of war.* A young man with long hair stood on the pavement playing "When the Saints Go Marching In" on a trumpet. And then on the final day Sonia opened her eyes and without moving from the floor saw through the window of the church hall where they had spent the night that the sun was shining. She was hungry. She had almost run out of money and had had to make do with a bag of chips for supper. She wriggled out of her sleeping bag. Beside her Dilys still slept, only a tousle of blonde hair visible. Sonia examined her blistered feet and applied her last two sticking plasters before pulling on socks and shoes and limping off to join the queue for the toilets.

There were tea urns and jam sandwiches. She wolfed a sandwich and found a spot near a window to drink her tea. Outside the morning sun bounced off grey brick buildings. When she turned she saw the kaftan girl again, heading for the exit with a large tapestry bag on her shoulder and her hair pulled back from her face by a deep blue scarf with trailing ends. The door swung shut behind her.

Half an hour later Sonia was on the street. She had left

Dilys reluctantly emerging from her sleeping bag muttering, I'll see you out there. There were bagpipes and drummers and brass bands and families with toddlers in pushchairs. Sonia drifted away from the university contingent and found herself under a banner reading "We urge disarmament everywhere," bold white letters on black. It was oddly polite, a solemn request, unlike the peremptory *Make your minds up now or never, ban the bomb for evermore*, sung loudly and not very harmoniously. Disarmament everywhere. Fat chance. She was walking among people she did not know. The march was carved up into small sections, stopping every few hundred yards to let traffic through. The streets were lined with expressionless police. From time to time a wave of chanting broke out and ricocheted off the tall resistant buildings.

In Trafalgar Square they were packed shoulder to shoulder, but when she glanced round Sonia found she was standing almost next to the tall young man, but she could not see the girl. Speeches boomed out through the microphone but she hardly listened to them. She found a sticky packet of mints in her pocket and offered them to those standing nearest to her. The tall young man took one and smiled. Didn't I see you with Cambridge University? he asked. His accent was from somewhere in the north. She nodded. Behind his heavy-rimmed glasses he had deep brown eyes.

People were leaving, the mass beginning to thin out. There was space between bodies. They were standing next to each other, Sonia and the tall young man. She took a deep breath. Well, he said, I guess I've had enough. I think I'm going to head off. Where's your friend, asked Sonia, suddenly bold. He rubbed his hand over his face before replying. Good question. We had words. She departed this morning. Sonia looked down at her grubby jeans and sore feet. She could feel the grime in her uncombed hair. Oh, she said. I better leave too, and go for my train.

They moved off together. Which station? he asked. Victoria. I'm for King's Cross. They walked to the tube together, and down the steps. Name's Tim Billings, he said. I graduated last year, Peterhouse, engineering, working for Burnley Council now, if you know where Burnley is. Lanca-shire somewhere? North of Manchester. I've never been to Manchester, or Burnley. In fact, I don't think I've ever been in Lancashire. You'll need to do something about that. He laughed. Still north and south, this country. Well, I'm south, I'm afraid, Sussex. Sonia Letford, first year, New Hall. They stopped where they would have to go their separate ways. Tim Billings held out his hand and Sonia took it. Nice to meet you, Sonia, he said. His leather jacket was undone and she noticed the cable knit of his jersey and a snag of wool. He was looking down at her, serious, not smiling. His hand was large and warm. She said, I'm sorry about your girlfriend. He let go of her hand and shrugged, his mouth relaxing into a slight, rueful, dimpled smile. He pulled off his glasses and rubbed them with a crumpled handkerchief. Not the first time she's stomped off. Bit of a drama queen, our Kathleen. She'll be back.

On the train Sonia took her copy of Coleridge from her bag but didn't open it. She stared out of the window but saw little. Shaking Tim Billings's hand, looking up into his serious brown eyes. But she would never see him again, of course. And anyway, Kath would be back.

She walked home from the station, slowly because her feet were sore. Her parents greeted her with relief and – was it pride perhaps? We saw it on the TV, they said excitedly. We looked for you, but so many people! She shed her dirty, damp clothes and lay for a long time in a hot bath as pictures of the last four days streamed through her mind. So many people, so many voices, so many songs. And Tim Billings, tall, lanky, with thick brown hair like a bottlebrush, and serious brown eyes. Miranda, home for a few days, smiled indulgently at her sister's account of the march. You don't seriously think it will have an effect? You're just annoying people. You don't have any real power. You're not exactly storming the bastions of Westminster.

It had felt like real power. Thousands assembled, voices in unison.

Back in Cambridge after the Easter vacation she had only weeks before prelims. A few days before the exams started a postcard arrived. It showed a stone bridge in a green valley and was addressed to Sonia Letford, New Hall, Cambridge. Good luck, it said and was signed, your friend from Burnley. There was also a return address.

Sonia sent a picture of punts on the river. Exams not too bad, she wrote, but was involved in a stupid accident. Not hurt but chastened. A reply: Taking risks OK, but not stupid ones.

The two things, the exams and the accident, seemed linked, as if one led to the other, as if they both in some way defined the end of her first university year. Something had changed. Had she herself changed? Had she grown up, perhaps, a bit at least? She looked round the room she would soon be leaving, a room that had grown into her own space. Books, notebooks, records, clothes, the markers of her small world. They would all need to be packed away, to re-emerge in the autumn in another space which would for a while become her own.

Summer. Term was over and Sonia went home. She did not tell her parents about the Ely escapade, or about Tim Billings. She helped her father out in the shop while his assistant was on holiday, then helped the assistant while her father made a trip to the Rhine. There had been a spike in demand for German wines. Miranda was home for a week before going off to Greece with friends, taking a break from working on her Oxford DPhil. Sonia envied her. She had arranged nothing herself for the summer vacation, though she planned to do a lot of reading. She tried to fight off the inadequacy that descended on her when Miranda was at home.

When she was not working in the shop she read George Eliot (*Daniel Deronda*) and Elizabeth Gaskell (*North and South*), in her room, on the patio, in the living room with the French windows open and the smell of summer drifting in from the garden. But her thoughts often took her away from the page. Might she go to Burnley? Could Lancashire be her holiday destination? But she didn't go to Burnley. She couldn't possibly go to Burnley, that would be ridiculous. But she thought about Tim Billings, his dark eyes, his long, lean stride, his Yorkshire voice. He seemed to live among the characters of *North and South*. She thought about the exotic Kath. She'll be back, Tim had said. Was she back? The summer dribbled past. September, the return to Cambridge, the start of another university year. She cycled along the Backs in her new yellow jersey and grey hipster skirt that revealed several inches of thigh, the fallen leaves skittering away from the wheels of her bike, her gown flying. She bought a second-hand typewriter and painstakingly typed her essays. The words on the page looked more authoritative, even with sentences x-ed out and later additions in ink.

There would be more postcards. No letters, just short messages exchanged for nearly a year. Then, Are you marching again at Easter? Shall we meet?

Sonia did march again. Not Dilys. Sonia didn't see much of Dilys these days, and anyway she had a new boyfriend who had political ambitions and believed in the nuclear deterrent. You have to admit, Dilys said, it does seem to work. On the second day Tim Billings appeared as he had appeared the year before, wearing the same leather jacket but without his exotic lady friend. He found Sonia under the Cambridge University banner. They walked together, but that evening in Slough Tim went off to the pub with old friends. Sonia was stung – how could he just waltz off when he had made a point of seeing her? She stretched out in her sleeping bag and did not see him return or locate his patch of floor. But there was no Kath. That, perhaps, meant something.

Tim found her again the next day and again they walked together. Her rancour melted away. She learnt that he came from Scarborough, that his father was a solicitor, that he did not much enjoy his work at Burnley, that he had his eye on a job with an engineering firm in Leeds. He had an older sister who was a teacher in Hartlepool. He had a good singing voice and knew the words of all the protest songs. Dad will be pleased that he can sing, she thought. Kath wasn't mentioned. On the final day she lost him in the crowd and again she felt let down, but there was another postcard soon after she returned to Cambridge.

That October Sonia voted in her first general election. She felt slightly nervous as she entered the polling station, as if half expecting to be told she had no right to vote. Her father had always voted Liberal, her mother Labour, but they never talked much about politics. In Cambridge in the weeks before the election, Sonia distributed leaflets for the Labour Party. As always, the town returned a Tory candidate, but that didn't matter. After thirteen years of Tory government, Labour squeaked to a narrow victory. Sonia lay in her college bed listening to her transistor radio as the results came through. She was hearing the names of towns and constituencies she had never heard of. I'm twenty years old, she thought, and I scarcely know anything about the country I live in.

December 1960
Sonia Letford's grandmother was making her a dress from a length of pale green silk that her husband had brought back from a wine trip to Italy. The silk had been in a drawer for years. Sonia was going to the sixth form Christmas dance, a joint event with the boys' school. Pale green suits you, her grandmother said firmly. She neatened the seams with a very fine needle. Opposite her sat her husband, his white

hands motionless on the arms of the chair, his head lolled at an odd angle and his eyes closed. He had survived a second stroke. He would not survive a third, which struck a few days into the new year.

Sonia's parents had given her a gold locket for her sixteenth birthday. She had a bath and put on the dress and combed her short hair. She smoothed the silk with her hands, pulling it tight over her insubstantial bust. The cap sleeves seemed to accentuate rather than disguise her bony shoulders. She fastened the locket around her neck and applied pale pink lipstick which Miranda had given her. I've gone off the colour, she said. Sonia put on the black T-strap shoes with two-inch heels she had bought the week before. The door of her bedroom was closed. She did not want to open it, to go downstairs, where she knew her family were in the living room watching TV but in reality waiting for her descent. Her father was going to drive her to the school.

She opened the door and descended the stairs slowly and as quietly as she could. She heard the television behind the closed door of the living room and hesitated again. Then gently turned the door handle, pushed the door open and stood motionless watching her parents. Her father sat comfortably back in his armchair, her mother was sewing a button on a shirt, glancing from time to time at the television screen. Miranda, home from Oxford for the Christmas vacation, was on the sofa writing in a notebook. They didn't notice Sonia at first, but then Mairi looked up. Come on pet, let's have a look at you. Oh my word, don't you look stunning. She was in the room and they were all looking at her. Her father got to his feet. Who is this gorgeous girl? He took both her hands in his and twirled her round. You'll sweep them off their feet. But her own feet, in her new shoes, were not entirely comfortable. Right, then, her father said. Are you ready for the off? Have a nice time, Miranda said without looking up, her pen still moving across the paper. She had lent Sonia her camel-coloured coat and didn't comment that it looked a little odd, with two inches of the pale green dress showing below the coat's hem. Grace Letford had insisted that the dress be a decent length.

The dance was held in the boys' school hall, which was swathed in paper chains and balloons, boys on one side, girls on the other. There was a Christmas tree in one corner, and on the stage a band played. Sonia found herself in a sea of newly made and newly bought dresses, blue and turquoise, red and yellow, navy and dark green, but no one else in pale green Italian silk. She was pleased that her dress was different, but at the same time wished that it was not.

For the first hour it was quicksteps and foxtrots and the Gay Gordons. Sonia stood with other girls from her class hoping to be asked to dance yet dreading that the lanky boy with spots or the boy with slicked down hair and sideburns might be coming for her. Her first dance was with a boy she knew from the Reading Club, her second with the son of friends of her parents. He was tall and looked down at her through a blonde forelock. She had never liked him. He had a way of holding back his head, which accentuated his height and gave him a supercilious air. Then there was a long gap. She found a chair and sat with her hands folded on her lap trying to look as if she was enjoying watching others dance. The band got more adventurous and played "Rock Around the Clock" and "Blue Suede Shoes". Dancers whirled past her. "Go Cat Go". The Reading Club boy came back for another dance, and suddenly she was enjoying herself. Out of breath and laughing, they went together for sausage rolls and soft drinks. He put his hand on the small of her back to guide her through the crowd. She felt its heat through the fabric of her dress. But when they reached the tables where refreshments were laid out he drifted away to join a cluster of boys at the far end. Sonia guessed that one or two of them had quarter bottles of vodka in their jacket pockets.

When she turned away from the table with a sausage roll in one hand and a paper cup of non-alcoholic punch in the other she nearly bumped into a boy called Miles. She knew him by sight because her friend Debbie had gone to the pictures with him a few weeks before and pronounced him nice but boring. But now he and Sonia were simultaneously apologising to each other, and then awkwardly laughing, and then, No harm done, no spills. I'd hate to be responsible for ruining your beautiful dress, he said. Oh, do you like it, she said without thinking, my grandmother made it. And then she blushed, because it seemed a rather childlike thing to say, and going to a dance in a dress made by your grandmother was not something to broadcast. It's lovely, he said, elegant, I noticed it before, when you were dancing. She smiled more warmly. I'm starving, he said, I'm going to get something to eat but don't go away. So she stood exactly on the spot, in the way of others trying to get to the food, until he returned with a paper plate piled with sandwiches. Egg and cress, he said, and ham. I'm not that keen on sausage rolls. He was wearing a pale blue shirt with the sleeves rolled up and a loosened tie.

They found two seats and sat side by side eating the sandwiches. You're Sonia, aren't you, he said, Debbie's friend. I'm Miles. Sonia nodded. I know. And that was how it started. They danced. As the evening drew to a close the music slowed. "It's Now or Never", "Cathy's Clown". The lights were dimmed and Miles held her a little more adventurously. Sonia took a long breath and tried to relax. Miles walked her home although Sonia had money for a taxi and her shoes were hurting. It was cold with a dampness in the air, and Sonia had no gloves as she had not expected to be walking home. Miles took her hand and tucked it into the pocket of his coat. It was agreeable but a little awkward. She felt she had to keep her hand very still. As they walked, Miles told her about his family and she told him about hers. When they reached her gate she quickly detached her hand

and went through it. She suspected he would want to kiss her and she was not sure she was ready for that. But she walked up the path with a light step, and when her waiting parents asked if she had had a good time she said Yes, great, and could not help smiling. And when she had left the room to go upstairs Ray and Mairi smiled at each other.

Debbie was right. Miles was nice, pleasant looking with neat brown hair and steady blue eyes. He was polite. He complimented Sonia often. He was reliable. If he promised to phone or come round at a particular time he always did. He worked weekends in his father's garage and so could afford to pay when they went out, which they did on Saturday nights, sometimes to the pictures – they saw *The Millionairess* and *The League of Gentlemen* – sometimes to the local espresso bar where they drank foamy coffee and fed the jukebox. He always walked her home, and they did kiss, and after the first few times he unbuttoned her coat and ran his hands over her back and her hips and briefly touched her breasts. She shut her eyes and did not stop him. All that winter and spring they saw each other every week, and in the summer, when their exams were over, they sometimes went for a walk on a Sunday afternoon if the weather was nice, and found a quiet spot where they lay in the grass together. Sonia liked having a boyfriend. She quite liked lying stretched against Miles exchanging kisses and feeling his hands on her, but Debbie was right. Although he could excite her body, at least a bit, Miles was boring.

In July Miles finished school. Sonia had another year to go. Miles would be leaving soon to start a traineeship with Unilever. His parents were very pleased and mentioned this whenever they saw Sonia. On his last Sunday Miles suggested they take a picnic to the Downs. Sonia made sandwiches and a flask of coffee and added some slices of her mother's home-made gingerbread. Miles bought train tickets to Lewes. They walked through the town and out on to the Downs. It was a warm afternoon, with clouds obscuring the sun from time to time, but it did not rain. There were families and dogs out for walks, and the grassy slopes were studded with wild flowers. Miles and Sonia walked hand in hand and climbed up to Blackcap. They looked south to the coast and the channel and north across the slightly hazy fields and woods of the Weald. On the north slope they found a secluded hollow with a little cluster of orchids, and they settled there to eat their sandwiches and drink their coffee. Miles put his empty plastic cup down and kissed Sonia, probing with his tongue. This was nothing new. She had been startled the first time but now she was used to it. She lay back and he pushed his hand under her checked shirt and unzipped her jeans so that he could reach down. She felt his shoulder blades and the muscles on his back.

She liked the feel of him but it didn't seem real. It seemed to be happening to someone else, even the sharp stab between her thighs when his tongue touched her nipples. She wouldn't part her legs. Please, he said, always polite. But her hand involuntarily was pushing against his chest. She looked up at him, saw the niceness of his open face and steady eyes, and put her hand up to muss his neat hair. It's not as if you were going off to war, she said. If I was, would you let me? If it was twenty years ago and tomorrow I was getting on a troopship and heading for France to fight the Germans, if it was maybe my last chance. But you aren't and it isn't. I might not see you again. That's all the more reason to be … careful. I'll be careful, I promise. I've got… you know, and he eased himself up so he could fumble in his pocket. I wouldn't hurt you for the world. Miles, I'm sorry, but I just don't want to do this. I love you, Sonia, I really love you. She stroked his hair and said nothing. If we could find a place to go… But she shook her head and kept on stroking his hair. It wouldn't make any difference. But I love you, he repeated again, almost querulous, as if annoyed that the words did not ignite the required response.

They returned home on the train, sitting side by side and

saying little. Would you let me? The words drummed in Sonia's head. That seemed to be what it was all about. She was being asked to allow Miles, as if it were understood that she herself was not an active participant. What would it be like to be the one saying please?

Miles walked her from the station to her gate. He did not come in to say goodbye to Ray and Mairi Letford, who thought Miles was a nice boy. Sonia put her hands on his shoulders, kissed him quickly and immediately drew back. Write to me, she said. But Miles did not write to her, did not even send her a birthday card. In December, when she again went to the Christmas dance wearing a different dress, a dress she had saved up her own money to buy, a silver-grey dress from Biba with black-striped sleeves, she thought of him. This time she had several dances with the captain of the cricket team when she was not sitting with Debbie and the others making usually scathing comments on the talent. How you managed to keep going with Miles for all those months I simply do not understand. What on earth did you find to talk to him about? Or maybe you had other things to occupy you. They all giggled. But he was nice, Debbie, Sonia said. I liked him. Not that nice, said Debbie. If he'd been really nice he'd at least have sent you a birthday card. Debbie stood up, put her hands on her hips and surveyed the room. What you need, she said, is someone to sweep you off your feet. But … she paused. But somehow I don't think that's going to happen tonight.

When Sonia was packing her suitcase to go to Cambridge she took the green silk dress from its hanger, but she knew she would not wear it again, even if she took up the hem. It belonged to the past, to school dances, to her first boyfriend whom she thought of kindly and without regret. She did not replace the dress on its hanger, but folded it and put it in a drawer. She laid the Biba dress out on her bed, but in the end that was returned to the wardrobe.

Sonia told Tim Billings about Miles. She told him about

the captain of the cricket team, though that had never amounted to much. And she told him about the young man with elegant hands and beautiful eyes who had made love to her in a drab bedsit on the far side of Parker's Piece and played honky-tonk on his landlady's out of tune piano. It was alcohol fuelled desire but at least it was desire, and it lasted most of her second term at university. Damp, bitter winds blew through the town and her fingers on the handlebars of her bike were numb with cold. It snowed, and as she cycled past Parker's Piece she noticed snowmen appear and survive a week or two, slowly thawing into shapeless lumps. The ponies on the piece of common across from the college had ice frozen in their manes and pawed at the snow to get at a few blades of grass. Her room was icy. She drew her chair close to the thin blue flame of the gas fire and read Shakespeare's sonnets. *The expense of spirit in a waste of shame.* Could that be right? At least she was warm in bed with Clive, the young man with beautiful eyes. When the thaw came the wheels of her bike threw grey slush on to her legs.

And Tim told her about Kath, whom he had met in the first week of his first term at Cambridge. She was my first real girlfriend, he said. We discovered everything together. No one else we knew stuck together for their whole time at university – we had a certain notoriety. The summer after we graduated we went off hitch-hiking round Europe. It wasn't good. I think we were just growing out of each other but didn't realise it until some months later. I went off to explore on my own and Kath sulked in cafés. It was a relief when we got back and went to separate jobs in separate cities. And then I met you. That helped. He took Sonia's hand and examined each finger.

Tim and Sonia lay side by side on the narrow bed, their hips touching. Sonia said, I guess sometimes people meet when they're eighteen and get married and stay together for the rest of their lives. Our problem, Tim said, mine and

Kath's, was that that was what people wanted us to do. Love's young dream, happily ever after. People wanted an exemplar of romantic possibility. Funny, really, when you think that now, a couple of years later, it's all about liberation and experiment. Is this liberation and experiment? Sonia asked. It's more than that, Tim said earnestly, isn't it? I mean, liberation is fine, but it's where it takes you that counts.

April 2014

I still have the postcards Tim sent, with their brief cryptic messages. It wasn't a courtship exactly as there were never any written words of affection. I wanted to write him proper letters, I wanted to tell him about my thoughts and feelings, but all we exchanged for a year and a half were postcards. In the summer of 1965 there was a picture of Highland cattle – he was in Scotland. That was followed by a Rembrandt self-portrait – he was in Amsterdam. I went camping in northern Spain with three friends and sent him postcards of Asturian mountains and Picasso's *Guernica*.

I was back home in Sussex in early September when the telephone rang. It's a man for you, my mother called. I was puzzled. Since Clive on the far side of Parker's Piece, I'd gone out, in a desultory kind of way, with a couple of boys but neither of them had my phone number. I'm in London for a few days, the voice said. Any chance we could meet? I'm here for work but I have a couple of free afternoons.

So we met on the steps of the National Gallery and he bought me tea and scones in the café. We wandered rather aimlessly through several galleries until Tim brought us to a halt in front of the Canalettos. This, said Tim firmly, this is what I like. For a long time we looked at Canaletto's *The Stonemason's Yard*. I'd like to build with stone, Tim said, but I probably never will. You don't build stone bridges any more. Have you been to Venice? No, I said. We'll do that one day. Will we? Of course. Tim continued to look at the painting. Water, buildings, people at work – what more can you ask for in a picture? You know what you like, I laughed. He turned then and looked down at me. Yes, he said, and then after a pause, I like you. But I just kept my eyes on the picture in front of me, the warm stone, the almost purple clouds in the sky, and the little people at work. Will we go to Venice, I was thinking, will Tim Billings and Sonia Letford go to Venice? It seemed a momentous question.

We did go to Venice. It was the December before Jake was born, cold and bright, with vivid sunshine every day. Venice was luminous and eerily empty, with so few tourists we could hear our own footsteps as we crossed the Piazza di San Marco. We sat outside – it was just warm enough – and drank coffee as we gazed at the light-bathed dome of Santa Maria della Salute. The water threw the light back at us. It felt almost like drowning. We stayed in a tiny room in a dark hotel near the Rialto. At night fragmented light danced and shimmered sliced by wedges of blackness. Magical, Tim said, as arm in arm we stopped to look down at a crowded row of tethered gondolas shifting slightly in the water like restless horses. And sinister, he added, as we continued our walk through the night, avoiding the narrowest and darkest streets. Imagine what might be lurking in these dark places.

When we emerged from the National Gallery we stopped to look out across the square. There were plenty of people there, but nothing like the mass assembled at the end of the march. It all looks completely different, doesn't it, Tim said. I lost you, I said. He took my hand. *I once was lost but now am found*, he said. He bent to kiss me, a slight, momentary touching of the lips, then straightened, tightened his grip on my hand and said, Let's walk down to the embankment. The thing is, he went on, all this time Kath has been flitting in and out of my life. She likes to wring every ounce of drama out of a situation. But now I know it's really over, that I'm really over her. And anyway, she's met someone else, so that's that.

The sun was warm. We found a seat and sat for a long time looking out over the river with pigeons at our feet. I remember the dress I wore, midnight blue and sleeveless, and I remember the sense of him sitting close, his hand covering mine, and the smell of the river mingled with traffic fumes. He talked not about Kath but about a girl he knew when he was still at school, who used to watch him playing cricket for his school team. They spent a few Sunday afternoons loitering on the front at Scarborough, eating ice cream or candyfloss, and then he would walk her as far as the corner of her street where they would part. I always meant to ask her out properly, he said, but I was too slow. When school finished she went off on holiday with her family. I had her phone number and in my head I rehearsed what I would say, but I never rang. Her name was Chrissie. She wanted to be a social worker. Tim smiled. I fantasised that Chrissie and I would be together forever. I would build bridges and she would do her social work (although I have to admit I wasn't very clear about what that entailed) and we'd have children and live in York, perhaps, in a house with a big garden. And here I am now, five years on, with someone completely different, and completely different from Kath, and no idea what Chrissie is doing. We hardly know each other, I said. With someone, with? I was thinking. His smile vanished and his eyes became serious again. We're going to get to know each other, aren't we? I really want that to happen. Yes, I said, I do too. But I remember how small my voice sounded. It wasn't lack of conviction but the fear of hoping for the impossible.

Tim talked a bit about Burnley and the mills closing down, and sang a verse of "Dirty Old Town". Then he stood up and with both his hands pulled me to my feet. We walked along the embankment and up to St James's Park and all the way to Victoria Station. His sleeves were rolled up and he held his jacket slung over his shoulder. The heat throbbed up from the pavement. I could feel him holding back his long stride so that I could keep pace with him. So let's begin, he said. Tell me about your boyfriends. There's not much to tell. There was Miles when I was sixteen, who was nice but, well just but. Miles now seemed distant and bland, and I wished there was more of a story to tell. There was Clive, who didn't last long. I didn't dwell on Clive, but almost wanted to make something up. I sensed that Kath was a big story, but he didn't say much then. He squeezed my hand but I felt diminished. I had so little history. Nice parents, nice house, good enough school, no traumas, no serious disappointments. Two past boyfriends, one nice, one not very. I felt empty of everything except ordinariness. Even sibling rivalry seemed ordinary.

Under the departure board at Victoria he held me firmly. My head rested on his chest and I was breathlessly conscious of my body against his, with just the thin cotton of my dress and his shirt between bare flesh. I felt the tension in his bare arms. He moved his hand to the back of my neck.

I was about to start my final year at university. He said he would visit me and he did. The first time he stayed in a guest house in Adams Road. The second time he spent the night with me in my room in the college's house off the Madingley Road. We took off our clothes and lay together in my narrow bed. It was a cold, damp late November night, and at first all we wanted was to get warm. I briefly thought of Clive, but quickly dismissed him. This was different. We were shivering and holding tight to each other. But it was a closeness I could not have imagined, a closeness born of companionship as much as the desire that came as our bodies warmed.

Half a century ago. If I concentrate I can bring back, almost, the sensation of skin on skin, the growing warmth relaxing our limbs, Tim's fingers and the palms of his hands.

I remember the feel of his bony shoulders, his muscled back, his smooth pale flank. I remember a surge of love that caught in my throat and brought tears to my eyes. I remember afterwards lying in his arms and thinking, Has this really happened? Can it be true that this man I have ached for all this time really loves me? Or am I kidding myself that all this means something? I'd read enough books to know, or to think I knew, that men were different, that their tenderness of the moment could be heartfelt but short-lived. But I held on to that initial closeness. We became good companions, Tim and I.

At least, I think I can remember that cold November night. It was the first of many, many times that Tim Billings and Sonia Letford, later Billings, were united in sexual congress. How can I filter out one stream of memory from another? But it hardly matters. The first time counts for so much less than the sum of all the other times.

I had an urgent need to be wanted. More than Dilys, I was sure, who was so casual about men, who didn't care whether they were attracted to her or not, which meant of course that they were drawn to her like wasps to jam. Dilys who boldly claimed that if you went out with a man you should be ready to sleep with him – after all, wasn't that what they all wanted and wasn't it, well, just mean to let them think that was what they would get, and then deny them? And in those days Miranda was never far away, always at the edge of my mind brimming with sexual as well as intellectual confidence, Miranda and her admirers whom she hinted at but never named and certainly never brought home to meet her family.

In the room next to mine was a girl called Rosalind, plump and pretty with honey-blonde hair. We didn't see much of each other – she was a biology student and spent long hours in labs and on field trips. But at night she became an enthusiastic co-conspirator. She checked that the coast was clear so that Tim could use the bathroom and gently tapped the door if all was well. She seemed to like the conspiracy, the subterfuge – perhaps it was a welcome diversion from her studies. She was the first person I told that Tim and I were going to get married, as we stood in the kitchen downstairs waiting for the kettle to boil for late-night coffee. Our final exams, Tripos Part II, were approaching.

The second person I told was Dilys, as we found ourselves leaving the examination hall together after three hours of desperately scribbling our way through the last paper. We crossed King's Parade to Miller's where she bought me a pink gin. That tall fellow you met on the march? My God, you are a dark horse. Well, we've hardly seen each other this last year or so. There wasn't a chance to tell you. You're well-suited, she said. Your children will be lean and long-legged with high cheekbones. Brown eyes probably, or hazel maybe. I bet you're going to live in a big house and have lots of children. You've done better than me, anyway, and she told me that she had been engaged briefly to two different men. Not the future Tory Member of Parliament, you'll be glad to hear. I think I may become a serial fiancée, she laughed and drained her glass. I've got my eye on another fellow. Met him in the Easter vacation – not a student at this university I'm pleased to say. Shall we have another? I checked my purse. I had just enough for two more pink gins. It was three in the afternoon when we emerged from the dim interior of Miller's into the sunny street. We stood slightly dizzily on the pavement. I'm off to a party in Trinity, Dilys said. Want to come along? For a moment I hesitated, as cars and bikes and people flowed past, but I shook my head. She didn't try to persuade me, but turned away a little unsteadily and walked off with a backward wave of her hand. I never saw her again. I invited her to the wedding but she didn't come, although she sent us a little earthenware jug which I still have. It survived the Yorkshire purge.

I found my bike and cycled back to my room, along the

Backs and up Madingley Road. By the time I got there I was feeling slightly sick – I'd had nothing to eat since eight that morning and the gin was boring into my stomach. I thought I might make some toast, but lay down on my bed. It was evening when I woke. There were starlings nesting in the eaves outside my window and I could hear the young ones shrieking for food. My head throbbed. Apart from the starlings, the house was empty and silent.

I collected "a decent II.1" (my supervisor's words) and my parents came to my graduation. My mother wore a hat. I had not often seen her in a hat – it seemed to distance her from me, although it could equally have been the dark clothes and gown and mortar board I had to parade in. We were a long crocodile shuffling into the Senate House. Tim was there too and met my parents for the first time. Miranda wasn't there, which was a relief. I was nervous of the effect my glamorous sister might have on my future husband. Later, my mother said he was a nice young man. My father was more circumspect. You're very young, he said. Perhaps you should wait a bit.

I was invited to Scarborough with Tim to spend a summer weekend with John and Myrtle Billings. John Billings was tall with thick white hair and dark eyes behind spectacles similar to his son's. One day Tim will look like that, I thought. His mother was a rotund, heavy-breasted woman who was simultaneously gracious and uncertain. I felt she was as uneasy at the prospect of a daughter-in-law as I was at taking on that role. She took my hand in both of hers and smiled, then hesitated. Was she going to kiss my cheek? But no. Well, she said, well, we'll have tea shall we, and she led the way into a spacious living room and through French windows on to a neat terrace, where we had tea and fruit cake.

Tim carried the tray from the kitchen, loaded with floral cups and a large teapot clad in a cosy, and then sat down in a garden chair and stretched out his long legs. He grinned across at me. The sun was warm. Did someone take a photograph? I can picture it all so clearly, me in a carefully chosen olive-green cotton two-piece, Mrs Billings in a yellow and white dress and white sandals, Mr Billings in baggy corduroys – what he called his gardening clothes. Tim rolled up the sleeves of his blue checked shirt. Mr and Mrs Billings asked me about my family, about living in Sussex, about university, polite questions to which I gave polite answers. What were my plans for the future? It's not a bad thing for a woman to have a profession, John Billings said, looking at me over the top of his glasses. I can remember that. I can hear his voice, followed by the clink as he replaced his empty china cup in its saucer. And I looked involuntarily at Myrtle Billings who at that moment leant forward to offer more cake, smiling but saying nothing. She, I knew, had never had a profession. She was a solicitor's wife. During the war she had worked briefly issuing ration books, the only time she had earnings of her own.

After tea Myrtle Billings retired to the kitchen and cooked an elaborate three-course meal. She fussed over cutlery and napkins. At dinner she talked in little bursts, dropping scraps of news about family friends who meant nothing to me. John Billings was almost silent. He methodically ate everything on his plate, pushed it away when it was empty, and leant back in his chair. There's pudding, John, his wife said, but he ignored this and asked, looking from Tim to me and back again, Well now, what are your plans? We don't really have plans, Tim said mildly, except for wanting to get married as soon as possible. Hmm, was the non-committal reply. Oh but we'll need to have a proper wedding, Myrtle said brightly as she began to gather up the plates. A proper wedding? A marquee in the garden, perhaps. Mother, I think... She was smiling with the plates in her hands as she stood by the dining room door. Tim's sister, she said, isn't married yet so we've not had a chance to plan a wedding. I took a deep breath.

Our garden isn't really big enough, I said tentatively. Oh, of course… Yes, of course, the wedding will be in Sussex, won't it? She couldn't mask her disappointment, but smiled briskly before disappearing into the kitchen. We'll have some good wine, though, Tim broke in. Sonia's father is a wine merchant. John Billings peered at me over his spectacles with a flicker of interest. He let out a short, explosive laugh. How splendid, he said.

After dinner, as I was helping with the washing-up, Myrtle confided that Tim had never brought a girlfriend home before, not since Chrissie whom he was friendly with in the sixth form. A nice girl, she said, but of course they were still only children. It was never serious. I'll be glad to see Tim settled, but … well, it's important to be sure, isn't it, and to plan carefully. There's no rush. She had reined in her enthusiasm for planning a wedding. I'm sure your parents feel the same, she added. I'm sure your mother will want time to consider all the details. I took extra care with the dishes, examining each plate to check that no smears or crumbs had been overlooked. I needed to pass muster.

I was nervous all that weekend, careful, wondering where to put myself. Was it all right to pick up Mr Billings's discarded copy of *The Times*? Should I offer to help with lunch on Sunday? Should I be looking for ways of demonstrating domestic competence? Should I attempt to reassure Tim's parents that we were making sensible plans, preparing for the future? That I'm capable and reliable? After lunch Tim and I walked along the Scarborough front, past the shopfronts piled with buckets and spades and candyfloss and postcards. How can you possibly prepare for the future? We stood for a long time watching an elderly man throw a ball for two Jack Russell terriers. The exhilaration faded and I felt frightened.

A strange world, it seems now. It's April. After a week of grey, damp weather it has grown a little warmer and the cloud is breaking to reveal tentative blue. The dogs and I walk up beside the burn as far as the grassy edge of our favourite little loch. I sit there for a while, listening to the birds. There are primroses out, and celandines, and pale green buds on the birch trees. Cleo goes into the water and splashes out again. Jet lies beside me, his head resting on his front paws. He watches me. It's hard to believe that so much time has passed, that so much has slipped through my fingers, irrecoverable. Tim is dead and I am here, in a place Tim never saw, never thought of. He could never have imagined the way I'm living now, in a small place in a small country. And in this small place I am a very small person, not physically as I am slightly taller than average (though probably not as tall as I was) but insignificant, making little impression beyond the money I spend in the shops and an occasional spark of interest in the strange old woman in the railway carriage. Kirstie is my friend, and I talk to other dog walkers. Some of them know my name – they all know the names of my dogs and I can name their dogs, Sam and Tilly and Murphy and Bracken. But to most I am nameless, the white-haired railway carriage woman with Cleo and Jet.

Tim and I used to describe people in our village with initials. There was the LM, the limpy man who walked with a stick, and the BTL, the bad-tempered lady, elegantly dressed but sour-faced and never responding when you said good morning, and the DU, the dirty urchin who was always hanging about the village shop. I wonder if people around here refer to me as the RCW. The W could stand for woman or witch.

Tim would hardly know me now. My neat short-cropped hair, cut in the same style for most of my adult life, has grown to my shoulders. I don't go to the hairdresser, but trim it myself when it gets too long. I tie it back at the nape of my neck. Most of the time I wear jeans. I still have some of the clothes I wore when I taught my evening classes, but there is no need to wear them. They are folded away in suitcases under the spare bed. They come out on my rare trips to the south. Each time I hang them at an open window for a while and then iron them. When I put on these unfamiliar garments they feel awkward, and for a while I am not sure who I am.

Harriet and Matt came for New Year. They arrived in their car loaded with food and drink. I pointed out that there were good shops in the town and that there was not much you couldn't get. Matt plans to cook some special meals, Harriet said, and wasn't sure if he'd be able to get everything he needed. I handed the kitchen over to him. They squeezed into the spare room, where the double bed takes up most of the space.

Matt cooked a splendid Hogmanay dinner. There was just room for three to sit at my little table. Well, he said, as we ate his crème brûlée, have you decided how to vote? I shook my head. We don't want Scotland to abandon us. He raised his wine glass thoughtfully and put it down again. On the other hand, I can see the attraction of severance from that shower in Westminster and if I were in your shoes I'd be tempted. I don't like borders, I said. I want collaboration, not separation, not nationalism, but collaboration on equal terms. Equal terms! Matt laughed. In your dreams. You're not suggesting mum should vote yes? Maybe. Maybe, I echoed. Trident, Matt said. Yes, I said, indeed. But I want – it came to me suddenly what it was I wanted – I want a better Britain, not just a better Scotland. Yes, said Harriet emphatically, leaning forward, yes, that's it exactly. So you can't vote yes, mum. But maybe, Matt said, you have to have a better Scotland first. That's the dilemma, I said, that's what I'm not sure about. Matt placed both hands on the table, the candlelight glinting on his glasses. If I were living here, I could get quite carried away. Something different, something new, a nation reinvigorated. I think a lot of people feel like that, I said in what I hoped was a neutral tone. Sometimes I feel like that myself. Only sometimes? I'm not convinced that much would change. Worth taking a punt on, maybe, Matt persisted. Nothing's going to change if you don't. But I think, said Harriet, I think that having the debate will in itself encourage people to think about possibilities. And aren't they giving the vote to sixteen-year-olds? That could re-engage a whole generation. Yes, I said, I hope it will. Whatever the outcome, that seems to be a good thing.

We went out just before midnight, up on to the canal bank, to watch a brief salvo of fireworks above the town. I hugged my daughter – Happy New Year, mum – and my almost son-in-law. With the fireworks faded, there was a bright scatter of stars above us. In a few weeks' time it will be Harriet's fortieth birthday. I notice the first intimations of lines at the corners of her eyes and mouth. Too late for children, I suppose. I'd have liked a grandchild closer than Auckland. Could be the start of a momentous year, Matt said. No one in England is paying much attention to what's going on here, but I predict they will. I predict that this referendum will shake up the whole country. I looked at him in surprise, but he didn't notice. He was smiling, as if in eager anticipation of the shake-up.

When Harriet and Matt left two days later I felt unusually alone. As I watched their car roll away down the narrow road I was almost tearful. The Turnbulls' house was empty, although they usually come for New Year. This time they'd gone somewhere exotic. The big house seemed to expand its emptiness into the garden as I crossed it followed by the dogs. I stepped into the railway carriage and felt a palpable absence. It was good to claim the space as mine again but it didn't feel quite right. There was something missing. Not some*thing*, I reproved myself, someone, my daughter, my daughter and the man she lives with. I heard her voice. Why so far away? Matthew's voice. We wish we could see more of you. Yes, I was fond of Matthew. His voice. Nothing's going to change if you don't.

I sat for a long time on the sofa with the dogs beside me. When I finally got to my feet I was stiff. I had to get out. We walked along the canal, not in the direction of the town but the other way, to the western shore four miles distant, where I stood and looked out at the dark islands and the boats swinging idly at their moorings. Cleo as usual went into the water, scuffed by an erratic wind, while Jet sat close beside me. This was what I had chosen and I didn't regret it. To have turned my back on the derelict railway carriage would always have been the road not taken. I'd have been haunted by imagining a different life. To have stayed in my much-loved red brick house, where my children grew up, where Tim and I had made a decent fist of marriage and had never stopped loving each other, would have been no road at all. The walk back along the canal was a weary trudge against the wind.

Of course love changes its shape and its colour and its clothes. But its core of warmth and kindness was never eroded. Through most of my thirties I was too exhausted to enjoy sex much, but when the children were older there was a rediscovery that seemed equally urgent on Tim's part. A couple of times we were able to have a weekend away. Once when Tim was advising on a bridge repair job in Shropshire I joined him for a weekend in Church Stretton. We stayed in a guest house and walked in Carding Mill Valley and out on to the hills which that March were covered in snow. We came on a herd of shaggy-coated ponies that peered at us through frosted thickets of mane. And we went back and made love on a soft, wide bed and watched the light fade through the uncurtained window. Later we pulled on our coats and scarves and tramped through the snow to find a pub where we ate scampi and chips and drank indifferent white wine and then tramped back through the snow and the cold to shed our clothes and slide back into the warm, wide bed.

And now it's April in the Scottish Highlands. There are

lambs in the fields and Kirstie comes to tell me her cat has had five kittens. Would I like one, or even two? Her daughters want to keep them all, which of course is impossible but it wouldn't be so bad if they go to neighbours. I look at the dogs. I'd have to think about that, I say. But I make coffee and we sit outside on the garden chairs I bought at the charity shop. Kirstie holds her mug with both hands and says with a slight smile, I have other news. I wait. I've met someone. Ah, I say. Is that good? I think so, she says, I think it's good. Her smile widens. He's nice. The girls like him, I think. I'm watching them like a hawk for signs of an adverse reaction. I'll invite you to supper soon to meet him. Maybe he'd like a kitten, I say. Kirstie laughs. A blackbird is singing on a branch in the corner of the garden. Cleo is stretched on her side, her legs straight out, bathed in sunlight. Jet is lying in his usual posture, head on forepaws. From time to time his eyes open. Just checking.

1974

Tim and Sonia Billings had been in their spacious new house for four months. They were not used to having a garden to look after, and in January it looked bedraggled and unkempt. Dead leaves clogged the flower beds where remnants of the summer languished. It was a long, dispiriting month. Sonia stared out of the window into the gathering dusk and closed her ears to the shouts of Jake and Clare's wails. She looked at her watch. It was not yet four o'clock. The children's noise subsided as suddenly as it had erupted, and she turned heavily from the window to survey the scatter of bright plastic on the floor and the procession of toy cars that Jake, lying on his stomach, was pushing towards Clare. Clare, silent but with the corners of her mouth turned down, watched grimly as they approached. Sonia knew that at any minute there would be another wail. One by one Jake pushed the cars forward, a few inches at a time. His mop of fair hair almost reached his fiercely concentrating eyes. The nose of a yellow Ford was nearly touching Clare's bare leg. She opened her mouth. Let's do some drawing, Clare, said Sonia quickly. Clare shook her head. She stared intently, fists clenched, as Jake pushed the yellow car forward another inch so that it touched her skin. He looked up at her. She took a deep breath and let out a long, high-octane sound that seemed to shake the window. Jake smiled, reversed the yellow car and concentrated on bringing a blue Mini level with it. Sonia looked down help-lessly at the two small beings on the floor.

Three hours later Sonia was at the kitchen sink wash-ing the supper dishes. Clare was asleep. Tim was upstairs reading Jake a story. Sonia paused with her hands drip-ping soapy water. Something, more than the usual thumps inside her belly. A lurch, a pressure. She put her hands on the edge of the sink and leant forward. False alarm, surely. She had nearly three weeks to go. She finished the washing up and left the dishes to drain. She sat down in the living room and picked up the paper, but she did not look at it. All she wanted was to sleep. She closed her eyes, opened them again when she heard Tim's footsteps coming down the stair. Something again. She laid the paper down and waited. Tim came into the room. Out like a light, he said, and then saw the expression on Sonia's face. What is it? I think... It's too early. I know. I'll just wait a bit and see... False alarm? Maybe. Let's just wait. I can't take you. I know. An ambulance, or a taxi. Even if I phone my mother now she couldn't be here for, I don't know, probably a couple of hours.

Tim sat on the arm of her chair and put his hand on the back of her neck. She smiled up at him. It will be fine, she said.

It was almost not fine. Four hours later Harriet was born, in the local hospital but only just. It was nearly midnight when Tim called the ambulance, and soon after stood at the front door watching it depart while the children slept upstairs. Jake will be cross that he missed the ambulance, Sonia said as Tim had helped her into it. He kissed her fiercely. Don't worry Mr Billings, the paramedic said cheerfully. We'll get her there. But as they bowled along the dark road he held Sonia's hand and said, try not to push, and then made her laugh. You mothers, just as I was starting on a bacon roll, no consideration. She was laughing when the next contraction came and she held hard to his hand. Ten minutes after arriving at the hospital Harriet made a smooth if peremptory appearance, and afterwards Sonia said that she wished the other two had been as easy. There was no time for anything to dull the pain but the relief of giving way to the baby's urgent progress was all that mattered. Half an hour later she telephoned Tim. Another girl, she said. The next morning she phoned her parents and her father answered. A girl? Well done, love. Very satisfactory. Mairi! It's a girl! Her mother's voice. That's wonderful, pet. And she's all right, is she? And you? She's fine and I'm fine, no problems though it was all rather quick. And do you have a name? Yes, she's Harriet. Not sure about a middle name but probably Grace, after Tim's mother. Harriet Grace, that sounds nice. And you're quite right, it should be Grace as you gave Clare my name. Now, pet, you must take things easy. Tim's mother is on her way over to help. Well, that's just fine. Your dad and I will come up soon, you just tell us when you're ready. I can't wait to see my new granddaughter. She's lovely, quite a lot of light brown hair.

Tim drove them home from the hospital. Grace Billings was at the door and from behind her two children burst out and stampeded to the car. Tim hauled them back from the car door and helped Sonia and little Harriet out. Let me see, let me see! Jake reached a hand up to the bundle in his mother's arms. Clare was jumping up and down, then stopped abruptly and stuck her thumb in her mouth. It's a girl, said Jake dubiously. I've made a hotpot, said Grace.

Harriet, in spite of her precipitous arrival, was a calm and gradually undemanding baby who grew into a calm and thoughtful child. Tim worried sometimes. It didn't seem natural, the way she could walk into a room full of people, seem to take their measure, and retreat to a corner with her book. She would do that even as a toddler.

The year before the birth of Harriet, Sonia began to teach evening classes in Leeds. She had not been gainfully employed since before Jake was born, when she worked for a couple of years in a Burnley estate agent's. At first it was only one class a week, a course on Victorian fiction. When the children were asleep, she reread her favourite novels and read a few that were new to her. Tim made sure he got home early on a Wednesday evening. Occasionally he was away, and Sonia had to arrange a babysitter. It was hardly worth her while teaching if she had to pay for books, travel and babysitting, but once she'd started she enjoyed it too much to stop. During the last two months of pregnancy she was very tired and driving was uncomfortable, but she continued to take her class every Wednesday. When she realised she was likely to miss the last session of the course she arranged an extra class so that they could discuss Thomas Hardy before the baby came. It seemed appropriate to be discussing *Tess* and *Jude the Obscure*, and she made a joke about it. Her class of mainly pensioners were not sure whether to laugh.

Tim was a good sleeper. The cries of babies rarely woke him. Sonia was awake at the first splutter, and out of bed to hush and feed and change the complaining infant. Sometimes she returned to bed with Harriet in her arms and sat propped against the pillow, Tim asleep beside her, humming very softly until Harriet too was sleeping. Sometimes she would carry Harriet into the room which Jake and Clare shared and look down at her sleeping children, Jake's thick fair hair ruffled by the pillow, Clare's hand curled beside her ear. Their faces pale and fragile. Sonia would listen to their quiet breathing, and herself breathe in the peacefulness which only came at night, when all the family slept and she walked alone through the house with her youngest and, she thought, her final child, in and out of the moonlight that pooled through uncurtained windows. On those nocturnal wanderings, the warmth of her child seeping into her, she discovered a deeper self. Only with her third child and only when there were no waking voices to draw her away did she locate something at the heart of her being that she could not find words for. A kind of intimacy with herself that the baby unleashed, but once those months had passed did not return.

By 6 a.m. Jake was bouncing on his parents' bed and Clare was demanding to be lifted from her cot and Harriet was bawling for sustenance. At 7.30 Tim kissed each child and then his wife and left for work. The pattern of sound was now so familiar that Sonia heard it in her head almost detached from the actual sounds of departure. The bang of the front door, Tim's footsteps on the gravel, the growl of the engine, the crunch of tyres, the rise and fall of the children's voices. Clare refused to sit in the high chair and sat with her chin scarcely clearing the table's edge spooning a mush of cereal very slowly into her mouth. Clare took her time to eat. Halfway through she demanded toast. Jake was on the floor with a parade of cars. Sonia buttered Clare's toast while she cradled Harriet in her left arm. Awkwardly, she cut it into triangles and took a sip of lukewarm tea. Clare took a bite of toast and then continued slowly spooning cereal. She held a triangle of toast in one hand, stared at it thoughtfully, and dropped it into the mush in her dish. Are you going to eat your toast, Clare? She shook her head. I didn't want triangles, I wanted squares. Sonia reached over for what was left of the toast and ate it herself.

By 8.45 Harriet was in the pram and Jake was standing at the door trying to open it. Clare had removed the shoes which Sonia had just put on her feet. Sonia picked her up, sat her in the pram where there was just space for her without squashing the baby, and put one shoe in each of her pockets. They set out for playgroup in the church hall, ten minutes' walk at Jake's erratic pace. Clare howled that she wanted her shoes on. After depositing Jake at playgroup Sonia fished Clare's shoes out of her pockets and put them on. Clare contemplated her feet for a few moments before pulling her shoes off and dropping them over the side of the pram. Sonia returned them to her pockets and Clare howled again and kept it up until they were back at their own front door, when she stopped abruptly.

The year of Harriet's birth was not a good year. There was a feeling of menace, of the world awry. Bombs went off, in London, Birmingham. The newspapers were filled with Watergate and Nixon's resignation. Tim and Sonia struggled, prices rising, electricity cuts, petrol in short supply. Sonia returned to her teaching a few weeks after Harriet arrived. They needed the money, but it was more than just the money. She had discovered that she liked to teach, and most of all she liked to read and think about the books she read. Teaching gave a purpose to activities she loved. She also discovered that without teaching an undefinable malaise spread through her. There were times when the children, even Tim, shape-shifted into a hostile company of adversaries.

The following October, shortly after her thirtieth birthday, Sonia began to teach two courses, Victorian fiction and twentieth-century fiction between the wars. For the next thirty years she taught evening classes on a range of topics: Shakespeare, First World War poetry, the Romantic poets, American fiction, an entire course on George Orwell. The faces changed, although some of the faithful attended year after year, sometimes following the same course twice. The older ones gradually disappeared, they got ill or died or lost interest or were too infirm to come out in the evenings, but new and younger faces took their place. There were some modest achievements which were a source of quiet satisfaction. A young woman in her twenties was persuaded to take A levels and went on to the University of Hull. A middle-aged out-of-work husband and father was writing a novel which he showed to Sonia. She encouraged him, and it was eventually published. A husband and wife in their eighties attended doggedly for several years. When they failed to appear Sonia made enquiries, and discovered that they had died within weeks of each other. But there was very little excitement, beyond the flurry of expectation at the start of the course when Sonia looked around the room and noted the new faces. Each term the thirty or so who attended the first session gradually dwindled to a reliable core of about fifteen. It happened every time, and every time Sonia was anxious that the numbers were too few for the class to be viable. But closure never came. Sonia was a safe pair of hands, perhaps not inspirational, but her students liked her.

There was one apparent exception. One year a tall, good-looking young man who had dropped out of university signed up for her course on George Orwell. He sat at the back and made dry, cynical and sometimes aggressive comments. Orwell was so preoccupied with his own class background he couldn't see straight. Saint George, he said, tipping his seat back, was clearly a misogynist. He posed as an anti-fascist but wrote books that were a gift to the right wing. You're all determined to put him on a pedestal, he sneered. A retired trade unionist rose to the bait, and the young man, sitting at an angle with his long legs splayed out to the side, smiled. You have no idea, said the trade unionist, you don't know what you're talking about. Of course he wasn't perfect, not a saint, but by God he said things that needed to be said. He grasped nettles that no one else would grasp. Another voice joined in. Grow up, it said. The young man looked slowly round the room, still smiling. Do I detect resentment of the younger generation? he asked. I've probably seen more of life than all of you put together.

At least Saint George didn't live a safe little life. At least he got out there, did stuff, took risks.

At the end of the class he got lazily to his feet and, as the door was at the front, was the last to leave.

Sean, said Sonia, still gathering her books and notes. He stopped in the doorway and turned with a look of disingenuous polite enquiry. What are your plans for the future? For a moment he seemed puzzled, then recovered his detachment. I don't make plans, he said. That's a pity, said Sonia mildly. You have more years in front of you than most of the class. It's a shame to waste that potential. She slid her pile of books and papers into a capacious bag and smiled at him. She noticed the fleeting look of – anxiety, fear even? – that clouded his eyes. He was carrying paperbacks of *The Road to Wigan Pier* and *Homage to Catalonia*, which he shifted from one hand to the other. The gesture seemed to restore his confidence, and looking at Sonia directly his sardonic smile returned and he said, I'm going to be a journalist. Ah, said Sonia, excellent. She slung her bag on her shoulder and walked towards the door. He stepped back. She took a last look around the classroom and switched off the lights. Reading Orwell is a good preparation for a career in journalism, she said pleasantly. He did not reply, but walked along the corridor and out of the building a few steps ahead of her. He held the door for her and she thanked him. When she got to her car she turned and watched as he took long strides down the street, his hands in his pockets. She never saw him again.

Tim was promoted and was away more often, but never for more than two or three days. He went to a conference in Milan and to Vilnius to observe and advise on a project there. Why don't you come too, he said on these occasions. But the time was never right. She saw him off on the train to Heathrow, excited for him. Most of the projects he worked on were modestly utilitarian. The dream of creating some spectacular structure, a bridge, perhaps, that would be remembered for generations, never materialised. After he died, Sonia found a drawer full of sketches and diagrams and notes on materials. She could see at once that they were for structures that were never built.

May 2014

I was in the garden tonight with the dogs, still light after ten, the first nasturtiums glowing red and yellow. The potatoes and broad beans are in flower and the runner beans are twining up their stakes. I found a colony of snails near the spinach and dropped them into the bucket of saltwater I keep for the purpose. I have learnt cruelty to snails and slugs. I wonder if those who are brutal to humanity can so readily close their minds to what they are doing. The news is full of tales of unimaginable cruelty, out of anger, or fear, or despair, or conviction. I thought of this as I collected slugs in a flower pot and shook them into the bucket.

There was a shower of rain earlier and the smell of warm, wet earth lingered. I climbed a little way up the slope to watch an amber sunset while the dogs snuffled in the long grass. Like Stevenson's child, I find it difficult to go to bed when it is still light and now I am sitting inside while the dusk thickens beyond the window. The dogs have settled into their usual positions on the sofa. They know that the day has come to an end. Cleo watches me with soulful eyes. The little table in front of me is piled with newspapers, catalogues that keep arriving in the post, library books and a couple of recent paperback novels I bought from the local bookshop. Earlier I was reading, but I don't feel inclined to read now. I just sit, perhaps only half awake, knowing that the next thing I do will be to get to my feet and prepare for bed. There seems a disconnection between my brain and my limbs, my brain anticipating my next move, my limbs refusing to receive its message. I suppose these chasms are likely to increase.

When at last I move the last silvery gleam in the sky has almost gone. There is just enough light inside to see where I am going. Each dog gets a scratch behind the ears. Cleo gives me a resigned look and closes her eyes, Jet doesn't stir. I relish the insignificant action of slipping into bed, relaxing against the pillows, pulling up the duvet. I switch on the lamp and open my bedside reading. It's a book about Scotland's future. Scotland should be in better shape. Scotland could be in better shape if her government could be disconnected from Westminster. I read somewhere recently that a survey had found that a majority of respondents felt that only those who were born in Scotland should be considered Scottish. I would not anyway have considered myself Scottish, nor do I want to be considered Scottish, but I wonder at that. My mother's Scottish birth and ancestry should be sufficient. But it is irrelevant. I live here. I am registered to vote here. I expect to die here. That's what counts.

Should the place where you die have a bearing on identity? I think of soldiers who die on foreign soil, of my uncle, my mother's brother who died at about the time I was born. In her memory, his death in Holland was part of who he was. So for my children, will my death in Scotland affect how they remember me? Will it matter more than the years, however many they may be, that I have lived here? I didn't come here to die, but it will be, probably, a collateral of my transplantation. Some people go home to die, or hope to – *the hunter home from the hill.* Stevenson wanted to die among his own hills, although to readers now his Samoan death is so meaningful. Perhaps some atavistic pull brought me here, latent until triggered by the accidental sighting of a half-ruined place of residence. A carriage which will never again go anywhere, at least not in one piece or on its own wheels.

I should know more about my Scottish origins. Who knows, it might be useful one day if I can demonstrate my heritage. My father and grandfather were both railwaymen, that I am clear about, and here I am in a railway carriage. My mother's mother was a Gaelic speaker from Lewis who came to Edinburgh to a job in one of the city's big hotels, and here I am in an area thick with Gaelic names. But I cannot pretend to belong here. I am an incomer who has purchased a piece of Scotland, a very small piece, although the garden I cultivate is not mine. I have a very small home (I can confidently call it my home now) and a few square metres of space around it. I am not sure exactly how much of the space is mine, but I think I can circumnavigate my railway carriage on my own ground. I exchanged a larger piece of England for this small fragment of Scotland. Incomers who buy pieces of Scotland are not well liked, of course they're not. But I cannot take my little bit of Scotland away. I cannot parcel it up and lay it out in another territory, though I could, I suppose, transport a handful of earth. People have done that. A jam jar of Sussex earth to Yorkshire, of Yorkshire earth to Argyll, of Argyll earth to – where? Or perhaps a single jar with all the soil shaken up together.

Was my railway carriage Scottish-built? I know it's possible. I'd like to think that it was constructed not too far away, but I'm not sure why it matters. I know there were Scottish-built locomotives to be found all over the world. Like Clyde-built ships, they were a symbol of Scottish industry and enterprise, and now it seems that is all gone and we must find reasons for its departure and connect those reasons with forces beyond our control. Now there are those who believe that we can regain control, in this very different world. Tim would have been up for that, I think. His whole life was based on a practical connection between aspiration and the materials to hand. On the day he retired, as we were returning home after his farewell dinner in Leeds, he said, I may not have achieved anything spectacular, but at least nothing I've been responsible for has ever fallen down. He lost his son, though. That was beyond his grasp of cause and effect. There were times when I dreamt, wildly, of scattering Jake on the mountain that killed him. I would never have dared to mention the possibility to Tim.

I am urged to think of Scotland's future, of the society I would wish for my children and grandchildren. My children are elsewhere, my son and his children far elsewhere. I fear that if Scotland separates from England, the England where I have, as yet, no grandchildren, will be a worse place. It is the country of my birth, the country where I have spent most of my life although now I choose not to live there. But perhaps I am making too much of my personal circumstances. I should step away from the past, think of the children I see every day in the town, of Kirstie's teenage daughters. Potentiality. It's a word people use. There is always potential, wherever people are. In the worst situations you can imagine there is always potential. Is potential different from potentiality? Anything that may be possible, not *is* possible but may be. What are the verbs you can bring together with potential? You can unlock it, release it, realise it. You can stifle it. In my dictionary, potentiality is assumed to have the same definition as potential. Independence will set free Scotland's potential, or potentiality? It's a seductive thought. Anything is possible.

My mother didn't exactly choose to live in the south of England. I wonder if my father ever considered setting up business in Scotland. You'd have thought Edinburgh or Glasgow would have had plenty of potential for an off-licence. I might, after all, have grown up Scottish, never gone to Cambridge, never met Tim. We might have made annual visits driving south to Sussex, with my father triumphantly shouting England! as we crossed the border – which he never did when we returned from Scotland. There was only my mother's regretful, Scotland farewell, until next year. Our house might have escaped the bomb. You think about these things when you're approaching seventy. You think about the other lives you might have led.

I am not reading my book. I have laid it down while my thoughts freewheel. Eventually I will fall asleep, but just now I am imagining how it might be if I had grown up in this country, gone to school here, married here. I would still have had an English father. I'd have visited my English grandparents, become at least a little familiar with the southern county they inhabited. I would have felt connected in some way. I would perhaps be feeling that it was impossible for me personally to sever myself from my father's England. But it's only a vote, and in reality, how much disconnection is there likely to be? How possible will it be to separate Scotland's future from the rest of these islands? And will the act of voting make any difference, to me or to Scotland?

All I know is that I will vote. I cannot break the habit of a lifetime.

Tomorrow I am going to have supper at Kirstie's, to meet her new man. His name is Clem. The only Clements I know of are Clement Attlee and Clement Freud and I cannot imagine Kirstie with either of them. But I like the name, perhaps because there is a slight echo of Tim. A monosyllable ending in M. He's something to do with forestry. Maybe like Tim he is a practical man who understands the materials he works with.

There is an email from Lucas. He says he plans to bring the boys over for two weeks at the end of September. He won't make it in time for my birthday, as school doesn't finish until a week later, and Lettie has used up nearly all her leave so won't be able to come, but we could have a delayed celebration. Lettie says she hopes I'm voting yes, that voting for independence isn't necessarily a vote for nationalism. I can see her smile, her bright clothes, hear her New Zealand voice. Lucas himself does not advise on how I should vote. They'll spend a few days with Harriet in Cambridge, then hire a car and drive up to Scotland once they've recovered from jet lag. A surge of anticipation rushes through me. I wonder if I can fit Lucas and two growing boys into the railway carriage. Would it be reasonable for the boys to share the double bed and Lucas to sleep on the sofa? Or perhaps I could ask the Turnbulls if I could borrow space in their house, pay them rent perhaps. How will I entertain the boys? What if it rains all the time? What do the boys like to eat? I reply straight away. Dear Lucas, I write, I'm so pleased to hear about your plans and hugely looking forward to having you and the boys here. There's plenty of time to sort out the details – the important thing is that you're coming. I'm sorry Lettie can't manage to be with you. I tell him things he knows already, about the dogs and the garden. I hope the boys will like the dogs. I tell him I am still undecided as to how to vote.

I change my jeans and baggy shirt for clean trousers and a black top, and choose a bottle of wine to take to Kirstie's. I'll walk the half mile to her house and although I plan to leave before it gets dark I'll take my torch. The dogs will come with me and I'll feel quite safe. I've never felt uneasy here, even when my daughters do their best to make me nervous with their constant anxiety at my solitary existence in an eccentric residence with, most of the time, no near neighbour. They reprimand me for not locking my door. But I always do at night, I tell them. I would be annoyed if someone stole my laptop, but the prospect does not alarm me enough always to lock my door. Is it principle? A need to signal a difference from the way life used to be? All my years in Yorkshire saw the same ritual. Keys – check. Back door locked – check. Front door locked – check. On a few occasions I forgot to check that I had my keys and pulled the front door closed and heard the Yale click just as I thought, keys, and fumbled in my bag and pockets to no avail. But I kept spare keys under a stone in the garden. As teenagers the children often found themselves locked out and used the emergency keys. Sometimes they neglected to replace them. Once I came home to an empty house without keys and found nothing under the stone. My neighbours gave me a glass of sherry as I waited for Tim or one of the children to return. I'd left a note on the door. It was Lucas, coming in late from his music practice, who appeared. What are you doing here, mum? Someone didn't replace the emergency key, I said. Wasn't me, he said, showing me his own key on its football key ring. I knew it wasn't Tim. I can't remember a time when Tim forgot his keys.

I am at Kirstie's house. I am sitting at the table opposite Clem, a spare, wiry man with a beard and thinning hair, while Kirstie stands at the stove keeping watch over a risotto. Clem tells me he grew up in rural Aberdeenshire. I am sufficiently attuned to Scottish accents now that I might have guessed that. He worked in Brazil for many years and returned to Scotland after his divorce. His children are growing up Brazilian, more proficient in Portuguese than in English. I'd like them to be Scottish, he says rather wistfully. I'd like them to be with me and to make their homes in an independent Scotland, but they are with their mother. And he adds, Odd, isn't it, that a shrinking world makes it easier to divide families. It would have been so much harder to leave them if I'd thought I would never see them again. I probably wouldn't have returned to Scotland. I left a good job.

In a corner of Kirstie's kitchen there is a cardboard box lined with an old sweater from which comes a thin mewling sound. The kittens are still tiny, but their eyes are open and they clamber over each other. They are a mix of grey and tabby. Their mother lies patiently as they scrabble to feed. There is a grey one with white paws which takes my fancy. The girls tell me they think it's a boy and they've called him Ash. The other grey kitten is called Smoke. I wanted to call them Smoke and Mirrors, Clem jokes, but the girls wouldn't let me.

I think it's about right, Kirstie says. Jess is outside playing with the dogs and comes in reluctantly. Ellie is already seated. She is allowed half a glass of wine. She is just sixteen, and will vote for the first time in the coming referendum. I'm voting no, she says airily as we start to eat. I don't want to live in a tartan and bagpipes country. Clem laughs, shaking his head. Independence doesn't mean tartan and bagpipes, says her mother. It might even mean less of both. This is about political control, Ellie, self-determination. And it may be our only chance of a fairer society. Well, I don't buy it, Ellie says. What makes you think independence will bring fairness? I don't trust our lot any more than the Westminster crowd. You're an idealist, mum, she continues knowingly, a romantic idealist. Kirstie laughs. In my day it was the younger generation who had ideals, I say, and Kirstie says, I'd rather be an idealist than a cynic. She pushes her heavy hair back from her tanned and freckled face. Besides, if you don't believe that things can be better, nothing will ever change.

Ellie shrugs. We discuss possible homes for the kittens. Kirstie clears the plates and puts a rhubarb tart and a jug of cream on the table. Ellie has finished her wine and is looking speculatively at the bottle on the table. None of my friends is going to vote yes, she says. Jess leaves the table and goes out with the dogs again. Clem says, From the way some people talk you'd think a vote for independence would mean a physical severance. Scotland with her flotilla of islands would be ripped away from England and would drift north and east towards Norway and Denmark. Her southern border would become a jagged coastline. Better a coastline than barbed wire, some might say. But let's not be ridiculous. It's not ever going to come to barbed wire and armed guards. How do you know? Ellie says. She surreptitiously pours more wine into her glass, but her mother notices and takes the bottle from her. Jess comes in and cuts herself a large piece of rhubarb tart, adds a lake of cream, and then sits on the floor with her legs straight out. She holds her plate in one hand and with the other piles the kittens on to her lap. With the kittens heaving like a miniature furry earthquake she eats her rhubarb tart. Cleo sits beside her with her tongue hanging out.

Clem is still talking. Look at Scotland's resources – water, for a start. He opens his hands, fingers spread. I have a vision of a parched planet desperate for water, the south of England a desert and looking north to Scotland's rain and lochs and rivers. People are already fighting for water, Clem is saying. The world turns on oil and water. I wonder, I say, if there are any circumstances in which England, or what remains of the United Kingdom, would invade an independent Scotland? Clem laughs again. For our oil and water? It's not that hard to imagine.

Well, says Ellie, our most valuable exports are helping to destroy the planet and people. We all look at her. Oil, obviously, and whisky. Everyone knows that petrol and diesel kill loads of people. And do you know how many people die of alcohol-related diseases? How many, Ellie? Kirstie asks. I don't know the exact figures – but a lot, especially in Scotland. So, the economy of an independent Scotland will depend on killing people. She gazes round the table triumphantly. The girl has a point, Clem says.

It's a feeling as much as anything, isn't it? Kirstie says slowly. I mean, most people don't sit down and carefully work out how much they would gain and how much they would lose, although so often that's how arguments are presented. It's not even a heart and head thing, so much as a gut thing.

That's not very grown up, Ellie says. Perhaps not, but when I was little there was a wee burn that ran at the back of our house and my brother and I used to make dams with mud and stones and sticks. And I used to think then that it was our burn and our dam, our mud, our stones, our sticks. But of course they weren't ours. And I guess there are a lot of people who will vote yes because they think it will give them a sense of ownership. A false sense, Ellie says. Maybe, but the feeling's important all the same. Maybe it's attachment rather than ownership. Plenty of people left Scotland in search of the opportunity to own their own land, Clem says. Some of them ended up in Brazil.

I listen to this with a growing sense of fragility. My jam jar of mixed earth lying shattered, fragments of glass among the crumbs of dirt. Bombs. I never expected to belong, but I would like to feel less precarious.

Clem is watching Kirstie with a slight smile. She picks up her fork and pushes at a few grains of rice. So mum, Ellie says, leaning back in her chair, you're going to vote yes because you have a childhood illusion about owning your own mud and sticks. Maybe. But maybe not, because I have another gut feeling, a conflicting one. I have a problem with the United Kingdom, because Scotland would still be part of the UK, or part of a not quite so united kingdom but still with the same head of state. And that just doesn't make sense to me, and I don't think it would make sense even if I weren't a republican. If we still have a monarch and all that follows from that it will be a pretty pale sort of independence. There you are, says Ellie, the whole thing is pointless, a waste of time and money.

No, Ellie, Kirstie says earnestly, it's not at all pointless, because people in Scotland are thinking about the future in a way they've never done in my lifetime. And you've got a chance to vote, so don't waste it. It's fine if you vote no. It's a secret ballot, Ellie, Clem says. You don't need to tell your mother how you vote. Ellie grins and takes a swallow of wine. I won't, she says, and then she turns to me. How are you going to vote, Sonia? I smile. It's a secret ballot, Ellie, I say. But I'm interested, Ellie persists. You're not Scottish and you've not lived here all that long. It must seem different to you. Your family don't live in Scotland so your closest connections are somewhere else. That's true, I say, but my mother was born near Edinburgh and I probably have Scottish relatives, I just don't know who or where they are. You could find out though, Ellie says, suddenly interested. It would be fun to search for them. There are all kinds of records online now.

Kirstie is dividing up the rest of the rhubarb tart. I am looking at Ellie and wondering at her apparent insight into my thoughts of the night before. She plants her elbows on the table and leans forward. What were your grandparents' names? My grandfather was William Ewing. We used to visit him in the village near Edinburgh where they lived. I never knew my grandmother, but her name was Elizabeth and she came from Lewis. When were they born? Oh, I don't know. Late nineteenth century, I guess. I think my grandfather was born in Dalkeith. We could look up the 1911 census, Ellie says, see if there's a William Ewing in Dalkeith. What about aunts and uncles? My mother had an older brother but he was killed in the war, no wife or children so I had no Scottish cousins. There must have been great aunts and uncles, though. They must have had children. So your mother must have had cousins. Yes, she did, though I don't think I ever met them. One went to Australia to work on a sheep farm, I do remember that because as a child it sounded like a big adventure. There you are then, Ellie says triumphantly. If we can track down William Ewing and his brothers and sisters – people had big families back then – we might find you some second cousins, or whatever they're called.

Jess carefully lifts the kittens from her lap before getting to her feet and taking her place at the table. She helps herself to another slice of tart. I am glad of the interruption. In a way I'm enjoying Ellie's enthusiasm, but in reality I am dubious at the prospect of finding long-lost family. It is one thing speculating, quite another facing the possibility of real people. I don't see that I could possibly mean anything to them. Through the window of Kirstie's cottage I can see that the blue of the sky is deepening and a pale orange rim is gradually spreading.

The thing is, I say, I am not sure that even the discovery of dozens of Scottish kinfolk would make me feel that my vote is legitimate. Why shouldn't it be? says Kirstie rather fiercely. You live here. This is your home now. I guess so. Yes, I know I have the right to vote. And I will vote. But my presence here is … fragile. What do you mean, fragile? Ellie asks. Well, I don't really belong here, do I? And I may not be around for much longer. I'm not really part of Scotland's past, and in the nature of things am unlikely to be around for much of Scotland's future. Crap, says Clem, on both counts. I smile at him. I'm an incomer, a migrant. So what? Clem leans forward and thumps his hand on the table. You're part of Scotland's present. You have a responsibility to vote for what you think is best. Who knows if any of us will live to see the consequences? Clem's right, says Kirstie, and I nod because I believe he is, yet my sense of a tentative, frangible presence doesn't go away.

All this stuff about identity and belonging, says Ellie, is a waste of time. You live where you live, and you vote to try to make it a better place. The hard bit is figuring out how that can happen. Yes, it is hard, says Clem, watching her thoughtfully.

When I leave an hour later the blue is darker, the orange more intense. The air is very still. A flight of oystercatchers screech overhead as the dogs and I head for home. There is a heron on the far bank of the canal, so still it could be painted on canvas. There are primroses, pale in the fading light, and bluebells, and half-hidden gatherings of violets. A yacht approaches slowly, heading east, its engine throbbing, and the heron rises heavily as if its wings are scarcely up to the job. The yacht overtakes me and the man at the wheel gives me a wave. It will no doubt tie up at the pontoon near the town. It must be too late for it to be going through the locks. As I approach the house a deer breaks suddenly from a patch of undergrowth and leaps away. The dogs are instantly after it, but Cleo gives up the chase almost immediately, and Jet soon after.

My railway carriage seems small and silent and empty. I'm not out very often in the evening. Sometimes I go to a concert at the community centre, and there are occasional meals with Kirstie or the Turnbulls, but it's rare that I return home this late. I pause before I close the door and take a last look at the sky. There is a thin pencil line of colour, which fades entirely as I watch. Behind me, the dogs are drinking noisily from their water bowl, and then pad to their usual night-time positions on the sofa. I sit for a while before going to bed. It's often after I've been with people that the spectre of loneliness takes possession, but however alone I feel it doesn't dismay me. Sometimes I am surprised at the ease with which I adapted to solitude. It's almost as if it were always my natural state, as if marriage were an aberration, an interlude, and I have now been returned to the place for which I was intended. Belonging. I wonder if sometime in the future Ellie will find herself in a place of unbelonging, and whether, if she does, it will make any difference to anything.

I read in bed for half an hour before turning out the light. I've set myself to read contemporary Scottish fiction as a way of learning about my adopted country. I can't rid myself of the habit of purposeful reading. Recently, and a little guiltily, I've been enjoying a diet of Glasgow crime. I set the book aside, reach to switch off the light, and slide down under the duvet. I relish this moment at the end of the day, the comfort of it and the prospect of sleep, and since taking possession of my Scottish home I have missed Tim less intensely and have slept less fitfully. It may be the small space and the single bed. In the double bed we'd shared for forty years it was hard not to feel his absence. I often woke with an assumption of his presence, coming to with a lurch in the gut when his absence hit me. In all our time together there were probably fewer than a hundred nights that we were apart. Tim often slept with his hand on my shoulder, and often I could feel his breath on my ear.

The loneliness that creeps over me from time to time is less the absence of Tim than the weight of self-reliance. I'm not worried about an emergency – I have all the necessary phone numbers – but there are times when knowing that my day-to-day life is entirely my own responsibility brings something like panic. For most of my life what I did was shaped by other people, commitments to family, friends, students. My days revolved around the needs of others. I got up in the morning at the time required to get children to school and husband to work. It wasn't something I questioned – or at least not often. That was life. That was life for all the women I knew, except perhaps for Colette whose days could appear spontaneous and anarchic. I suppose that was why I liked her company so much. There was a vicarious pleasure in being on the margins of her freewheeling existence. She transmitted something of that freedom to those around her.

I have the dogs, of course. Their company and their need to be fed and walked and on occasion taken to the vet are reassuring. Against my better judgment I have agreed to take one of the kittens. I don't think the dogs would deliberately harm it, but I worry that they might hurt it accidentally.

An owl hoots. The wind is rising and through the open window there is a smell of rain. Underlying everything, just beneath the skin, the constant ooze of anxiety that something terrible could happen to one of my three remaining children, to one of my distant grandchildren.

1984

Clare Billings was twelve years old and making her mother a birthday cake. She had just started her second year at secondary school. Her brother Jake was two years ahead of her. Clare had shut the kitchen door and forbidden entry to the rest of the family. It was a Sunday afternoon and it was raining. In the living room Jake had the TV on and Lucas was on the floor with his father building a bridge out of Lego. Harriet was in the bedroom she now shared with Clare – Lucas occupied the room that was once hers. Their father had built a room divider in the girls' room so they each had their own space, but it didn't prevent outbreaks of discord. Later, the loft would be converted, and they would only have to share when there were visitors. Sonia was lying on her bed reading *Childe Harold*. She was about to start teaching a new course.

Clare had assembled all the ingredients on the kitchen table. She weighed flour, sugar and butter. She'd often made cakes with her mother and was confident she knew what she was doing. She turned on the oven and greased two baking tins. It was to be a chocolate cake in two layers. Concentrating hard, she cracked two eggs into a bowl and gazed in satisfaction at the two floating unbroken yolks before she punctured them with a whisk, ignoring the spillage of flour which could be cleaned up later.

The door opened slowly and Harriet's face appeared. Go away, barked Clare. Can I help? No. Can I help ice the cake? No.

Four years after Harriet, Lucas had made his way into the world. He came unintended, the result of carelessness with an elderly Dutch cap that should have been replaced. The knowledge that she was pregnant brought a malaise to Sonia that slowed her almost to a halt. Another child, another infant just when Harriet had started nursery, just when she had a few daylight hours to herself. In those first weeks her limbs felt heavy as lead and she found it hard to drag herself out of bed in the mornings.

Tim held her. We have a lovely family, he said, there's no

need for you to go through with this. Need, she thought, need, her face against his chest. No, we don't need another child, the world doesn't need another child. Tim was still speaking. I'd be delighted to have another little Billings, but not if it's too much for you. Sonia, love… And pulling her face away from his chest, she said, I can't possibly, I can't possibly… Tim was silent. Can't possibly what? Have the child? Not have the child? He looked down at the confused eyes of his wife. I don't know what to do, she said. And Tim also did not know what to do, or what to say.

The older children were delighted with their baby brother and brought in their friends to admire the pink creature who moved his tiny fingers like a wind-up toy.

Symmetry. Two boys and two girls. Very satisfactory, Mairi Letford said. How very organised of you, said Miranda, I couldn't have done it better myself. Sonia refrained from saying, You don't show any signs of doing it at all. There was no point, because to Miranda it would be meaningless.

Sonia was tired all the time. She took a term off teaching, but by the time she was home from meeting the older children from school her legs were shaking with weariness. She lifted Lucas from his buggy and sat with him as the others squabbled in the kitchen and got themselves biscuits and juice. With the baby quiet on her lap she closed her eyes and sometimes there was a moment of half sleep until the children erupted again and with huge effort she gathered the energy to send them upstairs to change out of their school uniforms. She would go up later and pick up the clothes discarded on the floor and check what needed to go in the wash.

It's not depression, she told herself, just tiredness. I am not depressed. At night she dozed in front of the television until it was time for the baby's last feed, but however late she fed him he was bawling for more at four in the morning. She lost her appetite. You need to eat, Tim said, worried. That baby's sapping all your energy. I am eating, she said brightly, but she knew he was right. Her milk was beginning to run out. Now she had to fuss with sterilising bottles and making up formula, but at least Tim could sometimes take over the feeding. Jake demanded to have a go, and then Clare and Harriet. They quarrelled over whose turn it was. I know how to do it, Clare said, shoving the teat into the baby's mouth. I am not depressed, Sonia told herself, but sometimes she struggled against a dark and paralysing wall of doubt.

A wet Sunday afternoon. Jake was at a friend's house. Clare had set up a shop in the kitchen and Harriet had been instructed to make purchases, which she did without complaint. Tim had plans spread out over the dining room table – there was a problem to be solved by Monday morning. I'm going to lie down for a while, Sonia told him, and went upstairs. She checked the baby – he was sleeping. She went into the bedroom, hers and Tim's, shut the door and leant against it with her eyes closed. For some moments the distance between the door and the bed seemed far too great to cross, but she forced her legs to move. She lay down on the bed and reached for the book on the bedside table, but did not open it. She closed her eyes again.

It could have been minutes later, but perhaps it was half an hour, when a thin wail reached her ears. She remained stretched motionless on the bed. The thin wail grew in volume. Soon Lucas was crying full blast, reaching a crescendo, then a gulp of breath, then another slow build to crescendo again. Tim, please, for God's sake, go to him, pick him up. The crying continued. There were footsteps on the stair, but not heavy enough for Tim. The door slowly opened. Lucas is crying, Clare said. Sonia opened her eyes and turned her head towards the small figure in the doorway. I know, love, she said, trying to keep her voice from cracking, I'm just coming. The figure retreated, and a voice said, It's all right Lucas, mummy's coming. Footsteps back down the stair.

She lay for another few moments. There was a pause in the wails but then they started up again. She pushed herself up to a sitting position and pressed her face against her raised knees. Lucas, please stop, please stop. But he did not stop, and at last she moved, got to her feet and walked unsteadily through the door Clare had left open, into the baby's room. She picked him up and the crying subsided into splutters. She went to the window. It was still raining, the sky an unrelieved grey. She carried Lucas downstairs and into the dining room and placed him on Tim's lap. He looked up in surprise. I'm going for a walk, she said. But it's raining. I know, but I have to go out. Tim sat, his arms around the bundled baby on his knee, and regarded his wife with puzzled concern. She turned and left the room, took her raincoat from the jumble of coats and hats hanging under the stair, found her wellington boots, and went out into the rain. With her hood up and her hands in her pockets she trudged through the village and out along the narrow road. The hood obscured her peripheral vision and she stared at the few feet of tarmac in front of her. There was nothing in her head but a kind of anguish, a clot at the back of her throat which might have become a scream. An occasional car passed, sending up a fountain of spray. She had walked for nearly three miles when she realised the rain had stopped. She pushed back the hood of her coat and looked around her. Raindrops hung in the hedge at the side of the road where there were still a few blackberries and rosehips. A thrush was foraging for worms in the muddy verge. Ahead of her she could see the sign of the Plough and Harrow; she had walked nearly to the next village. She turned and looked back the way she had come. There was a thin streak of pale blue sky to the south and a finger of sunshine caught the raindrops in the hedge.

When she got back Tim was in the kitchen with the children. They were eating toast and peanut butter. Lucas held a finger of toast in his small fist.

Sonia was scheduled to teach a course on Dickens and another on fiction in the 1920s. She'd taught both before, but in the occasional hour that she had to herself she reread *Our Mutual Friend* and several of Aldous Huxley's novels. She was finding it hard to excavate books she had once known well. She longed to be back at work, yet was filled with trepidation. She was not sure if she was the same person who had engaged so cheerfully with books and people. And there was a new head of adult learning.

It was resentment, perhaps, that a fourth child should make so much difference. Everyone assumed that she was a practised hand. The neighbours saw her come and go with her little tribe, Jake and Clare always on the move, Harriet solemnly keeping pace with her mother and the pushchair as they all walked home from school. It was no big deal, surely, to do it all a fourth time. And Tim was such a nice man. They saw him at weekends out with the older children on their bikes, pegging out the washing, digging the garden, kicking a football with his elder son. You're lucky with that man of yours, said Anne Watson from next door. My Brian still doesn't know where to find the teabags. And Sonia smiled, because she knew that she was, indeed, lucky. Lucas was crawling and emptying the kitchen cupboards. Sonia learnt to navigate her way round pans and dishes stacked on the floor. Then he was walking and attacking Jake's Lego. He scribbled on Clare's homework. Mum, Harriet said solemnly, if we put him in his playpen he wouldn't be such a pest.

Sonia went into the office in a converted Victorian house near the university to meet a woman a little younger than herself who welcomed her with a smile and a brisk hand-shake. The office had changed, freshly painted, its old clutter gone, the overflowing box files removed, plants in elegant containers on the windowsill. There was a name-plate on the door – there had never been one before. It said

Dr Marion Highfield. The young woman wore sleek black trousers and a multicoloured jacket, with heavy, square, shocking pink earrings. Her smooth brown hair was neatly coiled, but Sonia, mesmerised by the bright, chunky earrings, imagined that a single gesture would send it tumbling about her shoulders. The smell of her perfume almost obliterated the smell of new paint. Dr Highfield noted that Sonia was repeating courses she had taught before. Perhaps it was time for something new? Something a bit more contemporary? She smiled. I'm reviewing the entire syllabus, she said. I've asked Duncan to help me. He's come up with some interesting ideas. Duncan? Ah yes, the young man who ran courses on politics and society. And this is Dr Moulton's last term so we'll be refreshing the history courses. Refreshing. An apparently innocuous word. Refreshing can't be bad.

Dr Highfield picked up a piece of paper from the almost empty surface of her desk. Numbers are looking satisfactory for your courses – but we need to do more than just give people what they want, don't you think? I know you have a loyal following, and of course we do value what you've done over the years. She smiled again. But we owe it to them to offer a bit of stimulation, don't you think? And we need to widen our demographic, appeal to younger people. Contemporary women's writing perhaps? I'm not suggesting feminist theory, not yet at least. Both women had been standing. Now Dr Highfield sat down at her desk and gestured towards the chair opposite. Jim, the previous incumbent, had his desk under the window, so he could look to the pigeons for inspiration, he used to say. It meant that the desk did not loom between him and others in the office. His chair was always at a friendly angle. An electric kettle and carton of milk stood in the corner, and he was always quick to make any visitor a mug of instant coffee. He did not drink tea himself, and if a visitor asked for tea he would mutter, I know there are teabags somewhere, and the result was always that the visitor accepted coffee.

Would you like coffee? I'll ask Jill to make some. But Sonia shook her head. So you see the lines I'm thinking along? I want something fresh. We'll redesign the leaflet, aim for a different clientele. Clientele? But, Sonia ventured, there are regulars with expectations. Dr Highfield leant back in her chair and brushed something invisible from her jacket. I quite understand, she said, if you feel you'd prefer … well, if it doesn't suit you to introduce something new, especially now when there are other demands on your time. Another smile, but it did not reach her eyes. How many children do you have? Four? My goodness, I do admire you. How do you do it? She placed her fingertips on the desk. Give it some thought. I'm getting everyone together for a meeting, perhaps next week. Jill will be in touch.

Sonia nodded and got to her feet. Fine, she said weakly. She walked out into the street and into the nearest coffee shop. She knew she should not linger as she had left the baby with a neighbour, but she sat for a long time over her coffee which by the time she had finished was quite cold. She believed that Dr Highfield would be very happy if she were gracefully to accept that she was not the right person to assist with the new broom.

Don't be ridiculous, said Tim that night when the children were at last asleep. What does she know? You're just the right person to bring in younger students – you're young yourself. Not as young as she is, Sonia replied. It was a long time since she had felt young.

Sonia did not leave. She offered a course on women's fiction after the Second World War. The office received several requests for a repeat of her Victorian fiction course. Dr Highfield resisted. We're not doing our job if we just serve up what people think they want. We need to provoke, we need to challenge, we need to expand their horizons. The message was reiterated the next year, the year after. Dr Highfield's energy left Sonia feeling more tired than ever. Her fortieth birthday approached. Once she had said to Tim, in the early days of their marriage, I aim to make my mark before I'm forty. I'm not sure what that mark is going to be. She had laughed then, and Tim said, Maybe a black mark, and they both laughed. Anything seemed possible. Even black marks had a certain attraction. And forty seemed such a long way ahead.

She looked around at the faces in front of her as she urged the fifteen women and two men to consider the novels of Angela Carter. Time was running out. Already, time was running out. She woke in the night sometimes and asked herself what else she could do. She read books and she talked about them. She knew it would be entirely feasible for Dr Marion Highfield to question what she contributed to the sum of human knowledge. She should consider alternative avenues of employment.

Her fortieth birthday. Around the university all through the spring and early summer students were collecting for the miners. She dropped pound coins into their tins. Then on a late May evening, as she got out of the car on her way to her class, there was a young man in jeans and work boots and a hard hat hooked over his arm. He was on the other side of the street and on impulse she crossed over. Were you at Orgreave? she asked as she fished out her purse, were you hurt? He shook his head. My uncle was badly bruised, he said, pushed to the ground by a horse, lucky not to get trampled. One of my pals has a broken arm. She dropped a five pound note into his bucket. Look after yourself, she said, and crossed the road again, angry and guilty. A five pound note in a bucket did not make her feel better, and the petty anxieties did not go away.

June 2014

The canal bank is thick with vegetation, willowherb and thistles, foxglove and meadowsweet. The water is dark, with an almost ebony sheen. Cleo likes to swim, but Jet is not so keen. If I throw a stick into the water, Cleo plunges in and Jet stands on the bank, his nose thrust out, his paws sliding towards the water. It's warm – we're having a good summer. It's Saturday, and children are out on their bikes. A boy of about ten, I guess, skids to a halt and stares, whether at the dogs or at me I am not sure.

Today I've made a sandwich and we've walked all the way to the canal basin. Several yachts have passed us on the canal and we stop to watch two of them go through lock six. We watch the water sink until it reaches the right level, the boats carefully tethered like nervous animals. One of the boats bumps rather hard against the edge and the man at the wheel swears at the woman standing ineffectually on the deck. The lock gates open and the boats are set free. The people on board, jaunty in their sailing gear and sun hats, sometimes wave at the plodders on the canal path. Occasionally there's a dog that barks at my two.

The canal basin is busy with boats and visitors. I sit on the grass and eat my sandwich. The dogs get the crusts. It's good to get a dose of busyness from time to time, to see the boats go through the last lock and head out to sea, which today is a deep blue with the islands and mountains smoky grey in the distance. Families wander past, I hear American voices, German, something that could be Russian. How cosmopolitan we are, here in this little corner of Scotland's west coast. A man on a moored boat, intent on polishing, raises his head and catches my eye. He turns and says something to a shadowy figure in the cabin. I can't hear the words, but the voice is unmistakably English. The little café's outside tables are full. Two long-haired girls in shorts saunter past eating ice cream and speaking Spanish. I get up from the grass stiffly and reluctantly and start the four-mile walk home.

When I get back a black year-old SUV is parked outside the big house. The Turnbulls have arrived. As I pass the house someone – I can't see who – waves from the kitchen window and I wave back. I'm tired and the dogs are hungry. I feed them and make myself a mug of tea. I go and sit in the garden seat which I have placed in the far corner, near the vegetable patch and shielded from the house by a purple buddleia, now in full flower and alive with bees. I don't feel like talking to the Turnbulls just yet, and anyway they'll be busy, I tell myself, unpacking, unloading their shopping bags of supplies, their case of wine, their selection of malt whiskies. I've taken off my walking boots and stretch my aching bare feet on the warm grass.

Twenty-four years ago today Jake fell from the narrow ridge of An Teallach and broke his neck. He was dead when they found him. He and his two companions had started the climb in bright sunshine, and it was still clear at the summit, with views west across the Minch and north to the mountains of Assynt and east to Beinn Dearg which they'd climbed the day before. He'd phoned after that climb, a long haul, he said, but not a hard climb. It's been a good day. As he spoke I could hear the voices of his companions in the background, an expletive, laughter. We're in the pub, he said. I sensed their comradeship.

They were walking An Teallach's ridge when the cloud rolled in very quickly. Stuart and Mark came to the funeral but it was sometime later that Stuart came to the house and told us about that day, about setting off from the shore of Little Loch Broom where they'd camped, and the long walk in, and the heady views, and taking care as they made their way along the narrow ridge of rock, and then of a sudden seeing almost nothing. The cloud muffles sound, Stuart said. Jake was behind us, and all we heard was a slight scrape of loose stone and then, not a shout, something more like a stifled grunt, and we stopped and looked back and listened. We retraced our steps but there was nothing. He just wasn't there. He was gone. All the time Stuart spoke he stared at the floor, unable to meet our eyes, as if he were confessing some terrible misdeed. And we felt so sorry for him, Tim and I, and so grateful – but also dismayed – that something had compelled him to come and see us, unannounced, to take a train and a bus and walk in the rain to our front door and brace himself to knock and tell his tale. We thought maybe he was just unconscious, but really we knew.

We insisted that he stay for dinner, and watched Clare flirt with him, and saw him thaw a little. I asked him if he'd like something of Jake's to keep. Tim said very little and pushed forkfuls of shepherd's pie into his mouth with no awareness of what he was doing. It wasn't so much pain that I saw in his face as vacancy.

And yet at the end of dinner Tim said, I'll drive you back to York to get your train, and abruptly silenced Stuart's protest. I watched him get into the car with Jake's compass in his pocket and waited for Tim's return. I heard the back door open and the sound of the car keys being returned to their hook. Tim came in to the living room where I sat with my book. That poor boy, he said, it was brave of him. But, I said, maybe he feels better for the telling. And maybe, now we know, we'll feel better. Tim looked at me, a long and puzzled look, as if the prospect of ever feeling better was beyond imagination.

I pour the dregs of my tea on to the grass. Tim was not as brave as Stuart. I suggested it might ease things a little if we went to Wester Ross and saw the place where our son had spent his last hours. But Tim wouldn't go to the mountain where the bright day had so abruptly proved murderous. It was months before he would enter Jake's room. It was his sense of fairness that pushed him in the end. It wasn't fair to let me do it all, was what he said at last, and then marched into the room and at once began to go through the boxes that were on the floor exactly where we had left them. He was methodical and thorough. He sorted everything into neat piles, decided what could be thrown away. Tim was always careful, systematic, a safe pair of hands.

I walk barefooted back to my front door, the dogs following. Bad timing. Moira Turnbull is approaching across the
garden. She raises her hand in a little wave and calls out,
Just wanted to say hello. We're here for a week. How are
you? I tell her that I am fine, that everything is fine. Moira
looks around. The garden's looking lovely. It's so good to
get away from the office. We've been so busy, this is the
first chance we've had. She has smooth bobbed hair with
a strand which continually escapes to fall over her eyes.
Every few minutes her hand moves to push it back. She's
wearing flowered cut-offs and a pale blue top and her toe-
nails, visible in thin-strapped sandals, are painted scarlet.
My nephew and his wife are coming, she says, you must
come over for supper one night and meet them. I have
never invited Brian and Moira for supper in the railway
carriage and know that I should, but I don't have space for
four visitors so this time I'm off the hook. That would be
lovely, I say. The dogs are looking well. Moira gives Cleo a
pat. Jet is sitting at the door, out of reach. Well, I'd better
get on, Moira says. You wouldn't believe the amount of stuff
that needs sorting out. Every year we say, this year we'll
spend more time at the house, but somehow it never happens. She laughs, and with another little wave she returns
through the garden and goes into the big house through
the French windows. I see her through the glass, a blurred
figure moving back and forth.

1994

Sonia met him off the train at Leeds. She almost did not
recognise the lean, tanned young man who swung towards
her along the platform, his hair bleached even lighter by
the sun, a massive rucksack on his back. He was grinning
and his eyes seemed a deeper brown. In the eight months
he had been away, he had surely grown.

She was crushed by an enthusiastic but clumsy hug, burdened by the rucksack. He had not shaved for a couple of days and his cheek was rough against hers. She was so pleased to see him she hardly knew what to say, and mundanely asked, How was the flight? It seemed astonishing that this lean and confident young man was her son, her eldest child. In the car he talked of the flight, the hassle of departure, the need for a discreet bribe or two, customs at Heathrow going through his dirty underwear. Unshaven young men flying in from Tanzania are bound to be suspect. He laughed, rubbed his hand over his bristly chin. You're home now, Sonia said, as if she had to say it in order to believe that it was true. She touched his arm with her left hand as they waited at traffic lights. We've missed you.

All of a sudden he became serious. The lights turned green and she moved slowly forward in the current of traffic. He turned to her and said, I've had the most marvellous time, mum. The people, the work, making a difference. She smiled at that phrase. I want to go back. I have friends there now, and there's so much work to do. And I have to go up Kilimanjaro again. It's the most amazing mountain, rising out of the heat like a mirage. You climb through coffee plantations on the lower slopes – and then you're dazzled by the sun on snow. Sonia touched his arm again as the road cleared ahead and she accelerated away from the city, but she did not put into words what was in her head. To talk so soon of going back when he was not yet home, not yet returned to the house where he had grown up, where his family waited.

Sitting round the kitchen table on his first night back, Jake had talked, relaxed and happy, and then looked around at his parents and siblings and asked, Well, what's new? What's been happening since I went away?

Clare has a boyfriend, said Harriet quickly. No, I don't. Yes, you do. I've seen him, his name is Gary and he plays tennis. Clare goes to watch him play, which is just so boring.

Almost as boring as cricket. He's just a friend, Clare said, and tennis isn't boring at all. Neither is cricket – you just don't appreciate the subtleties. Her big brother grinned at her. There's nothing wrong with cricket, he said, we taught the boys at Moshi how to play. They loved it, and so did we. I was friendly with a cricket player once, said Sonia, and all eyes turned to her. Oh mum, tell us, tell us, but she just smiled and mentioned that Harriet had done very well in her exams. I'm not surprised, said Jake warmly. Harriet always was the brainbox of the family.

The next morning Jake spilled the contents of his rucksack on to the kitchen floor and stuffed most of it into the washing machine.

Over the next few days Sonia marvelled at the boy who had in eight short months – long months for her – grown up. He teased his siblings but did not quarrel with them. He helped in the kitchen without being asked. I'll give the hedge a going-over, he said one lunchtime, and spent the afternoon with the electric clippers, his sleeves rolled up to reveal his tanned and muscled forearms. The girls seemed a little in awe of him. Lucas was jealous. His brother was eighteen. It would be eight long years before he too could leave school and take off.

Three weeks, and then he was off again, to Newcastle to begin three years of studying geology at the university.

Clare was going out, with whom she did not say. She wore black leggings and a belted top and a baseball jacket she had found in a charity shop. Her long dark hair was halfway down her back. See you later, she called as she breezed out of the door, a capacious bag slung on her shoulder. There was something of Miranda about her, Sonia thought, watching her daughter through the window as she swung down the drive and through the gate. Should we be worried about her? Tim asked from time to time. He would shake his head, not in answer to his own question but in puzzled uncertainty.

A Saturday afternoon in late June. Tim was on his way back from an inspection on the other side of Manchester. Clare was having a driving lesson. Harriet was sitting in the garden reading. Lucas was on the computer now installed in the dining room, and at the other end of the table sat Sonia, files and papers spread around her. She was trying to put them in some kind of order. The telephone rang. Lucas jumped up, I'll get it, and went into the hall. Sonia paid no attention – when the phone rang it was almost always for one of the children – but Lucas quickly reappeared. For you, mum, he said and returned to the computer screen. Sonia went to the phone. Mrs Billings? It was not the usual salesman voice. Yes? My name is Detective Sergeant Fraser. I'm phoning from Inverness. Inverness? I'm very sorry, Mrs Billings, but I'm afraid… The accent, the tone. A splinter of fear ran through her. Your son, Mrs Billings, there's been an accident, a serious accident.

She heard and she did not hear. Something like an avalanche roared in her ears. Is there anyone with you, Mrs Billings? The avalanche weighed on her chest, froze into a blade of ice. Yes, she said, amazed at the sound of her own voice, yes, and thinking in another part of her being, you know there's someone with me, the someone who answered the phone. But she said, My daughter, my son. Jake. Just two weeks before they had driven over to Newcastle to see him and collect some of his things. His exams were over, his second year at university drawing to a close. He and two of his climbing friends were off to the Scottish Highlands for a few days before coming home. Their talk was filled with the names of mountains. Later she found them on the map, Liathach, Beinn Eighe, Beinn Dearg, An Teallach. In her Yorkshire garden the sun shone and a light breeze moved a few knots of cloud. An Teallach, the voice was saying, an accident, An Teallach, an accident.

Another year of university, then back to Tanzania. That was the plan. His eyes so deeply brown, his father's eyes, in

151

his lean, tanned face, his stride so confident. He's my son, my firstborn, and we're so proud, Tim and I, so proud of him. We brought him home from hospital in our old green Mini, and up two flights of stairs to our flat in Burnley, those shabby rooms with a view out to the moors. He slept all the way and did not wake when Sonia tucked him into the cot that waited for him, along with neat piles of folded nappies and baby clothes. Tim and Sonia looked down at the sleeping baby and then at each other, disbelieving, scared. They crept out of the room and put the kettle on, and then Jake woke and cried and Tim lifted him and walked up and down, his hand cradling the back of the baby's head against his shoulder, until Jake's eyes closed and the mouth relaxed. It's the heartbeat, said Tim, the reassuring rhythm of the heart. You can't hold him against your heart forever, Sonia said, watching her husband and her child with a sense of wonder.

Every day Sonia pushed the pram down and up that blessed hill because Tim needed the car for work. He was a good baby, by and large, and then Clare was born and there were two of them to carry up and down the stairs because when Jake saw her carrying his baby sister he wanted to be carried too, until Tim got the job in Leeds and they moved to the red brick house, the lovely house with big rooms and a garden, Clare walking by then and Jake kicking his ball into the daffodils, and a big kitchen with space for the pine table they bought in Habitat and Clare's high chair. Jake ran through the empty, echoing rooms. And Sonia was pregnant again. Mrs Billings, are you all right? Is there someone with you? Oh yes, she said, but you've already asked me that. She could hear the click of the computer keys. Is your husband there? She shook her head, then remembered, No, he's at work. Would you like me to call him? No, oh no, don't do that. He's not... He's in the car. She put her hand to her face and stared blankly at the front door.

Slowly and carefully she replaced the telephone receiver

in its cradle. Through the open door of the dining room she could see Lucas frowning at the computer monitor. She walked into the kitchen and looked out of the window. There was Harriet in a deckchair with her book. What was she reading? Oh yes, Huxley's *Brave New World*. Sonia stood at the window for a long time. She's only sixteen. I can't tell her. How can I tell her? How can I tell Tim? She looked down and was surprised to see two white hands gripping the edge of the kitchen sink. She breathed in a deep lungful of air, then let it out very slowly. And again. Why was there not enough air? If she could not get air into her lungs she might scream, but without air in her lungs she could not scream. When she turned away from the window her legs began to shake and she had to sit down. There were crumbs and a little eddy of coffee on the table. She got up again, reached for a cloth and wiped the table. Her legs were steadier. She walked back into the hall and stared at the phone. But she could not phone Tim. She looked at her watch but failed to take in that it was nearly four o'clock. He said he would be leaving at lunchtime, but she could not remember where he was leaving from. She put both hands to her head and shut her eyes. South of Manchester. How far away was Manchester? How long? She looked at her watch again.

Mum, what's wrong? Lucas stood beside her. Twelve years old and tall for his age. Oh, Lucas. She held him, pressed his warm living body against her. He resisted, awkward and puzzled. Oh, Lucas. Your brother's had an accident. Her voice breaking, the dam that held back the scream beginning to crack. Is he dead? But his head was pressed against her and he could not see her wordless nod. Is he dead, mum? Yes, love, she whispered, Jake's dead. The voice muffled, tremulous.

Harriet was standing at the open kitchen door, her mouth open, her book in her hand. She had heard her mother's whisper. She watched her younger brother clench Sonia hard, then pull away, his eyes washed in stricken disbelief. Harriet dropped her book. She felt very cold, all the garden's sunshine gone.

Tim flew to Inverness. It was normal for Sonia to be in the house with her three younger children, Tim at work, Jake at university. Sonia got up in the morning and went through all the necessary motions, kettle, fridge, toaster. Clare, Harriet and Lucas appeared in their school uniforms, got in a tizzy about missing socks, asked for dinner money, argued. But now they moved about the house in near silence, hardly ate, and did not slam the front door when they left. And they each of them, one after the other, gave their mother a hug before they departed. Normality was there, but veiled, dimmed.

On the first day Clare got as far as the gate and then returned to the house. Are you sure you're all right, mum? I could stay at home. Now that exams are over we're not doing much. No, said Sonia, it's best to go to school if that's what you've decided. She spoke calmly – how was that possible? It will be harder if you put it off. You've got the note? Clare nodded. I've said you would all prefer no special treatment. Clare nodded again. Sonia put out her hand and smoothed her daughter's hair, then suddenly kissed her cheek.

She could not work. Her files and papers were spread on the dining room table just as they had been when the phone rang two days before. From time to time she went into the room and gazed at them, picked up a page of notes, let it fall again. In the kitchen half-empty mugs and barely touched bowls of cereal were untidily scattered. She took a mouthful of lukewarm tea, but her stomach instantly rebelled and she spat it into the sink. She cleaned the kitchen and washed the floor. She needed to make phone calls, but wouldn't it be better to wait until Tim returned, until arrangements had been made? She needed to be able to say something more than the brutal fact. Jake's school friends.

Some of them she knew only by their first names: Sean, David, Chris. Some had been in and out of this house. And upstairs in Jake's room, which she could not enter, were the boxes and bags they had brought back from Newcastle. Just leave them, Jake had said, and I'll unpack everything when I get home. And he had stood on the pavement outside the narrow and chaotic terrace house which he shared with four others and waved as the car pulled away from the kerb and his father and mother set off on their drive back to Yorkshire.

On 14 February 1993 at about 6 p.m., Sonia Billings returned home from a meeting in Leeds. She turned the car carefully through the rather narrow gate and noted that Tim was not yet back from work – the company car was absent. Only her fourteen-year-old son Lucas was at home. As she opened the front door she could hear the TV. When she looked into the living room to say hello he nodded but did not take his eyes from the screen. Sonia went into the kitchen to unload the shopping she had picked up on the way back. Without taking her coat off, she began putting things away. To her surprise, Lucas appeared and stood in the doorway grinning with one hand behind his back. What's up? she asked. He slowly withdrew his hand and held it out with a flourish. In it was a single red rose wrapped in cellophane. Happy Valentine's Day, he said. Sonia looked at the rose and then at her son, puzzled. She put down the jar of coffee she held in her hand. Is this from you? Lucas shook his head, still grinning. There's a card inside, he said, but I wasn't able to read it. Where did it come from? It was delivered next door. Mrs Watson came round with it. Here. It's definitely for you, has your name on it, look.

Sonia took the flower and stared at it through the cellophane, a long stem studded with thorns and dark red folded petals. She put it down on the kitchen table next to the coffee and the tins and the bag of oranges she had removed from her shopping bag. She slipped off her coat and dropped it on a chair. Tim had sometimes bought her flowers, but never like this, an Interflora delivery on Valentine's Day. Go on, said Lucas, open it. She untied the ribbon that fastened the cellophane and slowly extracted the rose. A small card fell out. She picked it up. Neatly written on it in blue ink were the words, "Soon we will be together." She frowned. Who's it from? asked Lucas. It's not from dad, is it? She turned the card over. It doesn't say who it's from. There's no name on it. She stood looking dubiously at the rose lying on the table and gathered up the cellophane which she crushed and dropped into the bin. You better put it in water, mum, Lucas said. She nodded and went to a cupboard for a narrow vase, ran water into it and added the rose, which tilted sideways. She stood with the vase in her hand, looking round the room. The windowsill above the sink, alongside the washing-up liquid and the little pot of dying miniature daffodils? The shelf crammed with jugs, two candlesticks, a "present from Whitby" jam pot and postcards? Or in the living room? What was appropriate for an anonymous Valentine rose? She put the vase down on the table, the rose askew, and finished putting her shopping away. She still had her coat on.

At the sound of the front door Lucas and his mother both turned. Tim was home. Mum has a secret admirer, Lucas said as soon as his father came into the kitchen. What's that? A secret admirer? How exciting. But if it's secret, how do you know? Sonia gestured towards the rose in a vase that was not tall enough. It came for mum, Lucas said, watching both parents with interest. Sonia picked up the card and handed it to Tim. How intriguing, he said. No guesses as to who it might be? He looked again at the card, turned it over. Sure it's for you? Had mum's name on it, Lucas said, Sonia Billings and our address. So, Tim said, his head on one side, someone who knows you and where you live – one of your students maybe? Sonia looked up sharply. As soon as Tim said the word "student" she saw Stephen Wright, always in the front, a pleasant-faced, neat man in his mid-forties, she guessed, with attentive blue eyes. She had noticed his eyes because he always watched her, an unnerving, unblinking stare, and although he had an open notebook and a pen in his hand he seemed never to write anything. He wore a sober tie and a navy V-necked pullover.

Sonia looked at Tim, who was watching her with his eyebrows raised and a slight smile. I'm sure you have lots of admirers, he said. I'm sure your students think a great deal of you. It isn't just a token of appreciation though, is it? Sonia reached out and straightened the rose in its vase, but it leant to one side again. Stephen Wright, she said, I think it might be Stephen Wright. Who's Stephen Wright? All last term he never missed a class. He never says anything but he does listen, or seems to.

The back door opened and Harriet came in, pulling off her cycle helmet and dumping her school bag on the floor. She shook her mop of hair, flattened by the helmet. Rain's started, she said, then noticed three pairs of eyes looking at her. What's up? You mother's been sent a Valentine's present. A rose. A rose? Harriet saw the vase on the table. A single red rose? How romantic! Not from you, dad, I take it. Unfortunately not. I wish I'd thought of it myself. Tim passed her the card. Soon we will be together, Harriet read aloud. Oh my God, mum, who is this? I don't know. Harriet scrutinised the card. Well, he's very sure of himself, whoever he is. Mum said Stephen Wright, said Lucas. Who's Stephen Wright? One of her students. It's probably not him, Sonia said hurriedly, it was just a thought. Why Stephen Wright? Tim asked. There's something about him. He looks at me all the time. He never says anything, but he looks at me. Well, laughed Tim, just shows how attentive a student he is. No, but it's… There's just something about him.

They ate supper in the kitchen and had not long finished

when the telephone rang. Lucas, always quick off the mark, answered it and called for his mother. When she went to the phone a voice she did not recognise said, I've made all the arrangements, for next Wednesday, after the class. What arrangements? She spoke calmly but her heart had started to race. Train tickets, the hotel for Wednesday night. The flight is early on Thursday. Who is speaking? I think you may have the wrong number. Sonia, the voice said, you know that this is what we always planned. I made a promise – I would never let you down. It's taken longer than I expected, but you know for a while I wasn't in a position… Well, I was ill for a bit, you know, hospitalised. But I'm fine now, they let me go home, and I knew when I saw you again that you were ready. The pleasantly measured voice stopped and there was a pause before Sonia was able to speak. It's Stephen, isn't it, Stephen Wright? There was a quiet laugh. Of course it's Stephen. Who else would it be? Another pause. You got my rose – a statement, not a question. You remember, that was to be the sign, that was what we agreed all those years ago. A red rose. I've been faithful, Sonia. You've never been out of my thoughts. There's never been anyone else.

Sonia gripped the phone and took a long breath. Stephen, what do you mean we agreed it? I'd never met you before you started coming to my class. Now Sonia, the voice said sharply, don't be ridiculous. I know it was a long time ago, but you haven't forgotten. You can't possibly have forgotten. When we said goodbye at Willow Street Primary and I went away to boarding school – you know I didn't want to go but my parents had decided. It was out of my hands. But we made our vows, in the school playground where we played together every break time. I said I would send you a red rose and now I have. It's time, Sonia. You haven't forgotten, I know you haven't.

Sonia looked up to see Tim standing at the end of the hall. She took another long, slow breath and tried to relax her grip on the receiver. Stephen, I've been married for twenty-five years, happily married. I have four children – she did not correct herself. And I was never at Willow Street Primary School. I went to school in Sussex, where I grew up. I didn't come to Yorkshire until after I was married. The voice interrupted, but calmly, as if trying to reassure a worried child. We were in the same class at Willow Street, Sonia. We were inseparable. We played together all the time. And I know you're married, but that's all right. I know it was just while you were waiting and I don't blame you. I didn't think it would take so long. But now it's all fine, I'm quite well, and everything's arranged. Your children don't need you any more, Sonia – and besides, one of them died, didn't he? Your son Jake. Tragic accident, I know, it was in the paper. And your daughter Clare's away at university, isn't she? Cardiff, I believe. And the other two are nearly grown up. Your husband doesn't need you now. You've done well, I know you've been a good wife, a good mother. You're a good woman and you wouldn't let them down, I know that. And I know you won't let me down. Pack your case and bring it with you on Wednesday. Don't bring much – I have money for anything you might need. I've ordered a taxi to take us to the station. You won't fail me, Sonia, I know you won't. The line went dead.

Tim came up behind her and put his hand on her shoulder. What was all that? Are you all right? She turned to him, white-faced, and shook her head. He's mad, she said. He knew all about me, the children, Jake. He's mad. Stephen Wright? He thinks I'm going away with him after my class next Wednesday. I don't know where, but he's booked train tickets and a flight. He says we've known each other since primary school, that we made a vow to be together. Her hands were shaking and Tim grasped them. We should phone the police, he said. Oh no, we can't do that. He needs help, Tim. There must be someone we can contact who can help him. His doctor, maybe he has a therapist. He said

159

he'd been in hospital... Do you know where he lives? She shook her head. The office must have his contact details.

In the kitchen Harriet and Lucas looked at each other. They could not hear all that was being said, but they caught the intensity of the voices. It's beginning to sound serious, Harriet said. I hope mum's all right, her brother responded. His teasing grin had disappeared. The rose in its vase was still on the table.

Tomorrow you can get his details, Tim said to Sonia, and we can decide what to do then.

Sonia could not sleep. Her thudding heartbeat rattled through her body. In the morning Tim drove her to the office on his way to work and she searched the files until she found a Leeds address and telephone number. Tim still wanted to phone the police but she was adamant that he should not. He considered phoning without telling her, but rejected the idea. When Sonia left the office it was still early, not long after nine. She had intended to take the bus home, but the prospect of spending the day alone in an empty house was unsettling. She walked for a while along a street that was familiar, but without noticing where she was going or how cold it was. The university's campanile and red brick buildings seemed strange, alien almost, and she felt unsure of where exactly she was. Half an hour later she was in a café in the centre of the city with a coffee in front of her. She took a book out of her bag and opened it but did not read.

By lunchtime she was at home. She had got on the bus and sat staring out of the window as it wound its way through brown fields and scattered villages. She had got off at the right stop and walked the quarter mile to the house with the white gate and the car in the drive. A part of her noted that the car was badly in need of a wash. She had taken out her key and unlocked the front door and removed her coat and sat down at the kitchen table where the red rose still leaned askew in its little vase. Her legs were shaking. I'll wash the car, she said out loud, but she did not move.

When Tim returned home she told him that she had Stephen Wright's address and had found out where Willow Street Primary School was. But it doesn't help, really, does it? You can't go and stake out his house. The weekend came. Harriet and Lucas were unusually quiet and watchful. Lucas went to his Saturday morning orchestra practice without being reminded. Harriet shut herself in her room and wrote an essay on Victorian factory reform.

Okay, said Tim on Sunday night, here's what we'll do. I won't phone the police, but I'll come to your class on Wednesday night. Unless your Stephen Wright is a six-foot bruiser I think I should be able to handle any difficulty, but maybe we should warn the janitor that there might be trouble. He's medium height and quite innocuous looking, said Sonia. Okay, good, said Tim. Can I come? said Lucas. No, you cannot.

Sonia looked at her husband with more than usual attention. He was standing with his hands in his pockets, his back against the kitchen door, staring thoughtfully at the ceiling. He was wearing an old pair of heavy cotton work trousers and a rather faded cord shirt. His hair was as thick and brown as when they first met, but parallel grooves had developed on either side of his mouth. She looked at him but said nothing. He lowered his gaze and when their eyes met he smiled. It will all be fine, he said. He took off his glasses and rubbed them on his shirt. She wanted very much to believe him, to believe that Tim would look after her and solve the problem that faced them. She turned back to the sink and pulled on rubber gloves and started to scrub out the pans in which she had cooked their meal.

On Tuesday night during supper the phone rang. They all looked at each other, then Lucas jumped to his feet. I'll get it. No, said Tim sharply, I'll get it, but Lucas was too quick for him. They heard his voice when he picked up the phone in the hall. Lucas Billings speaking, he said crisply. No, I'm afraid she's not available at the moment, can I give her a message? Yes, I'll tell her. You're looking forward to seeing her tomorrow and she's to remember her passport. I'll pass that on.

He returned to the kitchen. You're to remember your passport, he said, and he noticed how pale and drawn his mother's face was.

Her Wednesday night class was on late nineteenth-century fiction and they were to discuss *Dr Jekyll and Mr Hyde*. Sounds like the perfect topic, in the circumstances, Harriet said, but Sonia had not found that funny. On Wednesday morning she dug out her notes but struggled to concentrate. It was a two-hour class. Normally, she would talk for half an hour and then ask for prepared contributions from a couple of the students. She would suggest a topic the week before and ask for volunteers. Occasionally she had to prod the less forthcoming to offer something. She was aware that Stephen Wright, although so attentive, had never volunteered. She thought about that now as she tried to apply herself to preparing for the class. She realised she had avoided asking him directly to contribute. She realised that there had always been something about him that made her uneasy.

She arrived as usual ten minutes before the class was due to start, and arranged her books and notes on the desk. Her heart was thumping. They had agreed that Tim would slip in to the back of the room at the last minute, and as soon as the class ended would come to the front. Sonia greeted her students as they came in. Stephen Wright was, as always, prompt and sat in his usual place at the front. He looked at her directly with an almost imperceptible smile and took out his notebook. She nodded in reply and said nothing. He took a fountain pen from his breast pocket, unscrewed the top, examined the nib, and then replaced the top. She pressed her hands on the desk to stop them trembling. She was going to have to speak for half an hour and was not at all sure what she was going to say. There was a ripple of chat, someone dropped a book, someone else was writing rapidly. She began to speak, *Jekyll and Hyde*, the novel that catapulted Robert Louis Stevenson to fame. Why did it make such an impact then? Why has it remained so popular? And what relevance does it have now? To her surprise, once she got started there was plenty to say. She did not look at Stephen Wright or at Tim, but she felt Stephen's stare.

The clock at the back of the room told her that it was ten minutes to nine. There had been, to her relief, an animated argument about the nature of evil. Stephen Wright had as usual said nothing. She sensed his detachment from the discussion. Doubles, split personalities, depths of darkness, delusion, power.

The door to the room opened a few inches. I think Jack must be wanting away early tonight, Sonia said brightly. Any other comments or questions? No? Everyone clear about what we're doing next week? We'll be looking at *Jude the Obscure* and you might like to think about whether there is any link with the theme of *Jekyll and Hyde*. She smiled as she always did at the end of a class, a smile that she hoped was encouraging and inclusive.

Talk broke out and chairs scraped as people gathered themselves to leave. Sonia reached down for her briefcase and out of the corner of her eye saw that Stephen Wright had not moved from his seat. Two students came up with questions – she was glad of the distraction. Tim made his way slowly from the back of the room and stood a few feet away. The students, Glenda who never failed to come up with a question after the class was over, and Norman who seemed perpetually anxious and in need of reassurance, gave him a curious look but carried on talking as Sonia collected her notes and her books. She put on her coat. She spoke to them both and they seemed satisfied, said goodnight and moved away. The room emptied and Stephen stood up, smiling slightly. He paid no attention to Tim, or to Jack who was just inside the door. Where's your case? Stephen asked, I left mine in the hall. We'll collect them – the taxi should be waiting. He put his hand on Sonia's arm. She froze.

Have you got everything? Tim's voice, quiet. Ready for home? Stephen quickly turned, his blue eyes hardened. Sonia isn't going home, he said, tightening his grip on Sonia's arm. Stephen, Tim said, his voice still quiet, my name is Tim Billings. I'm Sonia's husband. She's coming home now with me. Sonia did not move, but she was aware that Jack had taken a few steps forward. Mr Billings, I know who you are but I don't think you understand. I have a taxi waiting. Sonia and I have planned this for a long time, haven't we Sonia? We are going to start our life together. I'm sure she's explained that to you. I know she's been married to you, but I'm sure she explained that that was only a temporary arrangement. She's with me now, Mr Billings. We've waited so long for this. Stephen, I don't want to have to call the police. The police? What have the police got to do with it? But there was a flicker of apprehension in Stephen's eyes. He did not notice that Jack was now standing right behind him. When Jack put his hand on Stephen's shoulder he started and swung round, but he did not let go of Sonia's arm. Come along, Mr Wright, Jack said cheerfully. You can hop into the taxi and go home. Or shall I tell it not to wait? Maybe you'd prefer to walk? I'm not going home, Stephen said truculently. Sonia and I have a train to catch. Sonia at last found her voice. I'm not going with you, Stephen. I never made any promises to you, you must know that really. In your heart you know that we never met at Willow Street Primary School. I didn't grow up here – I went to school in Sussex. Stephen stared at her, the anger in his eyes fragmenting into confusion. No, Sonia, he said. How can you say that? You know it's not true, you know we were at school together, that we spent every minute that we could together. Stephen, you've let your imagination run

164

away with you. Perhaps you've mixed me up with someone else. You must go home and ... go to your doctor. You need help. I think you've had help before, so you need to go back to your doctor. Sonia's right, Tim said. She can't help you, but there are people who can. I'm not going home, Stephen said steadily, then with a slight tremor, I can't go home. Doctors are no use, they don't know what they are talking about. You made a promise, in the playground, I know you haven't forgotten. The last words came out loud and angry. You made a promise.

For several moments there was silence. Then Tim reached out and covered the hand on Sonia's arm with his. One by one he prised the fingers loose. Jack now had a firm hold of Stephen's other arm. Come along, Mr Wright, he said again, let's get your case and find that taxi. Stephen looked at him as if he had never seen him before, and then pleadingly at Sonia. Go on, Stephen, she said gently. He opened his mouth, but resistance drained away. He allowed himself to be led out of the room by Jack. Sonia and Tim stood unmoving, listening to the sound of footsteps and a suitcase being wheeled along the corridor. They heard Jack's cheerful voice, but not what he said. They heard a door bang shut. At last they looked at each other and Sonia began to tremble. Tim put his arms around her and held her tightly. It's over now, love. Not for him, it isn't over for Stephen. Tim took her briefcase and with his arm around her shoulder walked her out of the building. Jack was standing on the pavement watching the tail lights of a taxi. Thank you, Jack, said Sonia, thank you. That's all right, Mrs Billings. Nothing like a bit of a challenge to make life more interesting. You were a tower of strength, said Tim. I'm not sure we could have handled it on our own. Oh he's not dangerous, said Jack. Sad, really. Wonder what will happen to him? I don't suppose we'll be seeing him again.

In the car, in the dark with the headlights guiding them along the narrow road, with her husband beside her, Sonia felt safe but she wanted to cry. What will happen to him? I feel guilty. I feel I have let him down. I feel I have broken my promise. But you never made a promise, said Tim. I know. But he was so sure, so convinced that I almost believed him.

July 2014

For a whole week the sun has shone and the dogs have been almost too hot. Cleo splashes into the canal to cool down. Jet slithers down the bank for a drink, but is reluctant to go into the dark water. Today we took our usual walk to town, to the chemist and the Co-op, where I picked up my usual newspaper but put it down again almost immediately. On the front page there was only appalling destruction. A passenger plane shot down over Ukraine, no survivors. Nearly 300 killed. A deliberate act by Russian separatists? A ghastly mistake? The wreckage is scattered over several kilometres. There is confusion as attempts are made to collect fragments of the dead. Armed men are preventing access. A child's rucksack is pictured in a field of sunflowers. There are suggestions that evidence is being removed. In the meantime, on another parcel of this earth, Israel batters the people of Gaza, a few of whom are attempting, without much success, to batter Israel. A population is being slaughtered in the name of another population's security.

I read the front page and put the paper down again. Enough. I lost a son who was at an age when soldiers and terrorists die – but what difference does it make, how death comes to a young life? But surely it does, it must, make a difference. What if Jake had come back in a body bag from Afghanistan? I lost a husband, not young but too young and suddenly, but he'd lived usefully. What if I'd lost my entire family? What if Lucas had been shattered by a shell as he and his friends were kicking a ball in the park? What if his sisters had run in terror from the sound of guns? The temptation of "what ifs" leading in other directions. What if Jake had decided not to set off on that beautiful day for the summit of An Teallach, but had gone to the beach instead, to have a swim in the cold loch and a doze in the sun before going with his friends to the pub for a cold beer? What if that plane's take-off had been delayed? What if those football-playing boys on a Gaza beach had run home ten minutes earlier, hungry or thirsty, or just wanting their mothers? I am walking down the main street, two dogs on leads panting in the heat, quotidian purchases in my backpack.

I go home without the paper. But the absence of news does not banish the thoughts that have taken possession of my head. The "what ifs" keep coming. What if a shell had landed on those boys just after they'd sat cross-legged on the floor to eat the dinner their mother had painstakingly prepared from what little food she could find? What if Israel's Knesset agreed to a ceasefire just as a Hamas rocket destroyed other young boys sitting round the family table? What if that delayed plane flew into a lightning storm and was struck down by natural causes? What if Jake returned home after several days of climbing and one lazy day on the beach and was hit by a speeding car as he walked home from an errand for his mother along the narrow road with no pavement that led half a mile to the nearest shop? All my life I have from time to time rehearsed the worst possible news, rehearsed my own reactions. It did not make it any easier when the worst news came.

I reach the big house and turn in through the gate. The grass needs cutting. The Turnbulls pay Gavin Duff to look after the grass and the hedges but he has taken his family to Majorca for a week. In the greenhouse Kirstie so carefully repaired, the tomatoes are ripening. I go inside and breathe in the delicious and reassuring smell. Even with the door open it is almost too hot, but I find it comforting nevertheless. The plants are reaching up against their trellis. A few almost fully red tomatoes glow amidst those that are still green and the scattering of little yellow flowers. There is an old stool in the greenhouse and I sit on it for a while. The dogs pant in the shade of the apple tree. I get up and take the watering can to the tap outside the big house and watch it fill with water. I struggle to carry it back to the greenhouse – when it's full it's almost too heavy for me. I water the tomatoes and the peppers. I'm feeling a little calmer now. Watering plants is a steadying activity. It's not good to allow thoughts of death to take hold.

The grey kitten with the white paws is curled amongst my tapestry wool. We think he's a boy. Cleo is very patient with him, sometimes pushing him gently with her nose but otherwise ignoring him. Jet is not so patient, and I worry that he might snap when Ash bats his tail.

I take my shopping into the railway carriage and open all the windows. In the afternoon I pick raspberries and put them in the freezer. I take my laptop into the garden and check my emails. There's a breezy message from Clare. London is hot and with the windows open her flat is noisy and dust and grit drift in. She's hoping to take some time off. There's a trip to Budapest planned for the autumn but before that she's hoping to get up to Scotland. She'll fly to Glasgow and then get a bus. Clare doesn't have a car. I reply, suggesting she waits until after the Commonwealth Games before coming, as Glasgow will be in chaos while the games are on. But I add that I'd love to see her, which is true, that she works too hard, and that it's important for her to have a break. As I write these maternal words I wonder if anyone else says these things to her, and I hope that when she comes she won't try to persuade me that four years is long enough for my railway carriage experiment and that Hat and Matt would love to have me near them in Cambridge. I look forward to seeing her, but I know that she'll be restless, that I'll be unsettled by the buzz of energy that always accompanies her. Jake had that same current of energy, but unlike his sister it was contained. He could sit quite still and convey a taut, latent vigour, while Clare was always on the move.

There are geraniums and begonias vivid in three old fish boxes ranged in front of my railway carriage. I'd found the fish boxes in the tangle of undergrowth behind the carriage. The orange-red montbretia is out. There's going to be a good crop of apples. The dogs have taken up expectant positions in front of me, reminding me that it's their dinner time. I've been sitting for too long and am stiff when I get to my feet. They bustle inside in front of me and their eyes follow every movement as I pick up their food bowls and carry them out to the lean-to and fill them from the big plastic box of dog food. I scoop some kitten food in Ash's little dish and put it on the kitchen table. I lift him up to eat it beyond the reach of the dogs.

Now the witch has a cat, but at least he's not black.

2004

Lucas Billings and his girlfriend Lettie Best got on the train at King's Cross and travelled to York. Sonia was at the station to meet them. She saw her son approach, long-limbed like his father and with his father's thick brown hair, and the thought intruded, as it often did, He's not at all like his brother, he's not neat and compact like Jake. They'd often wondered, she and Tim, where Jake had come from. He had his mother's cheekbones and light hair, but his body shape bore no resemblance to his origins. The other three looked like siblings, but Jake had always been different. Your father, I think, Tim would say. The mountain thing must come from him too. There were no more mountains after their honeymoon, Sonia said. Well, there was the war, wasn't there, and babies. And they were a long way from mountains.

Maybe, Sonia thought sometimes, maybe we shouldn't have taken the children to the Dales. The green slopes gave Jake a taste for climbing. Not the others, just Jake. She and Tim no longer speculated about Jake's passion for mountains. Sonia could not bear the bleakness that masked Tim's eyes when Jake's name was mentioned. She could not bear the reminder that Tim had changed. Some source of vigour had dried up. He seemed content with less, but perhaps that was true of Sonia also. Perhaps it was age, not grief, that was diminishing them. Perhaps the shrinking of horizons was inevitable.

Lucas had a small rucksack slung on one shoulder and was pulling a suitcase on wheels. Sonia's eyes moved to the young woman beside him, slim, dark-skinned, with long dark hair framing her face. She wore a flowered skirt and a denim jacket. Her outlined eyes were large and almost black, her plum-coloured lipstick gleamed. She smiled a wide, cheerful smile. Hello, Mrs Billings, and held out her hand which felt smooth and delicate in Sonia's own. I'm so pleased to meet you. Her son's girlfriend from New Zealand, the accent unmistakable. I'm so excited to be in Yorkshire. I've spent a whole year in London and never come this far north.

Sonia turned to Lucas and hugged him. This is Lettie, he said unnecessarily. Sonia felt that all eyes must be on the bright, shining Lettie.

Who was Lettie? What would Lettie become? Later, as they were getting ready for bed, Tim said, What an attractive girl, and Sonia laughed and agreed. And she's not just a pretty face. She's a research chemist, works in a lab somewhere. I'm not sure I've grasped exactly what she does, but she's clearly clever. You can tell she's part Maori, Tim said. Yes, does it matter? Of course not. Tim sat on the edge of the bed in his pyjamas and reached over to take Sonia's hand. Daughter-in-law material do you think? It would be nice to see one of our offspring married. Clare and Harriet show no signs of getting hitched. And then that bleak understanding, just for a moment, of the name not mentioned. He would have been thirty-four.

Sonia smiled at her husband – she had grown practised in creating a diversion. Harriet seems pretty much hitched, she said. Marriage doesn't seem awfully relevant to their generation. I wonder if parents are still expected to pay for their daughters' weddings? Tim held Sonia's hand against his cheek where she felt his sadness. She sat beside him on the edge of the bed. What about children, he wondered. Grandchildren. Are we ready for grandchildren? We mustn't load them with our own expectations, Sonia said. No, we mustn't do that, Tim said sadly. Sonia withdrew her hand and kissed him where her hand had rested against his cheek, and then his mouth.

It seems only yesterday they were little, she said, yet so much has happened. She stopped, but sometimes, however successful the diversions, the echoes of Jake could not be avoided, so she carried on. All of a sudden in our sixties. All of a sudden our children grown up and – she was going to say gone, but couldn't. Tim pulled her close and returned her kiss. I know, he said gruffly. And he did know. It was a deep, unfathomable knowledge entangled with guilt, yet he was the one who had said over and over, We could not have done anything to make it different, saying it to himself as much as to her.

Each of them felt the other to be the most in need.

The following day, Lucas came into the living room and found Lettie alone and examining the three photographs on the dresser. The small blond boy on a beach, his trousers rolled to his knees, grinning, eyes half closed against the sun. The teenager on an improbably narrow ledge beside a waterfall, one hand raised in salute. The tanned and relaxed young man sitting in this very garden, a glass in his hand. What a good-looking fellow, Lettie said. Yes, best of the bunch probably, or maybe it's just because he's gone that we think that – or mum and dad think that. He's not around to be a disappointment. They don't think you're a disappointment, surely. I guess not, Lucas said. He had picked up the last of the three pictures. Taken on my mother's birthday. We had lunch in the garden then, too. I remember that one because it was the first time I was allowed sparkling wine. It must have been … 1989. I was eleven. Jake was nineteen. Lunch in the garden if the weather was nice… It was a kind of birthday tradition.

For several moments Lettie looked at the photographs of Jake and then put her hand on Lucas's arm. It must have been terrible, she said softly. Lucas didn't reply at first, but then said, It still is. If you marry me, you'll be taking on the absence of Jake. I'm sorry about that, but it's part of the Billings family. I know that, Lettie said. I'll cope. And then she added, I guess every family has lost someone or something too soon. I had a cousin who died in a car accident. Lucas slid his arm around her waist. It's worse when I come home, when I see mum and dad, but it never quite goes away.

And now it was Sonia's sixtieth birthday. Clare and Harriet were on their way, driving up together. Sonia went out into the sunny garden and picked the last of the sweet peas. Is it warm enough to have lunch outside? Lucas and Lettie had been for a walk and were now in the kitchen drinking coffee and chopping vegetables for a Greek salad. I'll make a dressing, shall I? Lettie said, eager to be helpful. Tyres crunched on the gravel, and there were Clare and Harriet out of the car with bags and gift-wrapped parcels. Is it warm enough for lunch in the garden, Sonia wondered again, surrounded by people and hugs and parcels. Happy birthday, mum, happy birthday. Tim produced an armful of flowers from a bucket in the garage, too many for one vase. Sonia arranged them and put them in the living room. She placed the sweet peas on the kitchen table. She remembered the red rose.

Yes, let's eat outside, it may be our last chance this year. In

New Zealand, it's spring, starting to warm up. Was it a good drive? So how are you? How's the work going? When are you going to retire, mum? And dad, what about you? Matt sends his love – he's sorry he couldn't make it. We're going out for dinner, with a taxi home, one of those people carrier jobs, it's all arranged. The kitchen was full of people. Sonia opened the cutlery drawer and took out a handful of knives and forks. She paused, with the cutlery bristling, looking round at the four young people in her kitchen.

One more year, she said, so dad and I can retire at the same time. So have you planned the world cruise yet? Don't be ridiculous. And they all laughed at Tim's indignation, and looked out through the open door at the sky, blue with shredded cloud, and agreed that in spite of the breeze it was warm enough for lunch in the garden.

Clare carried out a tray of plates and glasses and Harriet brought the big bowl of Greek salad. Tim opened a bottle of Cava – a glass each, he said, pouring carefully. Lucas and Lettie came hand in hand into the garden where the rest of the family were assembled. Tim was pouring the wine. Sonia was sitting back in her chair, her hair very white in the sunshine, white trousers with a grass stain on the knee where she had knelt to pull out a handful of chick-weed. Clare leant forward to pick pieces of cucumber out of the salad bowl, dark glasses masking her eyes. Harriet had kicked off her shoes and was standing barefoot beside her father. With her faded jeans and ponytail she looked like a teenager. Sonia looked up as Lucas and Lettie came through the French windows. Oh Lucas, you're so like your father, she said. Tim handed Lettie a glass. Welcome to Yorkshire, he said, welcome to the Billings experience. And Lettie took the glass and smiled round at all of them, and said, It's lovely to meet you all. Thank you. And Sonia felt suddenly grateful for Lettie's bright and unfamiliar pres-ence. The Billings experience, Clare said. Do you think we can market it?

They sat round the battered garden table, with sweaters and cardigans round their shoulders. It was almost not warm enough. Sonia tore off a hunk of baguette and put a piece in her mouth as she listened to the voices of the younger generation eddy around her. Tim raised his glass and caught her eye. They exchanged the trace of a smile, like a whisper. Here we all are. But not quite. There was an absence and they all felt it, even Lettie. She had seen the photographs. Dad, said Clare, I think your birthday present is going to be some new garden furniture.

Lucas Billings and Lettie Best were married in London, with just the family and a few friends present. Lettie's parents arrived from Auckland, and a few weeks later Lucas and Lettie flew out to New Zealand. The other side of the world, Tim said mournfully. Our only married offspring goes off to live on the other side of the world. Lucas was given work by Lettie's father, and was soon in charge of updating his bus company's ticketing software. Lettie continued her career as a research chemist.

Miranda never married. She had a series of long-term but shadowy male companions. She had settled with apparent ease into an academic career, never moving from Oxford where she had collected two degrees. Her parents attended both her graduation ceremonies, and watched with particular pride as she moved across the platform in her gown, one of only a handful of women receiving a doctorate. They were charmed and baffled equally by Oxford. Takes after her mother in the brains department, Ray Letford said, taking the arms of his wife and his daughter, one on either side as they walked through the arched gate of Balliol on a post-graduation wander through the colleges. I've brought a rather special bottle to celebrate. They drank the wine out of paper cups beside the river and watched the punts slide by.

Occasionally work took Miranda to Leeds or York and

she spent a night with Sonia and Tim, but on those occasions she was always alone. She never stayed more than a single night. She always had a reason to depart, somewhere else to be. When the children were small the adults would have a late dinner after they were in bed. Miranda regarded the children with amused but distant toleration. She made no effort to engage with them and they were reluctant to approach her. Clare was the boldest. Sometimes she chose a book, sat herself on the sofa and with a winning smile invited Auntie Miranda to sit beside her and read her a story. Maybe later, Miranda stalled. Now, please, was Clare's firm reply. She sat with her legs straight out and the large picture book open across her knees. Miranda could not refuse to join her, and she made an effort to read with enthusiasm, but when the story came to an end she got quickly to her feet before Clare could demand another. She went out into the garden for a smoke. Once Clare persuaded her to play Ludo, but was not pleased when Miranda won. When I play with mum, I win, she said.

You must come to Oxford, Miranda would say to Sonia from time to time. Give yourself a break from the kids. She did not say, and from Tim. She regarded Tim in the same way she regarded the children, with distant amusement. She saw no appeal in Sonia's tall, amiable husband, her children, her life. There was very little in any of it that was of interest to her. She assumed that Sonia could not be entirely satisfied with her muddled existence. She looked for signs of discord. Tim's preoccupation with work? Jake's sudden appropriation of four-letter words? Clare's disappointing school report? Harriet's tantrums – how could a child normally so placid erupt without warning into red-faced screams? Lucas's bed-wetting? She noted the untidiness, the dirty fingermarks, the crayon drawings on the wall that were never painted over. She noticed the piles of washing everywhere, untidy heaps which she could not identify as clean or dirty. It was like visiting a foreign country with children as a foreign language. Come to Oxford for the weekend. Get away from all this, unspoken. There were times, of course, when Sonia was not happy and when the thought of escape to Oxford was very tempting. But she was troubled at the prospect of exposure to Miranda's silent criticism. She was troubled at the possibility that she could not cope with Miranda's life, or that she would envy it. It would only confirm the distance between the sisters.

But she did go to Oxford, only once, leaving the children in Tim's care. Miranda had bought a terrace house in a North Oxford Victorian crescent. The two rooms at the top of the house were let out to graduate students, always women and often American. The spacious high-ceilinged rooms were filled with art nouveau furniture and objects. A collection of lustreware was displayed in a glass-fronted cabinet. It was May when Sonia visited, and the garden was lit by lilac and laburnum. It was tended by a gardener who came once a week. Miranda had little time, she would say, for tending to flowers and shrubs, but in fact she had no interest. She liked the garden to be there, tidy and colourful, as long as she did not have to give much thought to it.

Miranda met Sonia at Oxford station straight from a meeting of the department of which she was head. In her late forties, she was still striking, her hair still thick and glossy. She stood slightly apart from the barrier, sleek and elegant in silk and linen, a briefcase in her hand, a jacket under her arm. Sonia knew she would be outshone by her sister, but had still given some thought to what to wear. The image reflected back at her that morning in the bedroom mirror revealed a slightly faded forty-four-year-old. She had a few grey hairs, although they hardly showed against the light brown. No make-up, although there were old lipsticks and eyeshadow in her drawer. Perhaps she should have pressed her navy trousers, but they'd only get rumpled again in the train. She was still slim, only a pound or two heavier than when she married, shoulders and cheekbones still prominent. She smoothed her newly purchased turquoise blouse and at the same time thought, I'm too old to be worried about this kind of thing. A striped scarf added a bit of dash. But the anticipation of Miranda at the station, attracting appreciative glances as of right, made her anxious. She had never stopped being uneasy in the presence of her older sister.

As the train approached Oxford Sonia combed her hair, smoothed her blouse, checked that there were no sandwich crumbs clinging to her trousers. But I have things that Miranda is without, she told herself against the anxiety, a husband, children. A husband who loves me, she amended. A husband I love. It could not be anything else, that core of warmth and understanding, of sanctuary. It was not the same, of course. They had had to accommodate the four growing individuals who occupied that same space, often with chaotic intrusion. Their love had to absorb all the demands of work and domesticity and the practicalities of care. But it survives, she thought as the train slowed. It flourishes, just about. We still make love in the bed we bought when we moved into the Burnley flat – what a business it was putting it together after getting it up the stair in pieces – not often maybe, but often enough. Often enough? Sometimes she wanted to shake Tim's sleeping shoulder, sometimes she pushed his hair back from his closed eyes. But Tim was a sound sleeper. He would murmur perhaps, reach out for her even, but did not waken. And sometimes, bone-tired, she would turn away when his questioning finger ran over the curve of her ear. She met the eyes of the stern-looking middle-aged man sitting opposite, and blushed.

Sonia knew that Miranda had never wanted a husband like Tim, or children (not that she disliked them, they were simply irrelevant). She preferred her lovers as appendages, part-time companions at most. Sonia knew that whatever she had did not figure in any way on Miranda's horizons.

The train came to a halt and Sonia was hesitantly on the platform, her weekend bag in her hand. Around her people surged towards the exit and she allowed herself to be carried forward. She did not see Miranda at first, motionless, a few yards from the barrier. Then there she was, smiling but not moving forward, waiting, composed. Sonia was taller than Miranda, but even without her high heels Miranda had an authority which Sonia felt she lacked. She could be a midget, she sometimes thought, but Miranda would always be my older, cleverer, more glamorous sister. And she knows it. Neither of us will ever question the status quo.

They exchanged a brief embrace. We'll get a taxi, Miranda said.

The guest room had a pale carpet and cream curtains, and an elegant tallboy decorated with carved ferns and flowers. At one end of the large kitchen was an old range, gleaming but merely ornamental, Miranda explained. There were copper pans hanging above it and a large decorated punchbowl on the hotplate. At the other end of the room was a table that could comfortably seat eight. The working part of the kitchen was cream and stainless steel.

Miranda had changed into jeans and her feet were bare. Sonia was still in her travelling clothes. Miranda was slicing a lemon. G and T? she enquired. Without waiting for an answer she assembled gin, tonic, ice and two tall glasses. We can sit outside, she said, the terrace gets the evening sun. So they sat with their drinks and talked about their parents, as it was one of the few topics they had in common. Some years before, Ray Letford had sold out to a chain and retired, though he still made trips to wine country on behalf of the new owners. Mairi had recently celebrated her seventieth birthday and Miranda, Sonia, Tim and the children had all congregated in Sussex for the occasion. They both looked well, didn't you think? Miranda said. Mum seventy. It's hard to believe. Borrowed time. Did she say that then?

She's lost weight, Sonia said. Her face looked thinner. Maybe. She was in good form though, both of them full of beans. Dad's got blood pressure problems, I know, but he's taking the medication and it seems to be working. It's good that he still plays the piano. After a fashion, Miranda laughed. He was never much good, was he? Those sing-songs. She gave an exaggerated shudder. Oh but I loved them, said Sonia. You did? Of course I did. They have nice voices, both of them. Well, maybe, said Miranda doubtfully, as if it had never occurred to her before. On her birthday, do you remember, we all sang, Sonia said. Well, maybe you didn't, but Tim and the children joined in, belting out "Annie Laurie". Tim sang "Scarborough Fair", he always sang "Scarborough Fair", long before it was appropriated by Simon and Garfunkel. Sonia stopped abruptly, closed her eyes for a moment, and then went on, Lucas seems to have inherited the musical gene. He's quite good on the clarinet.

But Miranda was not much interested in the abilities of her nieces and nephews, and the conversation turned to work. She would soon be attending conferences in Linz and Bologna. I'm just teaching the usual stuff, Sonia said, to the usual people. Although continuing education is expanding, lifelong learning it's called now. What happened to that impossible boss? Oh, she only lasted four years, went on to better things. It all settled down after she'd gone. It's not been so bad. I enjoy it. It allows me to read and think and talk. You can read and think and talk without what sounds to me like a pretty humdrum job. It suits me. I like the people – most of them. And it means I can contribute to the family finances. That's always useful.

Miranda drained her glass and fished out the slice of lemon which she nibbled at. Surely now the children are older you could aim a bit higher, she said. You mean, get a proper job? No, I didn't mean that, but something a bit more challenging, more rewarding. Maybe. But this was something Sonia did not want to talk about with her successful sister, who now pushed back her luxuriant dark hair and stretched out her bare feet. She shook the remnants of ice in her glass and regarded Sonia with a faintly amused smile.

I like what I do, Sonia said, feeling compelled to say more. And Tim's so busy. And Lucas isn't at secondary school yet.

Miranda gave an almost imperceptible shrug and got to her feet. She found it hard to imagine a life in which children took up so much space. Shall we go in? It's getting chilly. The sun no longer reached their corner of the garden.

In the kitchen Sonia watched as Miranda made a sauce for the sea bass she had bought. She managed to cook with a minimum of mess. She referred in passing to "Brendan" without explanation. He would have come that weekend but had been landed with some urgent work for the Ministry of Transport. The last time Sonia had seen Miranda the man in her life was "Richard".

Miranda removed the packaging from a bought cheesecake. I'm afraid I don't do puddings. When they had finished eating Sonia got up to clear the table and Miranda sat fingering her empty wine glass. By the way, she said, I had a lump removed from my breast a while ago. It's all fine now, I'm in the clear, so nothing to worry about. Sonia laid her fork down and stared at her sister. For God's sake, Miranda, why didn't you tell me? There was no need. They caught it early. It was just a little lump. She laughed. The treatment worked. It hasn't spread. I need to stay on the medication for a while longer, but I'm fine. She filled her own and Sonia's glasses from the bottle of Chablis they had been drinking. There was nothing you could have done. I could have been there with you. Miranda set the bottle down with her familiar smile and said, You have four children. And Brendan was around. Amazing really. I'd kind of expected him to bugger off. Don't bother with the dishes – they'll go in the dishwasher.

An unusual flare of anger reddened Sonia's cheeks. She

sat down, took a breath, started to speak, thought better of it. She swallowed some wine. You're sure you're all right? Of course. I'm having regular check-ups. I wish you'd told me at the time. It was pointless to worry you. But now you know and we don't need to discuss it. And before you ask, no, I didn't tell mum and dad, so don't mention it. There's no need for them to know – they'd only worry.

The next day Miranda and Sonia walked down Broad Street in the rain and through the main gate of Balliol College. Across the quad to the far corner where a staircase led up to Miranda's spacious book-lined room. At the bottom of the stair they shook out their umbrellas and breathed in the mingled smell of damp stone and damp grass. Miranda sat on her desk and watched Sonia move to the bookshelves and then to the window. Neither of them spoke. Sonia could not find a way to comment on the room's spacious comfort, the opulence of books. When they emerged twenty minutes later the sun was out and the stone's honey colour was restored. They passed other college gates, the Radcliffe Library, famous names casually mentioned by Miranda. Oxford seemed lighter and bigger and wider than Cambridge. There was a familiarity – Sonia had seen the pictures and the TV programmes – laced with strangeness. The traffic, the bicycles, the mix of ambling tourists and the university people briskly going about their business were like the other university town she had once known so well. Yet different. The stone softer, the air dustier.

They went to the Pitt Rivers Museum. Isn't it a delight, said Miranda with unusual enthusiasm as they wandered through the bombardment of rich and diverse objects displayed. Sonia agreed, but she was surprised, not just by the conjunction of extraordinary things but by Miranda's unguarded pleasure. Sonia turned her eyes from openmouthed masks from West Africa scored with deep lines and swirls to look at her sister, whose own eyes were bright.

The warmth and relish in Miranda's voice was something new. Isn't it an amazing place? I never get tired of it. After a tedious meeting or a session with dull students I come here and feel totally refreshed. The assault on the senses is like a massage of the brain, she laughed, and added, it's my secret indulgence.

It's hard to take in though, Sonia said. There's so much to look at. Don't try to take it in. Just submit to the ingenuity of humankind and the connections with different worlds. Weapons, musical instruments, pots, headdresses, baskets, masks, ornaments, amulets, figures carved out of wood and stone, shaped from clay, cast in metal. Such a concentration of skill and inventiveness. They wandered from display case to display case. But Sonia was thinking about her sister, about this new, uncalculating, appreciative Miranda. When had she ever spent so much time in only her company? When had Miranda ever stepped away from her protective colouring? Was it the cancer that had stripped away her camouflage?

I don't let everyone in on the secret of Pitt Rivers, Miranda said.

Three years later the sisters were together again, on either side of their father at the funeral of their mother. Miranda was dressed with perfectly judged sombreness, a dark trouser suit with a lilac-coloured top. Her make-up was meticulous. People might have commented that the sisters did not look much alike. Miranda's thick, glossy hair fell to her shoulders. Her eyes were dark, her mouth inviting. She was not as tall as her sister, but nevertheless had more presence, attracted more attention. On their father's other side Sonia, pale-faced, her crisp haircut more sensible than stylish, dressed in grey, her bony shoulders prominent. Next to her sat her four children, Jake, Clare, Harriet and ten-year-old Lucas, flanked by Tim, her husband. Lucas held his father's hand. He had never been to a funeral before.

When Tim's own mother had died two years earlier at the end of fifteen years of widowhood, Lucas was deemed too young to attend the funeral.

Sonia and Miranda spoke briefly, long enough to arrange that between them they would make regular visits to their father.

Two years later they were together at another funeral. Miranda for the first time in her life put her arms around her younger sister and hugged her wordlessly. What can you say when a sister loses her firstborn son? Jake, blond, dark-eyed, mountain-climbing Jake, had always been her favourite of her sister's children. She realised that now. She thought herself untouched by children, but Jake had touched her. A memory came to her suddenly of playing football with her five-year-old nephew in their Yorkshire garden. It seemed unlikely that she had ever done that, but she saw herself clearly running across the grass after a small boy and a large ball.

Between the two funerals Miranda had made one visit to the Billings home. It was late August. She had been travelling back from a week at the Edinburgh Festival with a man called Julian. It was the first time Sonia had met one of her sister's men. They arrived in a sleek BMW which parked alongside the family's elderly Volvo and Tim's company Ford. Unusually, the children were all at home, Jake about to start his second year at university, Clare her last year at school, Harriet year one of sixth form, Lucas his first year at secondary. They all assembled to watch curiously as their glamorous aunt arrived with a young man in tight jeans and rimless glasses who hooked the little finger of his left hand through the ring of his car keys and jiggled them nervously. He shook hands with each member of the family, including Lucas who looked puzzled and placed his shaken hand behind his back when Julian released it.

The house seemed very full. Each time Miranda and

Julian went up or down the stairs, or into the kitchen, the living room, the bathroom, they encountered Clare on the phone in the hall with her hair newly washed before a night out, or Harriet with the ironing board, or Lucas, or his friend Scott, or Tim in an apron rolling out pastry. I'm making a game pie, he said cheerfully when Miranda and Julian wandered into the kitchen not quite sure where to put themselves. I think Sonia's in the garden. I'll put the kettle on in a minute and we can have some tea. Or coffee. Would you prefer coffee? No? Tea then. Five minutes. The kitchen was filled with the smell of frying onions. I'll make some tea, said Miranda. The sink was piled with dirty dishes and it was with some difficulty that she filled the kettle. There was a pounding on the stair and the front door slammed. A moment later boys' voices were heard ricocheting round the garden. There are only two of them, Tim remarked mildly.

Teabags are in the blue jar marked "sugar". Yes, I know... But that's what happens when you find yourself with several jars labelled "sugar". Tim lifted the rolled-out pastry and placed it carefully into a pie dish. Miranda found a large teapot and looked for cups. Try the dishwasher, Tim said. I think the stuff in there is clean. Miranda opened the dishwasher and extracted four mugs. She peered into them. One of them did not pass inspection and she washed it again under the hot tap. Through the kitchen window she saw Lucas and Scott kicking a ball up to the far end of the garden, and her sister walking slowly across the grass with a few sweet peas in her hand. Her tightly fitting cotton trousers accentuated her hip bones and her long legs. There was a mindfulness about the blue-grey eyes steady beneath the neatly cut thick hair. She was smiling slightly, at the boys perhaps, or at some private thought. It struck Miranda as she stood with her fingers linked through the handles of four mugs that, contrary to what had been assumed for as long as she could remember, her sister Sonia was actually rather beautiful. Sonia's looking well, she said suddenly. Tim looked up in surprise. Through the window he saw his wife approach, unaware that she was being observed, flowers in her hand. Motherhood suits her, Miranda said. Tim lifted a pan from the hotplate and set it beside the pie dish. Just as well, he said.

The back door opened and Sonia was there in the kitchen. She appeared not to realise that the three other people in the room were looking at her. She gestured with her fistful of sweet peas. These are probably the last, she said. They're beginning to die back. Oh good, you've made some tea. Miranda put the mugs down and opened the fridge for milk. Tim filled the pie dish with the contents of the pan, releasing a rich gamey aroma, and added a pastry lid. He trimmed and crimped the pastry and carefully fashioned three leaves from the scraps, which he placed in the centre of the pie. He stepped back and regarded his creation through narrowed eyelids. I'm impressed, said Julian. Sonia ran her hand down her husband's back. What's in it? she asked. Venison mostly, plus pigeon and some bacon, onions, mushrooms, red wine, and redcurrant jelly. Sounds delicious, said Miranda. In theory, yes, said Tim. In practice, the proof of the pudding … as we engineers often say. He lifted the pie dish with two hands and held it aloft before relinquishing it to the oven, which emitted a blast of hot air as the door was opened. He stood for a moment with his hands on his hips. You can do everything right, he said, but when it's all done you still wonder if it's going to fall down.

The four of them sat down at the table and drank their tea amid the detritus of pastry making. Sonia cleared space for the biscuit tin and Tim helped himself with a floury hand. Jake came in, found a mug, filled it, and rummaged in the tin. No chocolate digestives? You've eaten them all, said Sonia. His hand came out with two hobnobs. He propped himself against the sink. The evidence suggests that we're having game pie, he said. Dad's signature dish.

The four sitting round the table were all looking at the nineteen-year-old youth munching biscuits, relaxed against the kitchen sink as if it were his backside's customary position. His thick fair hair was like his mother's but longer and less tidy, his brown eyes like his father's. He wore unevenly faded jeans tight on his lean hips and a black T-shirt. His bare arms were tanned.

After the game pie, when the children had disappeared and Julian had gone into the dark garden for a smoke, Miranda helped herself to another glass of wine. Tim was noisily stacking the dishwasher. It's come back, Miranda said casually, but with her eyes on Sonia to make sure she understood. It took her a moment. Oh. She reached out and covered her sister's hand with her own. It's all right, Miranda said, it's all under control. She withdrew her hand. Surgery as soon as I get back. All quite straightforward. She drank from her glass and smiled at her sister, as if daring her to make a fuss.

The children hadn't seen much of their Aunt Miranda as they were growing up. She appeared occasionally, with her sweep of dark hair and a whiff of perfume. Jake regarded her curiously, remembering that once she had given him a present of a London bus. She sent them all book tokens for their birthdays. He was always a good-looking boy, Miranda was thinking, fair-haired and dark-eyed, a winning combination. The others were nice enough kids, she supposed, but didn't have the same appeal. At his funeral she could not stop the tears, while Tim and Sonia were stonily dry-eyed. If any child had lured Miranda to thoughts of motherhood it would have been Jake.

It was all right for another nine years. Sonia got used to her sister as a survivor. Miranda's hair recovered its gloss and she recovered the weight she had lost. Her reputation grew. Dr Miranda Letford appeared on the radio and TV, was interviewed by the serious press. And then, very quickly, she was in hospital and when Sonia arrived she scarcely recognised the haggard, grey-haired woman who was still insisting that all would be well. Sonia knew that all was not well. She knew that her sister was dying, and that all she could do was to stay by her side until it was done.

When their first grandchild was born Tim and Sonia Billings flew to Auckland. It was an adventure, their first long-haul flight, with a two-day stopover in Singapore filled with an unreality of time and space that took them by surprise. It was as if they had forgotten how to relish difference – but the memory rapidly returned. They strolled through the streets around the harbour, got soaked in sudden rain, ate at food stalls and spent several hours wandering in the lush botanic gardens. It was their fortieth wedding anniversary.

In their hotel room Sonia stepped out of the shower and wrapped a large white towel around herself. She stood in front of the mirror and pulled a second towel from the rail to rub her wet hair. With her white hair sleeked back the face in the mirror looked gaunt, the eyes deeper set than she was used to, and hollows under the prominent cheekbones. A fashionable look for a younger woman, she thought, but not for me.

Tim opened the bathroom door and stood behind her with a hand on each damp shoulder. He kissed the nape of her neck. He loosened the towel which dropped to the floor. Their eyes met in the mirror. You're amazing, he said. But what she saw was lumpy flesh around her waist and unsightly grooves in her thighs. Tim ran his hands down her arms and pulled her back against his chest. His shirt was unbuttoned and she could feel the hairs on his skin. It had been a long time since they had paid much attention to each other's bodies. When they made love, not so very often, they took their familiarity for granted, but now Sonia was trapped under her husband's gaze. She closed her eyes, rippled by desire as his hands moved over her slowly and without urgency. When she opened them again she saw in the mirror that now his eyes were shut and his eyebrows were turning grey, though not his hair.

What better way to celebrate our anniversary, Tim said as later they lay on the wide bed. Sonia laughed drowsily and turned to kiss his cheek. Her hair was still damp.

They put on their smartest clothes and went to the Raffles Hotel where they sat rather self-consciously in the almost empty hushed lounge drinking Singapore slings. Waiters moved soundlessly and they felt constrained to whisper. Then out into the warm street where the darkness was punctured by bright lights and the pavements were crowded. They passed an outdoor café and stopped to watch a gang of monkeys swarm in and steal food from the plates of the people eating. Nimble fingers snatched lettuce leaves and tomatoes amid shrieks of protest. Tim and Sonia, holding hands on the periphery, laughed. Brilliant floor show, Tim said, and it's free. The monkeys scampered off, knocking over cups and glasses as they went, and stuffed their loot into their mouths, their darting eyes looking out for more opportunities. A furious young woman was on her feet shouting at them and then directing her anger at the helpless waiters.

Sonia and Tim walked on without speaking. There seemed no need to articulate their contentment, nor the intrusion of loss that would always be a part of it. They both knew it was there, that emptiness would always be present in every shared moment, every shared space, not shared in the sense of parcelled out, not his and hers. Ours, Sonia thought as they walked slowly back to the hotel. That insinuation of distance, that hint of retreat after losing Jake, it's ours, we share it.

They stopped often to look in shop windows or just to watch the people on the streets, but said nothing.

The next day Tim and Sonia were on a flight to Auckland. Lucas was at the airport to meet them. It was March, the end of the New Zealand summer but still warm and sunny. Lucas drove them through the city of volcanoes to a house with big windows at the end of a rising street in Parnell. Lettie was waiting for them with three-month-old Charlie on a mat on the floor. Sonia kissed her daughter-in-law and looked down at the little creature on the floor, bare feet in the air at the end of tartan dungarees. Meet Charles Anthony Billings, Lucas said. My God, said Tim, he really does exist. We really do have a grandchild. Lettie laughed. You won't have much doubt about that after you've been here a couple of days. Sonia knelt down and took hold of one of the little feet and shook it gently. Well, Charles Anthony Billings, how do you do? And now Lucas bent and picked the baby up and nuzzled his cheek and smiled proudly at his parents. Isn't he just perfect? And Charles Anthony Billings obligingly smiled too, his dark eyes round and wide under a slick of dark hair.

Every day for a week Sonia and Tim took their grandson for a walk in the Auckland Domain, pushed his buggy round the museum building and back through the trees, while Lucas was at work and Lettie slept. They stopped for tea at an outdoor café. They did the shopping and the cooking. Lettie's parents, who lived a couple of miles away, invited them to dinner. They sat on a sunny deck and ate barbecued lamb. They babysat to let Lucas and Lettie have a night out. When Charlie cried Sonia picked him up and took him to the window and looked out into the dark garden as she had done with Charlie's father on the other side of the world. She thought of that day in the rain when Lucas would not stop crying, when she walked along the road scarcely aware of her direction. And so many days, almost forgotten, when it seemed her grip on life, day to day, hour to hour, was too weak to hold.

At the weekend Lucas drove them to Mount Eden and they looked out across the sprawl of the city and the crowded water beyond. They went down to the harbour and took the ferry to Rangitoto and climbed the brittle volcanic trail to the summit. Sonia picked up a piece of lava and slipped it into her pocket. I don't think you should do that, said Tim. I know, she said.

You have to make a trip while you're here, Lucas said, as they were sitting on the terrace drinking white wine. You should go to Cape Reinga. There was a wail from the intercom. Lettie at once made to get up from her chair but Lucas said, I'll go, and got unhurriedly to his feet. You can get a bus, stop off in Whangarei and Paihia. It's lovely up there, amazing beaches. He came back down with Charlie and Sonia held out her arms to take him on her lap. The unreality that had wrapped them in Singapore still clung. Here was Charley, solid flesh and blood, his legs flexing and his little hands opening and closing, and Lucas clearly doing well, and Lettie, tired but delighted with her son, and the house, airy and comfortable. How had it all come about? How could her little boy now be a married man and a father, with a house and a car and a good job? How could it all be so respectable? Lettie was leaning back in her garden chair, her eyes closed, her bare brown feet stretched out. Without opening her eyes she said, He needs a feed I expect.

They took a bus north. They stood by the lighthouse at Cape Reinga and looked down at the collision of water that marked the point where the blue-grey currents of the Pacific Ocean swirled against the green waters of the Tasman Sea. There was a sweep of sandy shore, and an ancient tree clinging to the cliff from which, Maoris believed, the spirits of the dead slipped down into the water to enter the underworld. The ocean border churned ominously in the bright sun. It was, Sonia thought as she gazed from the vertiginous edge, an apt division between the living and the dead. What would it feel like to be caught in those currents?

A long way from Yorkshire. A long way from her mother's

Scotland, yet back in Auckland there was a whole district called Balmoral. The bus driver, according to the badge pinned on his shirt, was a Macdonald. Tim took dozens of photographs of the clash of seas. You can't draw a line in the water, he said, and yet the difference on either side is so clear. But it must shift with wind and weather and tide. A definable border, but unstable. I guess most borders are like that. They stood side by a side for a long time gazing at the restless water. When they looked at the pictures later they saw the clear division.

August 2014

My phone buzzes. Clare has sent me a text to say she has landed at Glasgow airport and is waiting for the bus to take her into the city. An hour later there is another text to say she is on the Argyll bus. I reply to tell her I'll meet her. My mobile is old and I'm not very adept at using it – it takes me several minutes to key in a short message. It is the fourth time Clare has visited me here, and I have been once to London since I came. I would like to see her more often. Harriet and Matthew have been here perhaps half a dozen times, but I mustn't make comparisons. Harriet and Matt come in their car and explore. Sometimes I go with them. Matt takes an interest in the sites of early churches and monasteries, which give them a focus for their expeditions. They took a two-day trip to Iona. I think they like to come here. I am not so sure about Clare. Perhaps it's just her lack of transport that curbs an interest, though I wonder if it is only a sense of duty that brings her here. Lucas has never been, though he and the boys will be here soon. I have a lurch of anticipation. Lucas didn't make it back for his father's funeral, but a few months later they were all with me in Yorkshire, Charlie a turbocharged toddler, Lettie pregnant again. I've never met my younger grandson.

I am early to meet Clare's bus and walk with the dogs

across the grass to the loch shore. The tide is in and way down the still, glassy water the Arran mountains are crisp against a pale sky. I turn back in time to see the bus pull in and half a dozen passengers alight. There is Clare in a red jacket, stepping down behind a woman I know by sight weighted with several carrier bags from Primark and Gap. Clare has done something to her hair – it's lighter and shorter than it was. She has made this journey before, but she is looking around as if it is all unfamiliar. She doesn't see me at first, but the dogs know her and rush ahead to greet her. She steps back from their onslaught. Hey, dogs! Then looks up as I approach, and smiles. Mum! We embrace, Cleo jumps up to join in while Jet circles us both. Cleo leaves a muddy print on Clare's red jacket. I've arranged a taxi, I say. I asked for it to meet the bus, and as I speak a Skoda slows and makes a U-turn to pull up on our side of the street.

You're looking well, I say when we're safely stowed in Dougie's taxi, the dogs crammed at our feet. So are you, mum, I can see you've had plenty of sun, but you've lost weight. You need to watch that, you know. Are you eating properly? I have to laugh, and Clare looks slightly disconcerted. It's all the exercise, I say. We've been having such a good summer. The dogs and I have been going for long walks and picnics. They like a picnic.

We are on the single-track road that leads to the big house. I don't have to tell Dougie where to go. Although I don't use his taxi often, he knows who I am and where I live. When we arrive he helps us out and carries Clare's case through the garden to the railway carriage. I suspect it's nosiness as much as a wish to be helpful, but I tip him generously all the same. I notice that he eyes Clare with interest. The last time Clare came it was his father Davey who was driving. Dougie is back home after a spell in the army. I've not asked him, but Kirstie says he's had two tours in Afghanistan. He has a small scar on his left cheek.

Clare looks round my little indoor space as if expecting, perhaps hoping, that something might have changed, that it might have expanded, but it is all just the same as when she was here nearly a year ago. Cup of tea, I ask, or something stronger? Oh tea would be lovely, she says, following me into the kitchen. Something stronger later. I make tea and feed the dogs, aware that she is watching me, as if assessing my ability to accomplish ordinary tasks. I'm sorry I can't make it for your birthday, she says. I have a job in Birmingham, quite high-profile – the company's expanding. We can't afford to turn it down. No, of course not, I say. I'm not planning to make a big deal of my birthday anyway. But it's a significant event, she says. It's just another year, I say. Not really. Threescore years and ten and all that. Well, yes, but that's just… I tail off, because I'm not sure what it is. Anyway, mum, Clare continues, how are you really? Really, I'm just fine. Bit of arthritis, that's all, a bit creaky. Takes me a while to get going in the mornings. Otherwise – I reach out to touch the kitchen table – otherwise, no complaints. Are you getting regular checks, you know, blood pressure and cholesterol and stuff? I am pouring boiling water into the teapot and get away with a non-committal grunt which she seems to accept as yes.

I put tea things and a plate of oatmeal biscuits on a tray and we go through to the sitting room. Outside clouds have gathered and minutes later there is a sudden shower of rain, but it doesn't last and the sun is out again before we've finished our tea, casting a golden light over the garden.

Clare spots Ash curled on the chair. Ooh, I didn't know you had a kitten. He's a new arrival, Kirstie's cat had five. She picks him up and after a squirm or two he settles on her arm and begins to purr. She gazes out of the window. It is nice here, she says, for a few days. She stands quite still, apart from a single finger stroking the kitten's fur, but I know she is choosing words. I don't suppose, she begins. I know what is coming. I don't suppose you feel it might be time to make a move. I'm not planning to move ever again, I say. She sighs. But we worry about you, mum. I know you do, but you shouldn't. I've chosen to be here and I intend to stay. Suppose, well suppose something happens, suppose you fall and break something, or get sick. How are you going to manage? With the dogs and everything, and now a cat as well. People look out for each other around here, I say, although I know that there is really only Kirstie and the girls I can call on in an emergency. But you have nobody nearby, Clare protests. We do have telephones here, I say, trying to keep the sarcasm out of my voice. And computers. Ah well, says Clare with a note of triumph. I've brought your birthday present, and I'm going to give it to you now.

She puts Ash back on the chair and rummages in her case which is still standing in the corridor, pulling out a gift-wrapped parcel. I want you to have it now so I can show you how to use it before I go. She hands it to me and stands over me while I unwrap it. Cleo stretches out her nose and gives a sniff, but goes back to sleep when she realises it isn't food. I've already guessed what it is, and sure enough a flat, sleek smartphone emerges from a rather large box. Make sure you always have this with you and you can phone or text or email at any time, as well as download all sorts of useful stuff. We all agreed that you need this. Ah. My children have been in cahoots. I look up at my elder daughter and smile. It's very thoughtful of you all. Thank you. Promise you'll use it. I promise, although… But then I change my mind, and don't point out that the signal can be erratic. Clare doesn't seem to notice the "although". The dogs are on the sofa beside me so there's no room for Clare to sit down there and then and demonstrate how the thing works. She hovers for a few minutes and then sits down carefully on the only chair and settles Ash on her lap. You'll soon get the hang of it, she says. I'm sure I will.

After a while I open a bottle of wine and make dinner. The fish shop had halibut and I searched my few remaining cookbooks for a recipe I remembered from years back. It was a favourite of Tim's. Clare talks about her work and a recent holiday in Cephalonia. She'd like to find a bigger flat and has seen somewhere nice but unaffordable in Hammersmith. I'm earning good money, she says, but you wouldn't believe house prices in London. I do read the papers, I say. Harriet was in London a few weeks earlier and they met for lunch. She's in good fettle, Clare reports. She's been asked to write a book, but I can't remember what it's about.

After dinner we sit by the window and watch the light fade.

The next day it rains almost incessantly, heavy downpours followed by short periods of drizzle. I put on my wet gear and go out with the dogs. We walk under the trees, my boots slopping through pools of water and soft mud. Clare stays in, busy with her laptop, but by mid-afternoon she is restless and stands at the window staring out into the garden where pools of water are gathering on the grass. What do you do with yourself when it's this wet? she asks. I read, I do my tapestry – that was a good choice and I'm improving all the time. I stitch away with some music on. I do sudoku and crosswords, I have the radio and the TV and I keep up to date with what's going on in the world. But the rain doesn't keep me in, as you can see. I have just come in from my walk and am pulling off my waterproof trousers. I've rubbed the dogs down but they are still damp when they jump up on the sofa. Clare doesn't comment but I can see that the prospect of another day cooped up with wet dogs does not appeal.

Do you miss your teaching? Clare asks suddenly. I am taken by surprise. Not much, I say, a little, perhaps. I'd have thought you'd miss the contact. They really appreciated you didn't they, the students? Some of them came back year after year. That's true, I say, but it was all a long time ago... Not that long ago. It was a different world. I like the world I'm in now.

The next morning we wake to bright sunshine and a sparkling garden. It is warm enough to eat breakfast outside, and Clare relaxes, leaning back in her chair with a second cup of coffee, her face raised to the sun. Later, she comes out with me and the dogs and we walk up the hill to the little loch. Clare stops suddenly and puts her hand on my arm. Look, she says, and points to three peacock butterflies each poised on a purple knapweed flower. Their wings are spread in the sunshine. First one takes off, then the other two, and we walk on, and realise that everywhere there are butterflies, mostly peacocks but I spot a few tortoiseshells and a smaller species, very dark with rusty spots. I'll have to look that one up, I say. And then we see a fuzzy caterpillar crossing the track, and Clare crouches down as she did when she was a child, and watches its progress across the stony surface and into the vegetation. And when she gets to her feet she is smiling and opens out her arms as she gazes round at the bright flitting scraps of colour and says, Isn't it wonderful? And I'm smiling too, watching my daughter while the dogs nose in the undergrowth, and seeing her way back when I had four children and Tim and I, when they were all asleep, used to imagine their futures. Jake and Clare are the adventurers, we'd say, Harriet the thoughtful one, and Lucas? It's tough being the youngest, Tim would say.

But by the time we drove Clare to Cardiff to start her first term at university there, we had only three children. We planned the trip with exaggerated enthusiasm, as soon as Clare's A-level results came through and we knew she had the necessary grades. We would both go, we decided. Harriet and Lucas arranged to stay with friends. It would do them good, we thought, to get away from the house for a short time. In the weeks that followed Jake's funeral they had moved about under self-imposed constraints. Their friends didn't come round. They didn't play their music. They only watched television if Tim or I had switched it on. They carried around with them an exaggerated thoughtfulness which I could hardly bear. They were trying so desperately hard not to let their grief show. We would only be away for thirty-six hours. Although neither of us put it into words, I think we both felt it would give them some normality. We felt we were a burden to them.

We'll take our time on the drive back, Tim said, forcing brightness into his voice. Get off the motorway and dawdle a bit. I had never been to South Wales, although we'd had a holiday once near Bala Lake, and Tim and Jake had climbed Snowdon while the rest of us took the mountain railway to the summit. It was Jake's first mountain. We had a picnic at the top, in a grassy hollow looking out over Glaslyn. It was a day of sunshine and cloud, and when the sun was obscured the steep slopes to the east darkened into sinister declivities. I remember Jake standing on a rock, hands held high with clenched fists. We all walked down together to Llanberis, Clare protesting loudly that she too could have climbed the mountain if she had been allowed.

Do you remember, I say to Clare, the day we went up Snowdon? Yes, she replies at once, Jake's first mountain. He was thirteen. And I was eleven, and very cross that you wouldn't let me climb. Jake was being impossibly triumphalist. And I smile at the memory of Jake prancing boastfully down the track as we made our descent. It was dad, I say. He thought the climb would be too much for you. And you would have let me? I think perhaps I would. But I would have said, once you start you have to keep going.

Clare and I pass the surviving gables of an abandoned croft rising out of a tangle of nettles and brambles. The stone is furred with moss. The heather is beginning to show its colour, the bell heather already out. At the lochside we see the prints of deer. The water is still – there is very little wind today – and the sun is warm. We sit down on a grassy bank and the dogs settle beside us. There is nothing spectacular to look at, no dramatic peaks or crags, no thundering waterfalls, no ospreys or golden eagles above us, just a small quiet loch and the trees and bracken and heather. There is a smell of earth and pine, and the only sound is a ripple of birdsong and the panting of the dogs. Clare lies back on the grass and closes her eyes. I watch her. I want her to like it here.

After several minutes she says, I do understand, mum, why you want to be here, but I'm still not convinced it's a good idea. I wouldn't want to be anywhere else, I say. I realise that, but – what I don't understand is how it all happened, why this particular place? It's not as if you have any connections here. She pauses. Jake wasn't here, was he? It isn't because of Jake? I shake my head. No... Although there are places where you can see Cruachan, which he climbed. There's a photograph... No, coming here was pure accident. Or fate, perhaps. When I decided to buy the railway carriage I didn't know about this loch or what it was like to walk up the hill and through the trees. I didn't know you could see Cruachan. All I knew was that there was a pleasant little town with a wonderful view down the sea loch – on a good day – and a canal. I could see hills nearby, and the Mull mountains in one direction and the Arran mountains in another. There was a Co-op and a post office and a bank and a baker's. And a dilapidated railway carriage that happened to be for sale. I wasn't looking for it, but I'm very glad I found it.

Clare sat up. Well, you know what Harriet and I think, you know that we worry. You shouldn't. This isn't the wilderness. There's a hospital. I do have to go to Oban for the dentist but I can get the bus, though sometimes Kirstie drives me. I reach out to scratch Cleo behind the ears. And Clare starts to say, what happens if... but she breaks off and looks at me with a shake of her head. Well, you know... she finishes. Yes, I do know, I say, I know you all worry but I wish you wouldn't. It's what I've chosen. Well, you've got your new phone, at least, she says. You must promise to have it with you all the time. As we walk back down the hill in the sunshine I am filled with pleasure, the warmth of the sun, the butterflies like a shower of sparks, my daughter companionable beside me. We walk all the way back to the railway carriage without exchanging a word.

Clare stays another day, which brings back grey skies and a drizzly rain. It clears in the evening, and she takes me out for dinner at the canal-side hotel half a mile away. Each time she has come we have walked along the towpath to have a meal there. When Harriet and Matthew are here with their car we go further afield. It is a treat to have a meal out, as I am only in a restaurant when my daughters visit.

Clare talks about her work, her unpredictable boss, her colleague with a drink problem. I want to know if she is happy, but do not ask her. I can see that she is successful and sought after. I tell her she works too hard. She laughs. We all work too hard, she says. It's just not possible to slow down. You have to keep pedalling faster and faster until something jams, and you hope that it's the machinery that jams, not you, because if it's the machinery you get some respite. I bet the workers in a Victorian mill were always hoping that something would go wrong. That the wheels would stop turning so they could have a rest. Is it as bad as that? Nah, not really. I do like what I do, mum, and I'm quite good at it. I'm quite good at taking the measure of people, assessing their capabilities, that kind of thing. Let's have pudding, shall we? She notices my worried look and adds, I do take holidays, mum. I can afford to go to nice places, with sunshine. And if things get really bad, well, I'll jump off the treadmill and take the consequences. I'm not saying I'm ready for a life of seclusion in a railway carriage, but there are other possibilities. Now, I seem to remember that the last time I was here they did a rather good lemon tart.

There's a nearly full moon and lingering daylight when we walk home along the towpath. As we go through the gate of the big house bats flit above us. Clare stops and watches them. I've never seen bats before, she says. I click on my torch to light our way through the shadowed garden. Jet begins to bark and when I open the door both dogs burst out. Clare bends to pat them, a hand on each wriggling body. It's nice to be welcomed home, she says.

We'd arrived in Cardiff in the late afternoon. The city was new to us and it took us a while to find the house in Canton where Clare was renting a room. A brightly blonde middle-aged woman greeted us. She let the two rooms at the top of her terrace house. We helped Clare carry her things up two flights of stairs while her new landlady made us a cup of tea. Her room seemed nice enough, and she immediately filled a shelf of the empty bookcase with the books she had brought with her. She unrolled two posters. I suppose I'll need to ask if I can put them up, she said as she let them roll back on themselves. Later, the three of us walked into the centre past substantial Victorian terraces and the looming walls of the castle, and found an Italian restaurant where we had a meal. It was dark when we walked back. Clare was silent. We'd booked a room at a small, faded hotel near her digs. We stopped at her new front door. It seemed strange to be saying goodbye on an alien doorstep, to see Clare slip her newly gained key into the lock. Shall we see you in the morning before we go? We asked. No, she said firmly, I'll have lots to do. She hugged Tim and then me, and turned decisively. With a wave that was more like a salute she was through the door. But then she stopped and looked back. Don't worry about me, she said, I'll be fine. And I remember nodding, and I remember that my eyes filled with tears as the door closed and the terrible claw of loss gripped me again. Tim and I stood for a moment before we continued on our way, but said nothing. We walked slowly and silently to our hotel.

So we left the next morning without seeing our elder daughter again, and she was fine. We drove up the Taff

Valley to Merthyr Tydfil. Coal and iron, Tim said as we sped up the valley road. Coal pouring down to Cardiff, shipped all over the world. Not a good life really, but worse for many now it's gone. The leaves on the trees were beginning to turn, and from time to time the intermittent sunshine lit up a splash of yellow or bronze. Beyond Merthyr the Brecon Beacons rolled bare and green on either side of the road. From Brecon on to cross the line of Offa's Dyke and the Wye and into England. The Welsh road signs abruptly ceased, though here and there a place name hinted of Wales. A crazy border, with Welsh names spilling into England and English names challenging the Welsh. Rivers and mountains don't make for sensible borders, I said to Tim. More sensible than straight lines drawn on a map, he replied, and I had to agree.

Twenty-four years ago, late September. The fields all harvested, some of them ploughed. Many of the fields were vast, stretching acre after acre, in the corner of one a monstrous combine harvester which had not yet returned to its home after doing its job. Mile after mile of peaceful landscape with occasional reminders of less harmonious activity. Our elder daughter way to the southwest in another country, our younger children waiting for our return, our elder son lost forever. We scattered his ashes in Swaledale, near where the old rusted lead mine machinery lay, near where he danced in the sunshine while his wet trousers were spread to dry on a ledge of rock.

We drove to Leominster, then northeast to Bridgnorth on the Severn. It was country new to me, but full of resonant names. The Malvern Hills behind us, Wenlock Edge to the west. *On Wenlock Edge the wood's in trouble.* Ah, Housman, said Tim to my surprise. We had an English teacher who was keen on Housman. *The tree of man is never quiet.* He used to glare round the class as if daring us to contradict him. The Wrekin to the north. Ironbridge and Coalbrookdale. We'll take a look at the bridge one day, Tim said, it's quite something. More than two hundred years old – demonstrated what you could do with cast iron. Why not today? Without taking his eyes from the road Tim said, I want to get home. We'll go when we have time to take a proper look. You've been there? Yes, of course.

But I never got to see the Iron Bridge, only pictures of its high single span. There's nothing to prevent me going now. It would be a different kind of pilgrimage.

We stopped at Bridgnorth and bought sandwiches which we ate by the river, once the highway for barges and boats from Bristol. The high town towered above the low town, with a funicular railway to connect them. A massive church dominated the skyline. Tim watched the funicular for a while, reluctantly deciding that we shouldn't take the time to sample it. Instead, we walked by the river for a while, and I remember saying to him, there's so much of England I don't know. So much of England I don't even know from books. We paused beside the powerful current of water empty of traffic. Imagine the pulling power needed to go upriver, Tim said. After half an hour he wanted to get moving.

We carried on northeast, dodging the Birmingham complex and heading for Stafford. At least I'd read Arnold Bennett and knew a little about the Potteries. We crossed the Trent. Then through Uttoxeter on the River Dove where Samuel Johnson's father had a bookstall, and where, as Tim informed me, the JCB company was based. From dictionaries to giant diggers, I said, and was pleased to see Tim grin in response. Ah yes, he said, connections. They are everywhere, but you need to look for them.

And then we were on the southern edge of the Peak District. Water, said Tim, water and hills. Without this huge chunk of the middle of England providing power and minerals there'd have been no empire, no London as we know it. Bridges are more than the structures built by people like me. And then we are on the motorway and only an hour from home, our own little bit of England, and another river, the Wharfe, rising in the Yorkshire Dales, joining the Ouse which carries its waters on through York and Selby to pour, like the Trent, into the Humber. I tried to reach back to school geography lessons. Did we ever look at England's rivers? Did we ever discuss the connections and divisions that water makes? We walked sometimes along the steep banks of the Wharfe, Tim and I. I remember a sunny October afternoon, some of the trees already bare casting stark and black reflections on the brown water. The path was muddy and on either side the vegetation was dying back. We tramped in our boots, side by side for a while and then single file when the path narrowed, Tim in front. When the sun dropped it grew suddenly chilly and I pushed my hands into my pockets.

Politicians don't understand the real sources of power, Tim said. They don't understand the past either, I added, or they choose to ignore it. And now I wonder if I understand my own past, the choices, the accidents, the unforeseen events that brought me here, to this place in another country where I and my daughter walk. It's easier to imagine a river barge loaded with coal or wool or sugar, or to reconstruct the tumbled walls of an old dwelling, or to invent a family living on the land we walk over, than to face our own histories. It's a great thing to enter other peoples' worlds. I've done it all my life. When I look at my own world my gaze constantly shifts.

Jake was always your favourite, Lucas said bitterly when he came home with disappointing exam results. Don't be ridiculous, was Tim's response, and what has that got to do with your exams? I'm not going to compete with him, I'm not even going to try. I'm not the same as Jake. And I saw how upset he was, fifteen years old and nearly crying. You expect me to be like my dead brother, but I'm not the same. I was standing at the kitchen table glancing through a pile of junk mail. Lucas... Oh shut up, I know you're always thinking about him, the golden boy. How do you know he wasn't into drugs and stuff? How do you know he wasn't leading a double life and had you completely fooled? We don't know, Tim said quietly. All we know is that he was our son and your brother, that he seemed a decent lad, we loved him and he's dead. A wash of bleakness passed over Lucas's face. He squeezed his eyes shut but couldn't stop two tears escaping and trickling down his cheeks. I put my arms around him and held him close. He was resistant at first but then dropped his head on to my shoulder. He was taller than me. Then suddenly he jerked upright, turned on his heel and left the room. Tim was staring out of the window looking desperately sad. I said, Maybe it's good for him to cry, but Tim seemed not to hear.

The taxi comes to take Clare to catch the Glasgow bus. The dogs and I pile in with her. At the bus stop Dougie helps with Clare's case and cheerily says, See you next time you come, as she takes it from him. We look down the loch but the cloud is low and Arran is obscured. Clare boards the bus and gets a window seat. Her face appears, as if through water. The dogs and I watch as the bus pulls away. Clare lifts her hand and I wave in reply.

September 2014

It's three in the morning and I can't sleep. Uncontrolled thoughts scud through my head until I am bludgeoned into complete wakefulness. I get out of bed and take my book into the living room, although I am too restless to read. The dogs don't move – they know it isn't time to start the day. I go to the window and notice that there are lights on in the big house. For a few moments I'm anxious – has someone broken in? Should I phone the police? But surely no burglar would have switched on the lights, even if he (in my imagination it has to be a man) does not know that someone is living in the old railway carriage at the bottom of the garden. It isn't the flickering light of a torch that

I'm looking at, but electric lights blazing in several different rooms. The Turnbulls must have arrived late, without me noticing. As I watch, the kitchen goes dark and a couple of minutes later an upstairs light comes on. I sit down beside the dogs and open my book, but I can't concentrate, and every few minutes glance out of the window. At last the house is in darkness, and I return to my bed.

The next morning I look for signs of activity in the house, but there is nothing to suggest that it is occupied. I begin to think I imagined the lights – perhaps I wasn't up at all in the middle of the night. Perhaps my head is starting to give way. If the Turnbulls are there, the car would be parked, as usual, at the front, out of sight. They could be having a long lie. No doubt Moira at some point will come tripping across the garden and knock on the door.

I decide to give my living space a serious clean. Using the vacuum cleaner is awkward as there is little room for manoeuvre and furniture has to be heaved about, so I don't do it very often. But I have left it too long and soft clumps of dog hair and dust have collected in the corners. I have the vacuum cleaner on and when the knock comes it is only the barking of the dogs that alerts me. As expected, it is Moira. There is a dishevelled look about her, her hair uncombed, her face pale. This is not like her. She is wearing slightly grubby chinos and a shirt with the cuffs unbuttoned. Lack of sleep, I think. They must have arrived very late. You're busy, she says, without her usual smile. I need a break, I say, come in for a coffee. She comes in, sits down in the armchair and looks vaguely out of the window. I go into the kitchen and make proper coffee.

When I return with two mugs she is still looking out of the window with her hands clenched on her lap and doesn't turn her head immediately. I put a mug of coffee down on the little table beside her and she murmurs an abstracted thank-you. She at last turns her eyes away from the window and looks at me. Are you all right? I ask. It is some moments before she replies. Not really. I wait for more. Brian has gone, she says in a voice so low I can hardly hear. Gone? Well, he hasn't gone yet, she continues, but he's going. Going where? To Mexico, with a woman called Annette. Who's Annette? Moira lifts one hand and lets it drop again. Annette... She joined the firm a few months ago. From London. She's very good at her job. Mexico, I say, is that work? Well yes, says Moira, and no. We were to have gone together, Brian and I. For work and then for a holiday. I always fancied a holiday in Mexico. Brian says it would be good experience for Annette. Moira gives a little wincing smile. It seems the experience he has in mind... She looks directly at me for the first time. I drink some coffee. Brian is leaving me.

Moira sits in the armchair with her hands clenched together again but she has found her voice. At dinner last night he said he thought it would be a good opportunity for Annette. He asked me if I minded if she came to Mexico. I said no, though I was rather surprised. I asked him if he was sure Annette was up to the job, if the company was prepared to pay for three. And then I saw his face. Well, no, he said, not three... And somehow, it all came out, not according to plan – there was bitterness in Moira's voice now. He hadn't intended to tell me last night but he'd had a few glasses of wine and perhaps he thought he should seize the moment. Annette is...well, who knows what Annette is or how long she'll be whatever she is? He talked for hours, or it seemed like hours. He said he'd been unhappy for years. He said that for years he'd felt our marriage was at a dead end. Dead end. That's what he said. Dead end. Funny words, really, aren't they? Dead. End. Can't be more final than that, I suppose. Moira's hands are twisting and her face contracts into pain and puzzlement. There is a pause. I want her to drink her coffee but she ignores it. She pushes her untidy hair away from her face. It seems, she goes on, that I was so obtuse, so selfishly bound up with my own concerns, that I failed to recognise that that was where

206

we were. So it's my fault, you see. My fault for not realising. I should have tried harder, I expect.

Moira, I'm so sorry, I say. But are you sure it isn't just … well, a temporary aberration? She barks out a laugh and leans forward slightly. You know what? After what he said last night I think I agree. Our marriage may not have been dead before yesterday, but by God it is now. Dead and ended. She picks up the mug of coffee, looks at it, puts it down again. Cleo, who had retreated when the vacuum cleaner was on, pads into the room and lies down at Moira's feet. Cleo can always tell when people are upset. Moira reaches down and absently strokes her head.

Anyway, she continues, by midnight Brian was rather the worse for wear after several postprandial whiskies. I went upstairs to our bedroom, packed a few things, made sure the papers I needed to work on were in my briefcase, collected the car keys and left. I was quite methodical, quite proud of myself that I remembered everything. I even remembered to take milk from the fridge so I could make a cup of tea when I got here. I took the car. That was a good move, don't you think? Another barked laugh. He doesn't have the car. My fault, of course – I always held out against a second car. I was very calm, organised. Moira Turnbull is always good in a crisis. She's dug a lot of people out of holes. That was my speciality, you know. I was good at getting clients out of fixes.

Have you had anything to eat? I ask. She shakes her head. I'll make you some toast. No, no, I really couldn't eat anything. But you must. She shakes her head again. At least drink your coffee. Oh … yes, and lifts the mug and takes a sip of its lukewarm contents. There is a long silence. I phoned the office, Moira says at last. Said I'd be working at home. Another pause. I have no idea what Brian is doing. When does he leave for Mexico? Next week. Another pause. I'll stay here until Sunday. Why don't you have supper with me tonight?

The vagueness returns to Moira's face. She tilts her head to gaze out of the window again. I think perhaps she hasn't heard me and am about to repeat the invitation when she says slowly, No, I don't think so. I think I'm better on my own. And with a jerk of her head she looks at me, the vagueness gone. I'll have to get used to it, won't I? But thank you. You're a good person, Sonia. I'm so glad it was you who bought the railway carriage. We thought it would be a weekender – like us. We thought someone would do it up, make it pretty, and hardly ever be there. We didn't think anyone would want it as a permanent home. I'm so glad there's someone properly living here.

I smile. I don't know about properly, I say. Oh but look, she says, and flings out an arm so suddenly that she almost knocks over the mug still full of coffee. You've made it so nice, so comfortable. And the dogs... And here am I rattling around with all those rooms. I mean, even with me and Brian... Far too big. I don't know what we were thinking of, buying that house. Just because we could, really. Just because we had the money, and no children to spend it on. You know when we first saw this house? We were on a friend's yacht going through the canal. We saw the house and the "For sale" sign, and we thought, wouldn't it be nice to have a house somewhere around here? Not that house necessarily, but a little place to escape to. And in the end it was that house. Her rush of words come to a sudden stop. She has a slightly wild look, her face pale without make-up, her hair askew. And now I've escaped, she says quietly. What do women do if they have nowhere to go? It must be awful. Suddenly she looks straight at me, her eyes focused. I do realise how lucky I am, she says. My father worked in the shipyards. My mother was a cleaner at the primary school I went to.

Cleo is still lying on the floor at Moira's feet, but she has raised her head and her large brown eyes are looking anxious. But Moira has taken another sip of coffee. I'll have to sell it, I expect. If it made no sense for the two of us to buy it, now… Well, it would be crazy to keep it, wouldn't it? She says the words as if she were giving a client some firm but kind advice. It should be a family home. Children and all that… Moira looks around at my small living space, intently examining the furniture, the curtains, the rug. She picks up the coffee mug and holds it with both hands, then looks at me with a brittle smile. This, now… The perfect country retreat for a single woman. It suits me, I say quietly. It does, doesn't it? She looks around again. But it wouldn't suit me, it wouldn't suit me at all. And I feel almost rebuffed, as if she is suggesting that there must be something lacking in me if I am satisfied with living in a railway carriage.

Well, I'd better get on, she says suddenly, and let you get on. Lots to do. She gets to her feet, but too quickly and has to grab the back of the chair to steady herself. Do you have food in the house? I ask. Oh yes, there's always something in the freezer. Brian likes his gourmet meals. She puts both hands to her face. I must look a fright, she says. You look fine, I lie, but you must take care of yourself. She nods. Moira… Her hand is on the door handle. She stops and looks back at me. Well, you know, I'm always here. If you need anything, if you want to talk. Again she nods, then opens the door and steps down from the railway carriage. She takes a few steps, stops, turns. Thank you, Sonia, she says, I'm glad it's you. Another few steps. She turns again. I've decided to vote yes. Brian will be very annoyed if he finds out. He thinks the surge for yes is mindless opportunism.

I watch from the door as she crosses the garden. She stops and seems to be staring at the house. A stab of something sharp and painful seems to enter me. Loneliness is a word I've banished, but for some moments, as I watch Moira continue her slow progress towards her big house, I feel overcome by loss. They all flood through me, mother, father. Sister and best friend killed too soon by cancer. Tim dead on the fresh spring grass. And Jake, long gone, my firstborn child. Never, ever am I allowed to think, now, as I approach the completion of my seventieth year, he would be forty-four, a husband probably, a father. But I am thinking it. As Moira reaches the French windows and pauses again, I am crying.

Almost the equinox. The light is filtering through my closed curtains. The dogs stir as soon as I do and pad into my bedroom. Ash, though still not reliably house-trained, is curled at the end of my bed. He raises his head and stares at the dogs, then drops his head and shuts his eyes again. When I move my legs he starts to purr. I get up and pull on jeans and sweater. When I go into the kitchen the dogs take up their usual positions, Jet at the door, his ears up, expectant, Cleo lying in the narrow passageway so that I have to step over her. When I open the door Cleo gets up, stretches, and they both tumble out. Jet goes straight to his usual bush and lifts his leg. Cleo circles the garden several times before choosing a place to squat.

Tim died on a Wednesday afternoon. It was a bright April day and he'd decided to dig out a self-seeded hawthorn that had taken root in a corner of the garden. When he'd retired two years earlier, he'd made a list of tasks that he'd been putting off for years. He started on them after our trip to New Zealand. He laid new floor tiles in the bathroom and replaced the badly stained kitchen sink. He sorted his photographs and slides. He cleared out the garage which had long since ceased to allow space for a car.

On that Wednesday I went to York for the opening of an exhibition which included paintings by the art teacher at the local school. She lived in the village and we knew her slightly, and when we received the invitation I thought it would be nice and neighbourly to go. I'd hoped Tim would come with me but I could tell he wasn't keen, and when the sun came out at lunchtime he announced that he would stay at home and do some work in the garden. So that afternoon I drove to York alone, bought a new pair of shoes, and at five o'clock went to the exhibition opening. I had a glass of orange juice, chatted briefly to the one or two people I knew, and conscientiously looked at the paintings, pale and abstract, which I didn't much care for. Shortly after six I left.

Tim had said he'd make dinner, but when I got home the house was silent and the kitchen empty. There was no sign of culinary activity. The back door was open. At first the garden seemed empty but as I stood looking out across the familiar green and the flowered borders something caught my eye at the far end. I walked across the grass. I am not sure at what point I realised that the shape on the ground was Tim, but at that same moment I knew that he was not alive. The whole garden was still, suspended, as if a breath had been taken and not let out. He was lying peacefully on his back, his eyes closed. He was wearing a dark checked shirt that I had bought for him years before and brown corduroy trousers, his gardening trousers. His brown hair, which had only just begun to show some grey, fell across his forehead. I'd been badgering him to get his hair cut. With extraordinary composure – it seems now as I look back – I knelt down in the Indian cotton skirt I'd worn for the exhibition opening and put my hand on his chest. I don't know how long I knelt on the grass, my fingers spread where a heartbeat should have been. But at some point I walked back to the house, in through the back door to the telephone in the hall. I dialled 999. When I replaced the receiver an icy shock went through me and my hands began to shake.

Tim, I was told, had all his life had an undetected heart defect which could have killed him at any time. Occasionally in a dream I am in that garden. There is a shape on the ground, but the shape isn't Tim, because Tim is calling me from the house. I keep on walking to the far corner of the garden, but I always wake up before I discover who or what the shape is. It is dread that wakes me, and dread that lingers long after I dismiss the dream. I want to be reassured by Tim's voice but it fades entirely away.

Lucas and the boys will be with me soon. There's a lot to do before they arrive. Moira is no longer in the big house and I have had no word from her. The house looms emptier now that I know that Brian has deserted her. She might be pleased to have it occupied for a few days, but I am reluctant to ask her. I stare at the telephone as if hoping that it will do the job for me.

Before the car gave out, when I'd been here for nearly a year, I drove down to Loch Sween and across a narrow strip of land to the west coast. It was an October day of bright sunshine. I left the car by a stony shore where there is a tiny hamlet, a little cluster of mainly new houses. The sky was a deep, intense blue which the water reflected back. A slight breeze rippled the surface. I walked up a track parallel with the shore, past a handsome older house in spacious grounds. I walked for half an hour or so, and then spotted a narrow path that twisted up to the top of a small hill. I clambered up. From the top I looked down at the water, quivering and sparkling below me. A small boat lay neatly at anchor, shifting almost imperceptibly. I was directly opposite Jura and the little white rectangle that was Orwell's house. I wondered if he had seen days like this. To the northwest loomed the mountains of Mull.

The air was cold but the sun was warm, and I sat for a long time staring out at the sea, the islands and skerries, the blue sky beyond. For a while I felt a part of it all, wrapped in the blue of sea and sky, held by the stern cliffs of rock. Behind me were slopes blanketed in trees flecked with yellow and bronze. I scrambled back down the meagre path. A young couple overtook me as I walked back to the car, striding purposefully in walking boots, sleeves rolled to the elbows and packs on their backs. They smiled and said hello. When I reached the car there was no sign of them, but some children were on the shore, throwing stones into the water. Though I had not walked far I felt tired, but also light-headed, as if a heavy weight had melted away, dissolved by the sun and the shimmer of the water.

A few days later, the weather closed in, and it rained relentlessly. But it wasn't so bad. I was sure now that I had made the right decision.

Today we set off after breakfast under a dull sky. It's warm and the air is very still. The dogs know we are going to town because I have my rucksack slung on my shoulder. They scramble up the canal bank and turn in the right direction along the towpath. A pair of mallards are making their way determinedly westward, trailed by a string of half-grown ducklings. It takes about forty minutes to walk to town. Once I get going, once the stiffness in my legs begins to ease, I walk quite briskly. I stop at the Co-op for milk and the paper, and at the baker's for rolls, then on to the polling station.

I look for signs that would suggest a special event, but there is nothing, the street is no busier than usual. I'd set off with a sense of occasion. I'd put on a clean jersey and my good jacket. I carry on with the dogs on their double lead. I like to walk down this street. Apart from the Co-op, the shops and businesses are small and distinctive. People may not know me, but some, at least, know who I am and stop to talk to the dogs. The people in my Yorkshire village also knew who I was of course, but there was no baker or butcher or post office and little reason to walk along the village street. Sometimes when the children were small we'd make a circle with the bikes, through the village and along a farm track and on to a path that took us alongside a small wood back to the road. Sometimes we would go as far as the river and take the path along its banks. When the children were older and lost interest in family walks, on a fine Sunday afternoon Tim and I would walk the same route and pause to peer into gardens and perhaps exchange a few words with neighbours.

I turn the corner, and to my surprise walking towards me is flame-haired Alison from the farm. I've never seen her in the town before. Off to vote? she asks. I nod. My Harry reckons it won't make any difference. They're all the same, he says, Westminster or Holyrood, what do they know? But I tell him, it's worth a try. It'll no be any worse, that's what I say, and it might be better. Cleo is nudging at the pocket of Alison's oversized jacket. Oh aye, she laughs, she knows what I've got in there. She pulls out a treat for each of the dogs and continues on her way.

Further down the street, at the corner, there is a man in a tweed cap standing quite still with a "yes" placard. He nods to me. We can make history today, he says. I smile but say nothing in return. I like the idea of making history and am quite ready to believe that each of us can contribute to its shape. But at the same time I know that history makes us, and that much of history is accident and coincidence. My father climbing the last few feet of Ben Lomond. A bomb that failed to kill my mother and my sister and my unborn self. Timothy Billings, tall and lanky in his leather jacket, tramping the tarmac into Slough. Sonia Letford on a June afternoon on an aimless walk beside a Highland canal.

At the polling place I tie the dogs to the railings. Cleo sits and gazes accusingly, Jet lies down with his head on his front paws. There are two middle-aged women in front of me, and a young man in work boots. I collect my voting slip, go into a booth and place my cross with the rather blunt pencil provided. As I come out an overweight man with a stick shuffles into the next booth. I fold the slip once and drop it into the large square box, under the eyes of the officials at the desk. There, it's done. There's something almost primitive about it, anachronistic, a plain cross with a blunt pencil in a drab space, and I wonder if there isn't also something anachronistic about the idea of independence. It belongs, perhaps, to a different world, a world left behind, or a world that should have been left behind. But I suppose as borders mean less and less we crave frontiers, delineations, more and more, and people will die rather than relinquish them. The officials probably are not local. They probably do not know that I am a stranger in this place.

On the other side of the world is Cape Reinga, where waters meet but appear not to mix. We stared down from the clifftop for a long time, mesmerised by the movement of oceans and the intensity of green and blue under the clear sun. And Tim – the memory comes on me suddenly – Tim put his arm around me and said, We've done all right you and I, haven't we? A grandchild. It's wonderful.

I walk out of the polling place more briskly than I entered.

As soon as they see me, the dogs get to their feet and wag their tails. We head back through the streets to the canal. The cloud breaks and there is tentative sunshine. The dogs leap up the steep bank in front of me and I scramble up behind as they stand at the top and peer down. It's steep and slippery and I have to use my hands. It's an undignified clamber for a seventy-year-old woman. Yes, it's my birthday. I was born in the early hours of the morning so have now reached my threescore years and ten. Yesterday, I got back from my walk with the dogs to find a large and elaborate bouquet of flowers on the doorstep, from Clare, my eldest surviving child. I remembered, with a sudden chill, the red rose. Sometimes I wonder what happened to Stephen Wright. Sometimes I think I treated him badly, that we all treated him badly.

If Tim had not died I would not be here. I would never have driven north, alone, on some undefined and unacknowledged quest. Tim and I never contemplated leaving Yorkshire, although sometimes he dreamt of building bridges in far-flung places where they were badly needed. We would let our imaginations race over a bottle of wine at the kitchen table. Work for Tim was all about making connections. I liked that idea too. Sometimes I was able to believe that my own work was also about making connections. The possibilities, Africa maybe, South America. Vistas took shape unimpeded by mundane realities. Deserts, jungles, raging torrents. So much to be done, Tim would say, so much to be done. When the children are older, I'd say. When they've finished school. When they've left home. And then Jake died.

I count the dead sometimes. How can you not do that when so much of life has passed? I am not lonely. If I cried when Moira vanished through the French windows, it was for her loneliness.

The leaves are turning and the water is a deep brown freckled with their bronze and gold. I spot a heron on the far bank, predatory and preternaturally still. The dogs escort me, Cleo in front, nose to the ground, Jet the shepherd behind ready to nip at my heels. Three score years and ten. Borrowed time. But it's all borrowed time, isn't it?